WE
MET
IN
DECEMBER

WE
MET
IN
DECEMBER

ROSIE CURTIS

𝒲𝓂
WILLIAM MORROW
An Imprint of HarperCollins*Publishers*

This is a work of fiction. Names, characters, places, and incidents are
products of the author's imagination or are used fictitiously and
are not to be construed as real. Any resemblance to actual events,
locales, organizations, or persons, living or dead, is entirely coincidental.

WE MET IN DECEMBER. Copyright © 2019 by Rosie Curtis.
Emojis © shutterstock.com. All rights reserved.
Printed in the United States of America. No part of this book
may be used or reproduced in any manner whatsoever without written
permission except in the case of brief quotations embodied in critical articles
and reviews. For information, address HarperCollins Publishers,
195 Broadway, New York, NY 10007.

HarperCollins books may be purchased for educational, business,
or sales promotional use. For information, please email the
Special Markets Department at SPsales@harpercollins.com.

Published as *We Met in December* in the United Kingdom in 2019
by HarperCollins Publishers.

FIRST U.S. EDITION

Library of Congress Cataloging-in-Publication Data has been applied for.

ISBN 978-0-06-296456-4

19 20 21 22 23   LSC   10 9 8 7 6 5 4 3 2 1

To Archie, with all my love
(and thank you for all the cups of tea, darling).

PROLOGUE

Jess

22nd December

Christmas and London are a match made in heaven.
There's a man on the street corner selling hot chestnuts
by the bag, filling the air with the smell of cinnamon
and vanilla. The ornate wooden windows of Liberty are
glittering with lights and decorations. I stop to look at
a huge tree swathed in ribbons and hung with a million
dancing fairy lights and—

'Watch out!'

A woman crashes into me, giving me a furious look
and weaving past, muttering loudly about bloody tourists.

I am not a tourist, I think. I am – or will be, in just
a couple of hours – an official Londoner. I step out of
the way of the thronging crowds, pasting myself against
a carved wooden window frame, and watch as a sea of
people scurry past.

1

I add 'stop dead on the pavement' to my mental list of Things London People Never Do. I know that already, really, but it's easy to forget when everything is so sparkly and festive. I pause for a moment and take a photo to share on my Instagram stories, because it's just so ridiculously perfect and my life has been so beige and boring for months – it's lovely to have something interesting to put on there. And then I take another of the street scene, because it's just so . . . London-y and Christmassy and perfect.

I look at the flowers in the doorway of Liberty, thinking that it would be a nice idea to take Becky some as a thank you (again) for offering me a room in a house that would otherwise be completely out of my reach. There doesn't seem to be a price anywhere though, which I think is weird, then I hear my Nanna Beth's voice saying, *If you have to ask, you can't afford it.* But they're only flowers, surely. How expensive can a bunch of flowers be?

'Can I help you?' The girl behind the faux-Victorian wooden flower stall looks at me. She's tiny and has huge brown eyes that match the expensive-looking Liberty of London apron she's wearing.

'I was wondering how much these are?' I lift up a ready-prepared bouquet – deep red roses mingled with silver-grey foliage and white lilies streaked with lime green, still not quite open. They're wrapped in thick, luxurious waxed paper and sealed with a gold Liberty sticker. They'll make the perfect thank you present for Becky.

The girl chews her gum for a moment and looks at me, taking in the fluffy pink coat I bought for my big move (if I'm going to be a London creative, I thought I should wear something that suits my new job), along with my denim pinafore, blue tights and my trusty silver Doc Marten boots. When I got off the train from Bournemouth earlier I felt quirky and artistic, but now under her supercilious stare I think perhaps I look like a kids' TV presenter.

'Forty-seven pounds,' she says. 'And five pounds extra if you want our gift-wrapping service.'

Ouch. That's a week's worth of my new food budget. I put the flowers back in the stylish metal bucket. I think Becky would understand.

'I like your coat,' she says, as I start to slink off. I turn, surprised, and smile a thank you.

'It's from eBay,' I tell her, patting my fluffy arm.

'Cool. It's really nice.' The girl lowers her voice, conspiratorially. 'I couldn't afford the flowers either, if it helps. There's a stall a couple of minutes away on Noel Street – he always has decent flowers.'

She waves her hand briefly in the air, but then another customer appears and she turns to them, greeting them with a cheerful smile.

'Thanks,' I say, in her general direction, but she's not listening.

So I take my phone out. My sense of direction is absolutely hopeless, and I still can't work out how people find their way around London. I've worked out bits of it, but

I can't seem to join them up. It takes me three tries, but I make it to Noel Street in the end. There I find a round-faced man wearing a Santa hat, singing along to Christmas songs from a Bluetooth speaker. His stall is piled high with fruit and veg, and – phew – surrounding it is a rainbow array of flowers, which look to my uneducated eye just as nice as the ones from round the corner at Liberty. Well, almost as nice. A bit gaudy maybe, but I can't afford to be fussy on my new London wages.

Five minutes later I'm back on Oxford Street looking at the Christmas lights with a bunch of (considerably cheaper) red roses, their cellophane wrapping crinkling in my arms. The lights – strung from one side of the street to the other – sparkle against the sky, which ten minutes ago had been the usual English winter grey, but now has shifted to an ominous bruised purple. I'm trying to figure out if it's easier to jump on a bus or get the tube to Notting Hill to meet Becky and my new house-mates. I'm standing on a street corner peering at Google Maps again when the first hailstones hit me on the head. And – *ow* – they really sting.

In seconds the packed streets empty, as everyone ducks into the nearest shop· or doorway to shelter, clutching their shopping bags tightly. Only the smug umbrella holders and the hardy few carry on, marching down pavements now clear of tourists and Christmas shoppers. The tyres of the red buses and black taxis hiss on the tarmac and the hailstones hammer on the metal awning over our heads. I'm crammed with a handful of shoppers in the doorway of – I look up to see a shiny brass plaque on the wall – NMC Inc, and then I frown at the screen of my phone once again.

'Are you lost?' a man says. He has Scandinavian-looking blond hair and a dark blue scarf wrapped round his neck. He's got a bit of an accent and now he's indicating my phone with a finger. 'Where are you trying to go?'

'Notting Hill,' I say, feeling like I've stepped into a film for a moment. Christmas is everywhere and there's a tiny split second where the noticing-things part of my brain is looking at me from the outside. The thing about being addicted to a certain kind of romantic movie is that you're always half-expecting that your life might just suddenly take a turn for the better. And handsome Scandinavian types who look a bit like Jaime Lannister are pretty much up there on my list of good things.

'I'm not sure which bus to get,' I say. 'Because I usually get the tube, but my friend said it was easy from here. Easy if you've got a sense of direction, I think. Which I definitely have not.'

And then I find myself telling this complete stranger, who has opened the Citymapper app on his phone and is tapping rapidly: 'I'm picking up the keys for my new house.' I can hear the little note of pride in my voice.

'Nice,' he says, smiling. He points to the bus stop on the opposite side of the road. 'If you get the 94, it'll take you straight to Notting Hill Gate. It'll take a bit longer than the tube, but on the other hand, it's a lovely view if you're new to the area.'

'Thanks,' I say. I'm not doing a great job at trying to look like a well-established local, then. A fresh torrent of hailstones batters the canopy above us. 'Might just wait a moment.'

'That's very wise.'

Obviously if this was one of those movies with woolly hats and kissing in the snow and hard-bitten business-women remembering the true meaning of Christmas, at this point we'd start a conversation, and he'd follow me onto the bus, and – well, you know the score. But this is not a movie, I am one hundred per cent single, and despite being as much of a sucker for a Richard Curtis movie as the next hopeless romantic, I remind myself that I am one hundred per cent not looking for anyone else. Because this is my new start, and my new life, and I am doing it On My Own.

The hail stops, and I try my best to stride across the road in the manner of an independent London girl living her best life, aware that the handsome Scandinavian person is watching and (obviously) thinking that I am the one that got away and wondering if he'll ever see me again. What actually happens is I almost get knocked flat by a bloke on a Deliveroo bike, fumble to find my card to swipe it when I get on the bus, and when I do climb the stairs and sit down on a seat, I look across the road to see the handsome Jaime Lannister lookalike beaming with delight as his boyfriend appears from behind the door of NMC Inc in an expensive-looking coat, kisses him on the mouth and runs an affectionate hand through his lovely blond hair. Ah well. It's just as well I'm not looking.

I sit wedged in against the window of the bus, wiping away condensation with my fluffy pink sleeve so I can stare out of the window all the way to Notting Hill. I watch as we pass Hyde Park, the huge trees' bare, branches reaching up to the grey sky. The bus stops, disgorging passengers, and I watch as a woman dressed in a red coat with a fur collar climbs out of a shiny black taxi, her arms full of expensive-looking paper shopping bags.

And then we pull away and I watch as the buildings get smaller and the grey sky gets bigger, and the bus takes me to my new house and my new life. I smile at a woman when she gets on and sits beside me, and I don't even mind that she opens up an absolutely honking tuna sandwich from M&S and eats it. Nothing is going to get in the way of this moment, because I've got a job in London and a room in a house-share I couldn't even begin to imagine. I squish my hands into fists of excitement when I see the words *Notting Hill Gate* flash up on the information board on the bus. I press the bell – my bell – and my heart gives a little skip of excitement as the bus pulls to a stop. This is London, I think. And now, London is home.

CHAPTER ONE

Jess

22nd December, 15 Albany Road, Notting Hill

I pause for a minute outside the house and look up, still
not quite believing that this terraced mansion is home.
It's huge, slightly shabby, and has an air of faded gran-
deur. Six wide stone steps lead to a broad wooden front
door, painted a jaunty red that is faded in places and
chipped away to a pale, dusky pink. Each window on
the road is topped with ornate stuccoed decorations – the
ones on our house are a bit chipped and scruffy-looking,
but somehow it just makes the place look more welcoming,
as if it's full of history.

Next door on one side is freshly decorated, the black
paint of the windowsills gleaming. They've got window
boxes at every window, crammed full of pansies and
evergreen plants. I can see a huge Christmas tree tastefully
decorated with millions of starry lights, topped with a

huge metal star. There's a little red bicycle chained to the railings and a pair of wellies just inside the porch. This must be the investment banker neighbours Becky talked about. The mansion on the other side has been turned into flats, and there's a row of doorbells beside a blue front door.

I rush up the steps and lift the heavy brass door-knocker.

'You don't have to knock,' Becky says, beaming as she opens the door. 'This is home!'

'I do, because you haven't given me a key yet.' I love Becky.

'Ah.' Becky takes my bag and hangs it on a huge wooden coat hook just inside the door, which looks like it's been there forever. There's a massive black umbrella with a carved wooden handle hanging beside my bag.

'Used to be my grandpa's,' she says, absent-mindedly running a hand down it. 'This place is like a bloody museum.'

'I can't believe it's yours.'

'Me neither.' Becky shakes her head and beckons me through to the kitchen. 'Now wait here two seconds, and I'll give you the tour.'

I stand where I've been put, at the edge of a huge kitchen-slash-dining-room space, which has been here so long that it's come back into fashion. It's all cork tiles and dangling spider plants and a huge white sink, which is full of ice and bottles of beer.

I think Nanna Beth would be impressed with this. With all of it. I've taken the leap.

'Life is for living, Jessica, and this place is all very well, but it's like God's waiting room,' she'd once said, giving a cackle of laughter and inclining her head towards the window, where a flotilla of mobility scooters had passed by, ridden by grey-haired elderly people covered over with zipped-up waterproof covers. The seaside town I'd grown up in wasn't actually as bad as all that, but it was true: things had changed. Grandpa had passed away, and Nanna Beth had sold the house and invested her money in a little flat in a new sheltered housing development where there was no room for me, not because she was throwing me out, but because – as she'd said, looking at me shrewdly – it was time to go. I'd been living in a sort of stasis since things had ended with my ex-boyfriend Neil.

Weirdly, the catalyst for all this change had been being offered a promotion in the marketing company where I worked. If I'd taken it, it would have been a job for life. I could have afforded to buy a little house by the sea and upgraded my car for something nice, and I'd have carried on living the life I'd been living since I graduated from university and somehow gravitated back home when all my friends spread their wings and headed for the bright lights of London, or New York, or – well, Sarah ended up in Inverness, so I suppose we didn't quite all end up somewhere exotic.

But Nanna Beth had derailed me and challenged me with the task of getting out and grabbing life with both hands, which is pretty tricky for someone like me. I tend to take the approach that you should hold life with one hand, and keep the other one spare just in case of emergencies. And yet here I am, an hour early (very me) for a housewarming party for the gang of people that Becky has gathered together to share this rambling, dilapidated old house in Notting Hill that *her* grandparents left her when they passed away.

'I still can't believe this place is yours,' I repeat, as I balance on the edge of the pale pink velvet sofa. It's hidden under a flotilla of cushions. The arm of the sofa creaks alarmingly, and I stand up, just in case it's about to give way underneath my weight.

Becky shakes her head. '*You* can't? Imagine how I feel.'

'And your mum *really* didn't object to your grandparents leaving you their house in their will?'

She shakes her head and pops open the two bottles of beer she's holding, handing me one. 'She's quite happy where she is. And you know she's all *property is theft* and that sort of thing.'

'True.' I take a swig of beer and look at the framed photographs on the wall. A little girl in Mary-Jane shoes with a serious face looks out at us, disapprovingly. 'She's keeping her eye on you: look.'

Becky shudders. 'Don't. She wanted me to come to Islay for a Christmas of meditation and chanting, but I managed to persuade her that I'd be better off coming when the weather was a bit nicer.'

Becky's mum had been a mythical figure to all of us at university. She'd been a model in her youth, and then eschewed all material things and moved to an ethical

12

living commune on the island of Islay when Becky was sixteen. Becky had stayed behind to finish her exams with a family friend, and horrified her mother by going into not just law, but corporate law of all things. Relations had been slightly strained for quite a while, but she'd spent some time in meditative silence, apparently, and now they got on really well – as long as they had a few hundred miles between them.

I look at the photograph of Becky's mum – she must only be about seven. She looks back at me with an intense stare, and I think that if anyone can save the planet, it's very possibly her. Anyway, I raise my bottle to her in a silent thank you. If she'd contested the will, Becky might not have inherited this place, and she wouldn't have offered me a room at £400 a month, which wouldn't have got me space in a broom closet anywhere else in commutable distance of King's Cross, where my new job was situated.

'Just going to get out of this jacket,' Becky says, looking down at her work clothes; then she disappears for a moment and I'm left looking around. The house is old-fashioned, stuffed full of the sort of mid-century furniture that would sell for vast amounts of money on eBay – there's an Ercol dresser in the sitting room and dining chairs that look like they've come straight out of Heal's. I take a photo of the huge potted plant that looms in the corner like a triffid, and then I wander into the hall. It's huge and airy, with a polished wooden banister that twirls round and up to the third floor where there's a skylight – dark just now, because it's midwinter, but I bet it fills this space with light in the

13

middle of summer. There's a huge wooden coat stand with a mirror by the interior door, and a porch with ceramic tiles worn through years of footsteps passing over them. The place must be 150 years old, at least. And – I push the sitting room door open – there's enough space for everyone to collapse on the sofas in a Sunday-ish sort of way. The paintings on the walls are draped with brightly coloured tinsel and fairy lights, and there's a Christmas tree on the side table, decked with multi-coloured lights and hung with a selection of baubles, which look—

'Hideous, aren't they?' Becky's voice sounds over my shoulder. 'I couldn't resist. They're from the pound shop so I just went to town a bit. If you can't be tacky at Christmas, when can you?'

'I love it,' I say, and I do. Becky disappears back into the kitchen and I can hear the sound of her warbling out of tune to Mariah Carey and the clattering of plates and saucepans. I stand in the hallway and look at this amazing house that I couldn't afford in a million years, and I think back to about two months ago when I saw an advert for my dream job in publishing come up and wondered if I should take the chance and apply. And how Nanna Beth had said, 'Nothing ventured, lovey – you never know what's around the corner . . .'

An hour later and we're in the kitchen and everything's been laid out so it looks perfect for the housewarming party.

'Stop!' I put a hand up in the air.

Becky stops dead and I leap between her and the massive old oak table in the kitchen. Her face registers alarm as I reach into the back pocket of my jeans and then she rolls her eyes as she realises what I'm doing.

With my free hand, I reach across, straightening a plate and moving a piece of tinsel so it sits jauntily beside the jewel-bright heaps of salsa and guacamole. 'There.'

Leaning over, I take a photo from above and step back, letting her put the tray of tequila shots down on the table.

'Since when were you the Instagram queen?' Becky tucks back a strand of hair that's escaped from behind her ear. She's had it cut into a sleek graduated bob, which makes her look like a proper grown-up, especially as she's still dressed in her work clothes of grey slim-fitting trousers and a pale blouse made of silky stuff, which I would definitely have spilled coffee on within an hour. But she's here at 6.30 p.m. looking as if she's just got out of the shower, instead of having battled her way home through London traffic after a long day doing corporate law stuff. I've taken off my pink fluffy coat because it was making me feel like a dislodged tree bauble, or a pom-pom, in comparison to Becky's minimalist chic.

'Hardly,' I say, fiddling with a filter and making the photo look nice before hashtagging it and hitting share. 'I just thought it'd be nice to show everyone back home what it's like living in London.'

'And make a point of what a lovely time you're having even though they all think you're insane to give up a

15

promotion in Bournemouth for a pay cut up here?' she says.

I nod, and pick up a tortilla chip, breaking it in half. 'That too,' I admit, making a face. 'And Nanna Beth is on there too – she's got herself an iPhone contract. I'm her only Instagram follower so far.'

'She's going to be sharing selfies with all the hot doctors in the nursing home, isn't she?' Becky snorts with laughter.

I turn the phone so she can see it. @nanna_beth1939 has posted a string of photos of her new ground-floor flat in the sheltered accommodation unit she's moved into.

'Oh, bless,' says Becky, taking my phone so she can have a closer look. 'Look, she's got that wooden carving you bought her in Cyprus on the mantelpiece.'

I peer over her shoulder. 'Ahh, that's nice.' I'm hit by a wave of guilt that I'm going to be up here and she's going to be down there. I've spent the last year living in her house, ever since Grandpa died, and it's going to be weird not having her there every night when I get home from work.

'She'll be fine,' says Becky, as if reading my thoughts. She clicks the phone off and puts it down on the table. 'And it's not as if you're miles away. It's a train ride, that's all.'

'I know. Just feels weird leaving her to the tender mercies of Mum.'

Becky makes a face. 'Yeah, well, she's not exactly . . . well, she wasn't at the front of the queue when they were giving out the nurturing quota, was she?'

I snort. My mother is many things, but maternal is

not one of them. I mean she's lovely, in her own way. But I'm not sure she'll remember to pop round every couple of days and check Nanna Beth's doing okay in her new place. Anyway. I square my shoulders and think of what Nanna Beth told me when she'd pressed a roll of twenty-pound notes into my hand yesterday morning. It was time for me to step out into the big world and let her do her own thing. Slightly odd role reversal, I know, but our family's always been a bit unusual.

In the kitchen, Becky's still singing out of tune and lighting the tiny tea-light candles that are scattered around. Even when we were living in university halls, she managed to make her room look good.

There's a clatter as someone opens the door, and a gust of air blows a couple of Christmas cards off the top of the fridge. I bend down and pick them up, catching the one-sided conversation that's going on in the hall.

'You said you'd be able to get away.' It must be Emma, the girl Becky's found to take another one of the rooms.

There's a long pause and I hover by the kitchen door, wondering if I should pop my head round and say hello. Becky's stirring spiced chicken and peppers, filling the room with a smell that makes my stomach growl. I haven't eaten since breakfast.

'What about me?' Emma says. My eyes widen. I shouldn't be listening in, but I'm a sucker for a bit of drama. I fiddle with my phone, trying to look as if I'm busy and not just eavesdropping. Emma's voice is in that middle ground, somewhere between angry and upset.

'I don't care what *she's* doing,' she says, and this time she's not keeping her voice down. 'I'm not waiting around forever.'

Becky turns round, frying pan in hand. She raises her eyebrows and looks towards the door. 'Uh-oh, trouble in paradise by the sound of it.'

I nod, and lower my voice. 'What's the story?'

Becky puts a finger to her lips. 'Tell you later. But it's very Emma. It'll be all over and they'll be loved up before you know it.'

A moment later, Emma appears in the room, her eyes sparkling in that suspiciously bright way that mine do if I've been crying and I'm trying to look like everything's okay.

'Hi, hello,' she says, and leans over and kisses me on the cheek.

'Sorry, just had to take a quick work call. You know what it's like. They pay us nothing, and expect us to be on call 24/7.'

I smile in a way that I hope suggests I haven't heard a thing.

'Emma, this is Jess, the university friend I told you about. She's taking the room on the first floor.'

'Lovely to meet you, Jess. God I need a drink,' says Emma, picking up one of the little shot glasses of tequila. I'm about to pass her a lemon slice, but she's too quick for me. The whole thing is gone in a second, and she winces in disgust. 'Ugh. Revolting. I hate tequila.' She takes another one and downs it as well. 'Cheers.'

I'm still holding the lemon slice in mid-air when the kitchen door opens again.

'Sorry I'm late,' says a low voice. I look up, and almost drop my phone in shock.

Standing in the doorway, taking up quite a lot of it, is a man. The kind of man that makes you feel like your stomach just fell through the floor. I mean I say that, but Emma's scrolling through her phone and Becky's running hot water over the fajita saucepan, so maybe they're immune or something but – wow.

I press my lips together, mainly to check that my mouth isn't actually hanging open. I suspect my eyes are cartoon circles though, and I can't press them shut without looking a bit weird, so I just sort of stand there, making a kind of mental inventory.

Scruff of beard – check. Broad, muscular shoulders – check. Twinkly eyes – check. Bottle of tequila in hand. He's wearing a grey shirt and a pair of jeans and he's got a scarf hanging round his neck and . . .

'Hey. You must be Jess,' he says, stepping towards me. He reaches out a hand to shake mine, and then leans forward to kiss me on the cheek in greeting. 'I'm Alex.'

He smells fresh, his cheek cold from the winter air against mine. I catch a faint scent of cedar wood and notice as he steps back that his sleeves are rolled up, showing off the sort of forearms that look as if he chops wood or does something outdoorsy for a living, only we're in the middle of Notting Hill and that's unlikely.

There's a moment where I think I've forgotten how

to speak, which is slightly awkward as I'm basically standing there like the human embodiment of the heart eyes emoji, suppressing the urge to put one hand to my cheek (because: phwoar, basically) and the other on his, to check he's real (because: well, ditto). And then I remember that I'm sensible, level-headed Jess, and this .is my new house and my new life and the number one rule that Becky told us all about in the welcome email was NO COUPLES. Which is absolutely fine, because I'm here to work and definitely absolutely not to fall in love at first sight with gorgeous men with cute beards holding tequila bottles.

'Hi.' I shove my phone back in the pocket of my jeans and try to force myself to do something practical, so I press my hands together in a workmanlike manner and say in an artificially bright voice, 'That's everyone, isn't it?'

I turn to Becky, who's halfway through what she'd later explain was a test fajita, a dollop of sour cream on her chin. She wipes it off, and tries to talk with her mouth full, so it comes out a bit muffled.

'Everyone except Rob.'

I watch Emma, who has helped herself to another drink, but she's added a mixer this time and she's actually drinking it, not downing it in one. She's sitting on the edge of the table, her long legs stretched out and crossed at the ankles. 'Ah, yes. The mysterious Rob,' she says, arching an eyebrow and smiling. She reaches over and takes a handful of tortilla chips. 'Have you met him, Jess? I'm beginning to think maybe he's a figment of Becky's imagination.'

20

'Yeah, Becky,' says Alex. He shoves the bottle on the wonky wooden shelf over the kitchen sink and grabs a plate, turning to look at her, jokingly. 'What's the story with Rob?'

'He is real, I promise you.' Becky shakes her head, laughing.

'Of course. Man of few words and many knives.' Emma points to the kitchen counter. 'Where are they, Becky? They were there the other day when I had breakfast then they disappeared.'

But Becky has her head in the freezer, trying to find a bag of ice, and doesn't reply.

I take a look at Emma while she's occupied with assembling a fajita wrap. She's properly beautiful. She has a very attractive, angular face, with an aquiline nose and huge doe eyes. She looks like she's made to swan about in Notting Hill, hanging out in expensive restaurants, being treated to expensive lunches. I pull up a chair at the big table and have a moment of feeling scruffy, freckled, and very suburban. Almost like someone who's been living with their grandparents and working in an office in a seaside town a million miles from London, which isn't surprising.

'So what we know is this: Rob's a chef, which means he works really long hours and we never see him because he's home when we're all out at work, and then out when we get back,' Emma begins. 'He turned up the other day, dumped all this expensive-looking kitchen kit on the table, then looked at his watch and said he had to run.'

'Then I put his stuff in the big larder cupboard,' Becky continues, banging a bag of ice against the edge of the table until the cubes separate. 'Because three blocks of intimidating kitchen knives sitting out on the work surface was going to give me nightmares and I had visions of a serial killer turning up and murdering us all in our beds.'

'I think a serial killer would probably have their own kit, don't you?' Alex says, looking thoughtful.

The three of them look at each other and laugh and I do too, but a split second behind. It's weird – like being back at school or when you start a new job and you have that new-girl feeling when you've missed the boat a little bit. I watch as Alex, Emma and Becky make themselves fajitas from the food laid out on the table.

'Dig in, Jess,' Becky says, shoving the bowl of guacamole towards me.

I'm still reeling a bit from the unexpected handsomeness of Alex, and trying not to look at him. Except I can't help taking a sneaky look when I think he won't notice, and he glances in my direction and our eyes meet and I think that there's a very strong possibility that I might inadvertently shout 'PHWOAR' by mistake because really he is very handsome indeed and the other two seem to be completely oblivious.

Becky's telling a story about something that happened at work and the two of them are listening and laughing. Becky's always been the most sociable of my university friends. We met in fresher's week and we've been friends ever since. I studied English lit, she studied law, but whereas I left and found myself back in Bournemouth working for a perfectly nice, safe little marketing company, and ensconced in a relationship with Neil, Becks headed to London where she got a job with a law firm and started working her way up the ladder. And then it all went slightly pear-shaped for me back home, and it turned out to be a (mostly) good thing and now, I still can't believe that this – I look out the window at the rainy street below, cars splashing past and the streetlights lighting everything with an orange glow – is my new life.

I let the evening wash over me for a while, and because they're all so chatty, nobody really notices that I'm not saying much. Emma hands me a drink. She's still in work clothes – very neat in expensive-looking boots and a shirt dress printed all over with tiny foxes.

'So. When are you joining us?' she asks.

She's very formal, I think, watching her as I take a sip. Alex and Becky have whizzed up some sort of pomegranate cocktail with the ice and tequila he brought. It tastes like something you'd drink by the pool, instead of on a rainy December evening in London.

'Not until after New Year. I've got a holiday booked with friends – we're going skiing.'

'Ooh, lovely. Christmas skiing.' She looks impressed.

'It's not quite as fancy as it sounds. My friend Gen got a last-minute deal through a contact of hers, so we're going to Val d'Isère on a coach.'

Gen's friend – an actor, like her – was working in a call centre for a travel company when the deal had come through. We'd been making promises to each other for years that we'd go skiing again, after a school trip to Andorra a million years ago, and when this came up it felt like the perfect time. As soon as I'd said yes, the prospect of living every moment on a twenty-one-hour-long coach ride had started to pall slightly, but that was a minor detail.

'Ouch.' Emma looked sympathetic. 'That's a whole day on a coach. Still, it'll be worth it for all the apres-ski and the gorgeous posh ski totty. You might meet a millionaire.'

I steal a quick look in Alex's direction, thinking that actually, I'd be quite happy with someone like him, thank you very much, but give Emma a smile of agreement. 'You never know.'

Becky fiddles with her phone, changing the music. She's wrapped some silvery Christmas ribbon around her head like a halo, and starts singing along as Michael Bublé begins crooning from the speaker on the shelf above the sink.

'Oh God, Becks,' I groan. 'Do we have to have Bublé *again*?'

'It's Christmas,' she says, pulling me up by the waist and waltzing me out of the kitchen door and into the hall. She puts a finger to her lips, shushing me before I can protest. The hall is painted an odd shade, somewhere between violet and grey, and hung with a collection of floral paintings that must've belonged to Becky's grandparents. There's a huge spiky-leaved plant towering over us in the corner by the stairs. I dodge sideways before Becky waltzes me straight into it.

'What d'you reckon?' Her voice is an urgent whisper.

'They seem nice.' I try to sound non-committal when what I want to know is why on earth she'd omitted to mention that one of our flatmates was ridiculously gorgeous. 'How'd you know Emma again?' I ask.

'Oh, she's one of those friend-of-a-friend people. You know, you're in the same pubs, vaguely know each other through a WhatsApp group, that sort of thing. I can't remember how we met in the first place. But she was looking for somewhere because the girl she was flat-sharing was moving her boyfriend in, and I had one room left. I'd already sorted you and Alex—' my stomach does a disobedient sort of swooping thing '—and it just seemed like she'd be a nice addition. Everyone's pretty chilled out, so it should be quite a nice laid-back sort of house.'

'She seems nice,' I say, lamely.

'God, I must pee,' says Becky, and leaves me standing in the hallway.

I hadn't noticed, but the carpet looks like someone threw up on a giraffe – it's yellow and brown with greenish swirls and it clashes so badly with the lilac walls that it must have been the height of fashion at some point in the 1970s. Nobody could choose that colour scheme just randomly, surely?

I head back to the kitchen, realising that I'm feeling a bit fuzzy round the edges. Emma's kicked off her boots now, and she's sitting at the table chatting animatedly to Alex, who is sitting opposite. He pushes out the dining chair next to him, beckoning me to join them.

'Come and get something else to eat.'

He passes me a plate stacked high with tortillas. I think perhaps it'll soak up some of the alcohol.

'So how do you know Becky?' He stretches across the table for the cheese, placing it between me and Emma.

I take a tortilla and spread it with sour cream. 'I feel like I should make something up that doesn't make me sound as tragic as this will.'

Alex raises an eyebrow. He really does have a very nice face. Emma gets up and goes and throws a load of ice and stuff in the blender, shouting, 'Sorry,' as she turns it on, drowning out my words as I'm about to start explaining.

Emma tips a pink slush into our glasses and Alex tastes it, pulling a face. 'Bloody hell, that's like rocket fuel. I'll make the next one, or we'll all end up with alcohol poisoning.'

'We met at uni,' I say, starting again. 'I was crying in the loos because I'd just dumped my boyfriend back home for someone who'd promptly cheated on me a week later.'

Emma laughs, but not unkindly. 'Oh God, we've all been there.' She picks at some slices of red pepper while I'm stacking a tortilla wrap with chicken and cheese and more sour cream, just for good measure. I roll it up and realise there's no way of eating it that doesn't involve half of it falling down the front of my top and

26

the other half spilling all over my chin, so I end up sort of dangling it in mid-air.

'So I took her out, bought her three vodka and limes, and told her the secret was to go out and lay his ghost,' Becky chimes in. I hadn't even noticed her coming back.

'The best way to get over someone is to get under someone else?' Emma says, taking a drink. She's one of those people who manages to just radiate cool. If I'd said that I'd have blushed extravagantly and probably got my words all tangled up into the bargain.

'I think so,' I say. 'I wish I could remember lines like that. I never think of the right thing to say until hours later, when I'm lying in bed reliving the whole conversation.'

'God, me too.' Alex looks at me and does an upside-down sort of smile, and the sides of his eyes crinkle a bit as he looks directly at me. I feel like we're on the same team for a second. It's nice. He lifts up the tequila bottle, waving it in Emma's direction. 'Oh go on,' he says. 'Throw caution to the wind. D'you want to make another one of those – whatever it was you just made?'

I feel like the world is starting to sway gently – or maybe I am. But I'm just the right sort of happily pissed where I feel like the edges have been blurred a bit and I don't feel as self-conscious as I usually do.

The other half a bottle of tequila later and we've managed to persuade Becky to put on something other than Christmas music. We're all sitting round the table, which is scattered with empty plates. The window isn't even open, but we can hear a gang of teenagers passing,

27

singing Christmas carols and laughing loudly. I get up and look outside, marvelling at the idea that outside there are eight million people, all living London lives, and in just a couple of weeks I'm going to be one of them. It's just an ordinary street, but to me it feels full of magic and promise.

I turn around to look at my new housemates. Emma's on her phone again, absent-mindedly twirling a lock of hair around her finger. I notice she has long, manicured red nails.

Alex looks up at me and grins. 'D'you think you can cope with living with us lot?' He starts stacking plates.

'No,' says Becky, firmly, tapping him on the hand. 'I'll do it in the morning. This is a get-to-know-each-other evening. When we're all in and settled, we can sort out a kitchen rota and all that boring stuff, but tonight is margaritas. The night is young. Let's play the name game.'

'Oh my God.' I roll my eyes at her. There's a point in every evening when she insists we do this. Before anyone else realises what's happening, she's got a packet of Post-it Notes out and she's handing them out. 'Everyone has to write the name of someone famous and stick it on the forehead of the person to their left.'

'And to think Rob's missing this,' says Alex, pressing the Post-it Note to my forehead. 'D'you want another drink?'

I feel distinctly head-spinny already, but I nod. This is my new London life. I can drink tequila and have avocado on toast and be cool. Well, cool-ish. Cooler than I was living back home. Not that there's anything wrong with back home, of course. I swallow a little gulp of sadness that sneaks up on me out of nowhere – just thinking about leaving Nanna Beth back there and me being all the way up here. She's already lost Grandpa, and now I'm going, too.

'Oh my God,' says Becky, seeing the name written on my forehead. She snorts with laughter.

'Am I a woman?' I say, when it's my turn.

'You're a phenomenon, I think you'd say,' Alex replies, grinning at me.

Emma guesses hers almost straight away (I think she's pleased she got to be Meghan Markle) and in no time there's just me and Alex, trying desperately to work out who we are.

'Do I have a unique blond hairstyle?'

We snort with laughter.

'Am I a megalomaniac? Am I the best president ever in the history of presidents? Is this the biggest Post-it Note, bigger and better than any Post-it Notes that have ever been before?'

Alex has already guessed, but he's making us laugh so hard with his terrible Donald Trump impressions that we're all doubled over, and mine falls off my forehead and onto the ground where I can't help sneaking a peek.

'Am I . . . Kim Kardashian?' I sit up, triumphant, waving the Post-it Note in the air.

'Yes.' Becky takes it from me. 'You're totally cheating, but you are definitely Kim Kardashian.'

'And I am definitely going to bed.' Emma pushes her

chair away from the table and stands up, looking at the kitchen clock. 'It's almost eleven, and I've got a killer day tomorrow. Back-to-back meetings.'

'But how can you leave us when we're just getting started?' Alex is standing by the sink now, brandishing a bottle of Prosecco and some sort of pink liqueur. 'I was going to make one of my signature cocktails.' He rummages in the fridge. I can't help but notice his nice arms again – I've always had a thing about nice arms, the kind that look like they'd wrap you up and make you feel safe. Oh, and the way that when he reaches up to get some orange juice from the top shelf his T-shirt rucks up, showing a strip of faintly tanned skin.

But I am absolutely not looking at any of this, because I am here to work, and he is my new housemate, and there will be none of that here. I blame the tequila for making my imagination run away with me.

But if I *was* looking . . .

'Night, all.' Emma picks up her phone and heads off. 'Have a great holiday, Jess. See you in the New Year.'

'You got any more ice, Becky?' Alex asks as he looks in the freezer.

'Nope.'

I know she's told us not to clear up, but I'm absent-mindedly piling plates and tipping leftover salsa into the bin. It's a distraction. The alternative is sitting with my chin in my hands staring with undisguised admiration at Alex, and that wouldn't be a good look.

'God I'm dying for some chocolate. I tell you what,

I'll go get some and grab some ice from Tesco Express while I'm at it.'

'We'll clean up.' Alex stands up from the freezer and turns around. 'And then I'll make cocktails. You don't think Rob will mind that we've borrowed his blender thing to crush ice?'

I pull a face. 'I dunno. I think it's knives chefs are funny about. Anyway, that thing's a monster. As long as we clean it out, I'm sure he won't object.'

Alex pokes an experimental finger at the huge behemoth of a blender standing on the worktop. It roars into life for a second and he steps backwards.

'Bloody hell. That thing could take your arm off.'

'Back in a sec,' Becky says, wrapping a scarf around her face and pulling on a bobble hat.

'Don't freeze,' I say, looking out the window. 'Oh look, the rain's turned to snow.'

'Really?' Alex and Becky join me, looking out. The snow is falling in flurries, swirling in the spotlight glow of the street lamp outside the front of our new home. It's disappearing as soon as it hits the wet pavement, but it looks gorgeously Christmassy and romantic nonetheless. For a moment we all stand in silence, watching it, all lost in our own thoughts.

Michael Blooming Bublé is playing in the background again.

It only takes me and Alex a moment to clear up the table, shoving the rubbish and recycling in the bins, and loading up the ancient dishwasher.

'My last place didn't have one,' Alex says, unwrapping a dishwasher tablet and shoving it in. 'This thing might be prehistoric, but it's a luxury. No more waking up in the morning to last night's dishes.'

'Were you in a house-share before?' I ask.

He pauses for a second. 'Mmm, sort of.'

I get the feeling there's more to it than he's saying, but I don't want to push it.

'And you used to work with Becky?'

I am standing by the sink, rinsing my hands, aware he's standing close beside me and putting glasses back on the shelf. I can feel the heat of his body and it makes the tiny hairs on my arms stand up. This is the tequila talking, I think. Tequila, and the fact that I have been single for a year and the only reason I fancy him is because I've been told there's no relationships allowed in this house so my brain is being contrary. He is Alex, a friend of my friend Becky, and my new housemate. And he is one hundred per cent off limits. I take a step sideways, drying my hands on the dishtowel and spending an excessive amount of time hanging it back up, neatly.

'I used to work with Becky, yeah,' says Alex, after a long pause.

I turn around.

'Turns out that thirty is the perfect time to have my first *oh my God what am I doing with my life* crisis.'

I find myself smiling. 'Me too.'

'So she's found herself a houseful of strays. That's very Becky, isn't it? She likes to think she's all corporate law

32

and hard as nails, but I reckon she's just as much of an old hippy as her mum. So what brings you here?' he asks.

'Oh God. It's a long story.'

Alex takes four limes from the fridge, then passes me two and a kitchen knife. 'Chop these, then, and tell all. It makes me feel better to know I'm not the only one making what everyone thinks is the biggest mistake of my life.'

He's taken a lemon zester and made a stack of bright green furls of lime zest, and he's putting them all together in a little grassy heap. I realise I've stopped chopping and I'm staring at his hands like some sort of weirdo.

'So I did English literature at uni. I've always loved books, and I used to dream of living in London and working in a publishing house, but it just seemed like you had to know someone in the business or have enough money to get an internship and work for nothing, and I had student loans to pay off, and bills to pay, and . . .' I pause, thinking of the responsibility of making sure that Nanna Beth and Grandpa were okay, because my mum was never around. I take a deep breath. 'Anyway, so I'd pretty much given up on that idea – I did look, but the money was terrible, and there was no way I could afford anywhere in London to live that wasn't basically a broom cupboard.'

He laughs. 'I actually know someone who lived in a cupboard. His bed literally folded down at night, then he'd fold it up, close the door, and go off to work.'

'Exactly.' Our eyes meet for a second and we laugh at the idea of it. London is strange.

33

'And then Becky came along?'

'Not quite. Basically, I was helping look after my grandpa and then he died.'

'Oh.' He turns to look at me, his brown eyes gentle. 'I'm sorry.'

I shake my head and curl my fingers into my palm, because I'm still at the stage where tears sneak up unexpectedly, and alcohol helps them along. 'It's okay. Anyway, my grandma – Nanna Beth – decided that she wanted to move into a sheltered accommodation place, and I'd been staying in their spare room.' I smile, as I always do, thinking about her. Everyone should have a grandma like mine. 'And then – when I'd moved back in with my mother, temporarily, Becky called and asked if I'd be interested in joining her house-share. My Nanna Beth kept telling me I should follow my dreams and do what I really wanted to because we only get one life, and I was trying to convince myself that actually, I was perfectly happy. Then I saw a job in *The Bookseller* – because I couldn't help looking, even though I knew it wasn't ever going to happen – and I thought I'd apply even though I had no chance, and I still can't believe they've given me it. And—' I stop and draw breath. It's all come out in a huge garbled sentence, just the same way that it all happened. 'One minute there I was thinking about it, and wondering how I was going to find somewhere to live and deal with my mother, and then next thing—'

'Here we are. That feels like fate,' Alex says, finishing my spoken and unspoken sentences.

'It does, a bit,' I say, trying to make a joke of it. 'What about you?'

'Oh I was all set. Law career on the up, nice – tiny – flat in Stokey, the lot. But I knew something was missing.'

I chop the limes into pieces, waiting for him to carry on.

'Anyway, I kept going for a while, but it was nagging away at me. I went into law to make a difference, but I realised that most of my life was going to be spent behind a desk pushing paper around, and it was boring me to death. And – some stuff happened.' He pauses for a second, and then says. 'And here *I* am.'

'So you're not doing law now?'

He shakes his head. 'No. That's how I knew Becky – we worked together. But unlike most other people, she was brilliant when I told her I was giving up. You need a friend like that on your side.'

'I agree,' I say, thinking of her insistence that I come and stay here, and the ridiculously low rent she'd suggested. I'd looked up Rightmove to see how much it would cost to rent a place like this, and I'd almost fainted. Basically a month's rent for a house this size was my annual publishing salary. When I'd mentioned it, Becky had just snorted and said something about redressing the balance, which had sounded suspiciously like something her mother would have said, so maybe the hippy stuff had rubbed off a bit after all.

'So,' I say, wincing slightly as a bit of lime juice squirts up and hits me in the face. 'What are you doing now?'

'Training to be a nurse,' Alex says.

'No way.' I put down the knife and look at him. 'That's amazing.'

'Yeah.' Alex gives me that same lopsided smile and looks relieved. 'That's not quite the reaction I got when I told people. It was more like: *Oh my God, why are you giving up a job that pays megabucks to be treated like crap, working for a failing NHS?*'

Not only is he gorgeous, but he's noble and ethical as well. He's like a unicorn, or something.

'Well I think what you're doing is brilliant.'

Alex tips the limes into a cocktail shaker and looks at me, his face serious. 'Thanks, Jess.'

I feel a bit wibbly. Like we've had a bit of a moment here together. Like we've bonded.

I pass him a glass, and we drink our cocktails and look out of the window at the Notting Hill street. He looks at me for a moment, just as I'm glancing at him.

For a second, our eyes meet again, and something inside me gives the sort of fizzing sensation that I've read about in books (oh, so many books) and never once felt in real life, not even in the four years I was with Neil, and he and I had talking about getting *married*.

I'm almost thirty, and I'd pretty much accepted that my secret love of terrible, brilliant, curl-up-on-the-sofa romantic movies had somehow cursed me. And yet here I was, looking directly into the chocolate-drop eyes of a man who looked like I'd ordered him online from the romantic movie store.

CHAPTER TWO

Jess

2nd January, Val d'Isère

'You got room in your case for these?'

My oldest friend Gen throws a bulging Tesco bag at me and I miss the catch. It bounces off the bed of the room we've been sharing for the last week and falls to the floor. I bend down to get it and emit a groan of pain. Everything hurts, and my head feels as if someone has hit me with a snowboard. I shouldn't have had that last cocktail last night. Or the one before. I stand up, holding the bag at arm's length. It smells like something died in it.

'What is it?'

'Don't ask.' Gen shakes her head. She should be even more hungover than me, but she somehow manages to look glowing and healthy, her skin bronzed after a week on the slopes where mine is scarlet and wind-chapped.

She's tied her hair back with a band, but spirals of red curls have already escaped and are framing her face. She's wearing an assortment of hideously clashing Nineties-style apres-ski clothes she found in a charity shop, and somehow it looks amazing on her.

I peer inside the bag and hold my nose. 'Ugh, honking ski socks.'

'If they ask if you packed your bag yourself, just say yes,' Gen says.

'And take responsibility for those?' I shove them in a corner of my case. 'They could probably walk home to London by themselves. Actually, I'm going to keep them,' I say, teasing Gen. 'When you're a famous actress, someone will pay a fortune for them.'

'Someone would pay a fortune for them now. There's a whole market for smelly socks on eBay,' says Sophie, who doesn't miss a trick when it comes to money stuff.

'That's disgusting.' I wrinkle my nose at the thought.

Being Soph, and therefore revoltingly efficient, she's already got her bag packed, and is sitting cross-legged on her bed, back against the wall, scrolling through her phone. 'Oh my God, Jess, that photo of us you've posted on Instagram is terrible. It looks like one of my legs is about to snap off.'

'It's not that easy to do a selfie on a ski lift,' I say, peering at her screen to remind myself. 'I was convinced I was going to drop the phone into a ravine.'

'Then you could have got Fabien to zoom down off piste and rescue it,' says Gen, making a dreamy face as

38

she mentions our gorgeous ski instructor. 'He definitely had the hots for you, Jess.'

'Shut up,' I groan. She's been going on about it all week, and I still haven't admitted to them that I've been daydreaming – and, if I'm honest, night-dreaming – about Alex, and accidental meetings in the kitchen where I'm dressed in a pair of cute PJ bottoms and a little vest top, my hair knotted up in a messy bun, just reaching into the fridge to get myself a glass of orange juice when his hands are on either side of my waist and he spins me round and looks at me with those incredible eyes and says . . .

'Jess?' Gen nudges me. 'You've been on another bloody planet all week. Come on, spill.'

I shake my head and zip up my suitcase. 'Just thinking, that's all.'

My phone bleeps and I look down at it. Both Gen and Sophie pick up their phones at the same time.

'Delay in coach pick-up,' we read in unison. 'You will now be collected from your hotel reception approximately two hours later than the scheduled time.'

'Oh God,' Soph groans. 'We could have gone skiing this morning after all.'

'Not without skis, we couldn't,' I point out, reasonably. 'We handed them back, remember?'

'Well, we can leave our bags here and go and have one last *vin chaud* at least.'

My stomach gives a warning lurch at the prospect. 'D'you not think we had enough of those yesterday?'

'And the day before, but one more won't hurt,' says Sophie, and we drag our cases down to reception and leave them behind the desk, collecting little tokens in exchange as they're locked away.

Outside there's no sign of the sun and the sky is thick with pale clouds, tinged with the faintest hint of violet. More snow on the way, it said on the forecast, after a week that had been absolutely gorgeous. The sun had shone so brightly that we'd sat at the piste café having lunch outside most days with our ski coats off, listening to the thudding bass of dance music, our skis standing upright in the snow. It feels sad to be leaving Val d'Isère, with its throng of holiday guests, swooshing past in their expensive-looking ski garb, heading up the chair lifts for another day of fun. We take a seat at the little wooden chairs outside the hotel and stretch our legs out in the sunshine. It's strange to be back in normal clothes, after a week of clomping around in heavy ski boots.

Celebrating New Year – and New Year's Day – in a ski resort has been amazing, but my liver feels like it needs to go on a rest cure. Not to mention my legs, which are aching so much I'm walking like a robot, and covered in bruises from a pretty spectacular fall when the aforementioned Handsome Fabien, the instructor we'd clubbed together to pay for, had tried to get us to go down a run that ended with *'une petit noir'*, except his idea of a little black run looked like a vertical drop. Sophie and Gen, who'd had more time on skis than me,

40

managed to make it down in one piece. I'd landed at the bottom, *on* my bottom, followed unceremoniously by one ski clonking me on the head (thank goodness for helmets) while the other one sailed past, over the edge of the piste and into the trees.

The waiter brings our order – hot chocolate laced with cream and a dash of rum for me and Gen, *vin chaud* for Sophie.

'It's amazing that we're all in the same place at the same time at the beginning of a year,' I say.

'Can't remember the last time that happened.' Sophie twirls a beer mat between her fingers, looking thoughtful. 'Wonder what we'll be doing this time next year?'

'Maybe I'll have had my big break,' says Gen, who has been saying that since she started drama classes back when we were in primary school.

'This is the year,' Sophie says, sounding determined. 'Rich and I are settling down. I'm going to be thirty. It's time. And I'm knocking these on the head, too.' She taps her glass with a neatly manicured finger.

'You're giving up drinking?' I look at Gen, and Gen looks at me, and together we look at Sophie.

'I don't want to take any risks.'

'You're not even thirty. *Nobody* has children when they're this age. You're the only person I know who is like a proper grown-up, Soph,' I say.

Gen nods. 'They'll make the house untidy and you'll have loads of plastic crap everywhere and you'll end up being one of those people who pisses everyone off in Pizza

Express because you turn up with a baby that screams the place down when we're all trying to have a nice hangover meal on Tesco points.'

'Thanks,' says Sophie, drily. 'I can't believe you spent so many years working as a mother's help. You're literally the most un-maternal person I've ever met.'

'I am not,' Gen protests, unconvincingly. 'I just don't understand why anyone would want to subject themselves to parenthood.'

'That's what she means,' I say.

'I am still here,' Sophie points out. 'As in sitting right here. Anyway, I won't have the sort of baby that screams in restaurants. If it does, I'll take it outside or something. But I've got it all planned out . . .'

There's a split second where Gen and I look at each other and make a face, and Sophie mutters something unrepeatable under her breath before we all laugh and she carries on. 'I'll get married this year. Then I want three kids and I want them before I turn forty.' She's actually counting this out on her fingers. 'If I have a two-year age gap, that's—'

'Soph, you're so *organised.*' Gen snorts with laughter. 'I don't even have a bloody house of my own, and you're planning everything out. I bet you've got a spreadsheet on Excel with all this stuff.'

'Shut up.' Sophie blushes a bit so we know that she absolutely does.

'Anyway, changing the subject.' Sophie purses her lips, but she's trying not to laugh. 'I'm so excited, Jess. I can't

42

believe we're all going to be in the same city. We can do lunches and go to the cinema and lovely girly stuff.'

'We can help you do fertility dances, or whatever it is you have to do to get pregnant,' says Gen, helpfully.

'Did you miss that class at school?' I say, and Sophie snorts. 'It's not fertility dances that get the job done.'

We all snigger, like we're thirteen again in science class with the biology teacher drawing pictures on the whiteboard.

'Ooh, we could help you find a wedding dress, Soph.' I'm imagining a montage of us, movie-style, all sitting around in the changing room of a wedding shop while she pops in and out with various different flouncy meringues on before she appears, radiant, in The Perfect Dress.

Sophie wrinkles her nose and looks a bit pink in the face. 'I've actually chosen one already.'

'No way.' My vision evaporates.

'Oh my God! I didn't know it was official!' Gen shrieks with excitement.

'It's not. But it's so gorgeous I decided it had to be The One.'

'Oh my God, this is so exciting,' says Gen, clapping her hands together. 'Have you got a photo of it on your phone?'

'I thought marriage was a tool created by the patriarchy to suppress women?' Sophie raises an eyebrow, keeping her phone curled tightly in her palm.

'Yes, yes, it is, but that doesn't mean I can't appreciate

a bit of dressing up, and that's basically what a wedding is, isn't it?'

Sophie opens her phone and scrolls down to show us a photo of the most perfect, understated, gorgeous dress. It's absolutely her, and I can see why she's fallen for it.

'Let's hope Rich doesn't have other plans,' Gen teased.

'Yeah, he might have run off with the girl in the flat next door while I've been away,' Sophie jokes, but we all knew there was no way that would happen. Rich and Sophie were the poster couple – the ones that were solid as a rock, the ones you could always rely on. Gen called them Mum and Dad sometimes, and I think Sophie secretly liked it. She's always wanted to be settled down, ever since we were little and playing together at primary school. Rich is the perfect match for her, and it was always a matter of when, not if, they'd get married. She met him at university and they've been smug (not) marrieds ever since. I reach over and give her arm a little squeeze.

'I'm so pleased for you, Soph. And I can't wait to be on Aunty Jess duty.'

Gen pulls a face, but we both know she's only teasing. She's happy for Soph even though she wouldn't like to be in her shoes. Her passion has always been acting, ever since the first time she stood on stage and played the starring role in *Bugsy Malone* in our primary school production. She's worked her backside off to get where she is – she may not be famous, but she's had a few decent roles in theatre productions off the West End, and

44

it's just a matter of time before she gets her big break. Gen believes in herself, that's half the battle, I think.

'And what about you, Jess?' Sophie looks at me thoughtfully.

'You're not still in mourning after Neil-gate, are you?'

'Gen,' says Sophie, 'if she was, she's hardly going to tell us now, is she?'

I shake my head. 'No, I am one hundred per cent definitely not in mourning over the end of my relationship with Neil.'

'Even though your mum thought he was *the perfect catch*?' Gen looks at me.

I shudder. 'Especially not because of that.'

I hadn't even been that upset when I found out he was cheating on me with someone else from the office – just slightly miffed that it was going to make work pretty awkward. After the initial shock of finding them together, I'd realised that I didn't really feel anything. That was a pretty good sign that it had run its course.

'Your mum just wants you settled down and happy,' Sophie says, kindly.

'Yeah,' I say, 'and she thinks because Neil dumped me for whatshername from accounts that I'm a complete failure as a human being.'

'That's not strictly true,' says Sophie, trying to make me feel better.

'Yes it is,' says Gen, who knows my mother as well as I do. 'She's weirdly fixated on the idea of Jess getting married and buying a nice house and having two-point-four children and a dog. Probably because she did the opposite.'

When I split up with Neil Mum had been absolutely horrified that I'd 'let him slip through my fingers'. I never knew my dad – she's never talked about him, and there's just a blank space on my birth certificate where his name should be – and she's absolutely determined that my life will be far more conventional than hers. It's weird.

'What's she saying about you moving to London?' Gen says.

'She's hoping I might meet a nice man and settle down.'

'Ironic,' Gen snorts, 'that your mother never did it but she wants it for you.'

'It's called transference,' Sophie says, thoughtfully. 'Or something like that. It's about wanting to live her life through yours, vicariously.'

'It's called being a total nightmare,' I say, scooping off some of the whipped cream on my drink with a spoon, and licking it.

'Oh she's not that bad,' says Gen, who has a soft spot for my mother because she's a fellow thespian. My mother's an actress too, but she's never made it to London. Instead she travels a bit, and she tries various schemes to keep money coming in, in between jobs working as a voice-over artist or being an extra on film sets. She's never really been the maternal type. It's lucky I've got my Nanna Beth to make up for it.

'No,' I concede. 'I think it'll be a lot easier to have a relationship with her when I'm ninety miles away in London than when she's breathing down my neck the whole time wanting to know what I'm doing with my life.'

The strange thing about Mum is that despite being unconventional herself, she's completely hooked on the idea of me doing a Soph and getting married, popping out a couple of grandchildren, and finding a nice house in the suburbs. It's weird. It also means she was Not Happy when Neil and I split up, and she thinks my plans for a new life in London are impractical and faintly ridiculous. I quote. Not that I'm still chuntering to myself over her saying it, of course.

'She'll be wanting regular relationship updates,' Gen says.

'There won't be any,' Sophie points out, shooting a quick look at Gen, 'because Becky has decreed that there's to be no relationships in the house.'

'She can't do that.'

'She can do whatever she bloody well wants if she's renting Jess a room in Notting Hill for £400 a month. I'd take a vow of chastity for that.' Gen takes a sip of her drink.

'Yeah but even so—' I watch Sophie giving Gen a fleeting look.

Sophie and Gen have met Becky a few times. They get on okay, in that way that friends do when you try and combine one part of your life with another part. I'm hoping that now we're all going to be in the same place they'll get to know each other a bit more, and even get on a bit.

47

'She isn't banning me from having sex with anyone,' I say. 'Just that there's to be no inter-house relationship stuff.'

'Just as well. You've got the whole of London at your disposal. You downloaded Tinder yet?' Gen asks. She curls one of her ginger ringlets around her finger, then lets it go so it springs back into place. Gen's never had a bad hair day in her life.

'Ugh, no.' I shudder. 'The thing is I'm not really a Tinder sort of person.'

'Mmm.' Sophie nods. I wonder what she means by that.

I sigh. 'Anyway the thing is there's a bit of a problem with Becky's whole plan. I mean, there's being practical, and then there's – well, do you believe in fate?'

Gen cups her chin in both hands and leans forward. 'Tell me more.'

'I totally do,' says Sophie. 'I mean look at me and Rich.'

I think about the two of them and catch a glimpse of Gen, who doesn't say a word but there's a split second when her nostrils flare, which is always a tell with her, and I know she's thinking *Sophie and Rich*, the most practical couple in the world?

'Come on,' Gen urges. 'Spill.' She looks at Sophie and they look back at me.

'It's not – I mean it couldn't go anywhere. I'm just being silly,' I begin. 'It's, um, Alex.'

'Ahhh,' they say, and exchange another glance.

'What d'you mean, *ahh*?' I cup my hot chocolate in both hands, holding it in front of me defensively.

'Oh, just Alex . . . as in the new housemate you've casually mentioned about fifteen times a day for the last week?' Sophie's eyebrows lift and she gives a snort of laughter.

'No,' says Gen, totally straight-faced. '*Alex*, as in the guy who's training as a nurse and isn't that amazing because he's given up being a *lawyer* to do something that really *matters* . . .'

'Shut up, you two.' I can feel my cheeks are going pink, and put my hands against them so my face is all squashed up, and I make a silly fish face at them to make them laugh and hide my blushes. I feel like I'm about fourteen again.

'Yeah, we wondered how long it'd be before you actually admitted to us that you've got a massive grade-A crush on him. I mean it's been pretty obvious. But—' Gen pauses to beckon the waiter, before asking, 'how does that work with Becky's no-relationships rule in the house?'

'I'm pretty sure that's not enforceable,' says Sophie, her brow furrowing. She's a stickler for rules and regulations and things. She takes out her phone.

'Don't google it,' I say, warningly, and she puts her mobile back on the table, making a face because I've caught her out. 'Becky's totally right. It would never ever work. Plus, I'm starting a new job, and I've got a brand-new life to be getting on with.'

'Yeah, and gorgeous men who wear nurses' scrubs and walk into your life completely out of the blue are ten a penny in London,' Sophie says.

'Totally.' Gen nods, earnestly. 'That's why I've been single for bloody eternity, and why you haven't had sex since Sad Matthew.'

'Don't,' I say, covering my whole face in my hands now. I'd had an accidental one-night stand with Matthew-from-school after Neil and I split up, and every time he got pissed he'd text long, drunken messages telling me how he thought we were the perfect couple, and how it wasn't too late. In the end, I'd blocked him, feeling only about five per cent guilty. The rest of me was deliriously happy to have him out of my hair.

'Anyway. You can't let him just slip through your fingers.' Gen looks up at the waiter and asks for some more drinks and a plate of chips to share. It's half ten in the morning and my stomach contracts with horror at the thought.

'He's hardly going to slip through my fingers. He's sleeping in the room next door.'

'And Becky's on the second floor. She'll never know,' says Gen, waggling her eyebrows. 'You can just sneak into his room after dark. That's quite romantic.'

'Or creepy,' said Sophie, pulling a face. 'Honestly, I'm sure Becky would be fine. Maybe when she said no couples, she probably meant it as in *no couples moving into the flat*, not that you all had to take a vow of chastity when you signed the lease.'

50

I make a face. I think Becky was pretty bloody unequivocal about it. 'I think that's probably just as well. I think keeping a vow of chastity with him in the room next door might be pretty much impossible.'

I think of Alex reaching up to get something from the cupboard and the sight of his bare skin underneath his T-shirt and the way it felt when I was standing beside him and my arms were all prickly with goose bumps and I give a tiny shiver of anticipation. Maybe when I go back, the best thing to do would just be to get it out in the open. Ask him out for a drink. There's nothing wrong with asking someone out for a drink, is there? And if it happens to lead to something else, well . . .

CHAPTER THREE

Jess

3rd January, London

I think there is a strong possibility that my body is going to be bent into this position forever. We've been on a coach for twenty-one hours, and I can't remember who I am. When I stand up, everything aches. I took a travel sickness pill and I've slept groggily for so long that I have to count on my fingers to work out what day it is. Victoria Coach Station doesn't look any more glamorous at 5.30 a.m. than it does in the middle of the day – in fact, it probably looks worse without people all around. It smells cold and damp and grey, but inside I feel a tiny fizz of excitement that I'm back home – that London, the city I've always loved, is home.

I've done what feels like the scariest thing of all in changing career when I was perfectly safe and secure. My stomach contracts when I think about it and all the things that could go wrong. It's a bit of a weird leap from managing a marketing company to working as Operations Manager for a publishing house where I'll be in charge of making sure books go from finished manuscripts to products on the shelves. It's still weird to think of books as products, if I'm completely truthful. I look at the posters on the bus station hoardings – half of them are for books. Someone like me helped that to happen. It feels like a huge, pretty terrifying responsibility. I swallow and turn back to the girls, who are organising their bags.

'I want ALL the details on what happens when you get back,' Gen says, hugging me goodbye before she hops in an Uber.

'Come for dinner next Friday?' Sophie kisses me on the cheek. Rich's waiting by the road to give her a lift home. Getting up at five in the morning to collect her from the coach is the most Rich thing he could do.

'Sure you don't want a lift?'

I shake my head. There's an early morning bus in ten minutes, and I want to stand up while I wait, stretch my legs, and think about what I'm going to do when I get home. And then I beam with happiness at a flock of unsuspecting pigeons. I think this year is going to be pretty bloody amazing.

Even though I'm so tired I feel like a zombie I can't help smiling to myself as the bus makes its way along the streets. London looks so pretty, dusted with the finest icing-sugar coating of frost. It sparkles on the top of stone walls and expensive-looking black railings, making the red telephone boxes look picture-postcard pretty. This is home. I squeeze my arms around myself, because I can't quite believe it's true. I feel warm and sleepy in my thick ski coat. My head leans against the cool of the bus window and I watch the city coming to life.

Two early-morning runners, clad in thermals with reflective stripes, zoom past as we wait for a traffic light to turn from red to green. Christmas trees still light up the windows of houses, which makes me happy. I always feel sad for the trees I see lying waiting for collection on the kerbside, piled up with heaps of black rubbish bags. When I have a house of my own, I'm going to have a tree in every room and the whole place lit up with millions of tiny, starry white lights. I think about growing up and how I used to decorate my bedroom, and how my mum couldn't wait to take the decorations down because she hated the mess and how Nanna and Grandpa used to make up for it with a tree they always let me decorate, hung with trinkets I'd made at primary school and riotous rainbows of tinsel. And then as we turn down into Church Street, my mind skips forward, imagining this time next year, and all of us celebrating Christmas in the house in Albany Road. Rob could cook – there had to be an advantage to living with a chef, surely – and I'd be there, dressed in something clinging and sexy, and—

I look out of the window, and realise I'm at Ladbroke Grove. After I get off the bus, I grab my bag and bump it along the street, the wheels sounding loud in the early morning silence. And then I turn the corner, and there's the street sign that announces I'm home. Albany Road. I live in London now, I say to myself quietly, stepping back to take it all in.

'Watch it!'

A man looms out of nowhere on a bike and speeds off, his wheel lights flashing. He's muttering something and I don't think it's very polite, somehow. But nothing is going to take the tarnish off this moment. The house is in darkness and I climb the stone steps, lifting the suitcase up so it doesn't make a noise. I'm aware that it's early and I don't want to wake anyone up. I stand at the huge red-panelled door for a moment.

I turn the key in the lock and open the door slowly. There's a sidelight on in the hall, and a pile of junk mail on the wooden dresser. Hanging on a hook there's a battered straw hat covered in tinsel. There's a tired-looking plastic Christmas tree, and three empty wine bottles that look like they've been dumped on the floor by the door, waiting to go out in the recycling bin. The house smells of stale beer and leftover pizza, like a student flat. I guess the New Year celebrations must have been ongoing. I creep upstairs and open the door to my room. Becky has made up the bed (I love her so much for that at this moment that I could run upstairs and hug her, but something tells me she wouldn't appreciate that) and the curtains are drawn.

I dump my case and my bag, and sit down on the edge of the bed for a moment. I feel completely wide awake, and as I sit there I realise that next door, with only a wall between us, is Alex. And – I hear a clonking noise, and the sound of footsteps – I realise he's awake. I could go and say hi. That would be perfectly normal, if he's awake. I mean admittedly it's – I check my watch – quarter past six in the morning, but maybe he's an early bird. I might just pop to the loo, and if I happen to bump into him . . . well, that's just coincidence, isn't it? Totally normal coincidence.

(Yes, I'll check my face in the mirror while I'm in there, wipe the eyeliner smudges from underneath my eyes, and fluff up my hair. I do that every time I go to the loo. Doesn't everyone?)

I open my bedroom door, and his door opens at exactly the same time. My heart gives a massive thump against my ribcage. This is *meant to be*.

And then *Emma* walks out, and heads towards the bathroom. She doesn't turn around, so she doesn't see me, and as the bathroom door closes I recoil backwards into my room like a snail into its shell, then floomp onto the bed with a groan. Why on earth is Emma coming out of Alex's room? If they've swapped bedrooms, that means he's across the other side of the stairwell, and I've been stealthily listening to her getting ready for work. She's exactly the sort of person who *would* get up at six a.m. She's probably done yoga already, and now she's going to drink some green juice and meditate before she does an hour of paperwork then goes into the office. She's a proper grown-up.

And then I realise that I'm still desperate for the loo,

so I stand up and open my bedroom door, just as Emma walks out of the bathroom.

'Oh! Jess. Hi,' she says in a whisper, smiling with her perfect teeth. 'Have you just got back? Did you have a lovely time?'

'It was amazing,' I say, and then I open my mouth again to ask if they've swapped rooms in my absence, and close it when I realise that she's walking past me, in a kimono-style dressing gown made of some sort of swishy silk material, and heading for the bedroom at the end of the hall. Her bedroom.

I lean back against the door of my room, and it sinks in. Emma, our beautiful housemate, has spent the night with Alex.

CHAPTER FOUR

Alex

3rd January

Oh. My. God. My head feels like someone used it as a punchbag. I reach down the side of the bed where Past Me has thoughtfully left half a bottle of Coke. It's completely flat and tastes like crap, but it washes down the double dose of ibuprofen and paracetamol I'm hoping might crack this hangover. What the hell was I thinking last night? Today's going to be a killer – a twelve-hour shift in A&E, full of half-pissed Christmas casualties (and that's just the staff). Oh bollocks – and I've just remembered that effing assignment I was supposed to do last night on Modern Nursing Practices and the *Something of Something*.

I rub my chin. And I need to get my beard sorted before I tip over into looking like someone who's been lost in a cave for a month. God, I should've been working that essay last night and yet instead I found myself sharing a bottle of red with Emma. And another one. And – I open one eye carefully, because it feels like someone's shining lasers in my direction – how the hell did I end up in bed with her, when I'd made a resolution that the last time was the Last Time? Capital letters, no going back.

I stumble to the bathroom and stand under the shower for ages, trying to wash off the hangover and straighten my head out. I didn't even mean to start something with Emma. In fact – I run my hands through my hair and groan again – it's probably best to not think of it as a *something* at all. Definitely not the sort of something that would get in the way of Becky's no-couples rule. After all, we're just two people, who'd ended up in a bit of a situation, and who were looking for the same thing. People do that sort of thing all the time.

Not me, admittedly, because I've never been a one-night stand sort of guy, but then – well, that all got screwed up last year when Alice walked out and I swore I was going to focus on work and absolutely definitely not on relationships. Not that I was planning on being a player or anything – that's not me, either. Just that I was going to focus on work, and studying, and leave the complications out of it. That's why Becky's no-relationships rule didn't make me flinch, even if it did seem a bit weird. To be honest with you, I'd have taken a vow of chastity for the next five years if it meant I could get a place like this for the ridiculously low rent she was willing to take.

Just as well she didn't make me take one, mind you. I switch off the shower and think back on how it all happened as I'm drying myself off.

I'd been working a late shift, and when I'd got home at eleven the house was empty. Rummaging through the fridge, I'd found a beer, cracked it open and sat down at the table, scrolling through my phone. The thing was just about falling over with a million notifications from friends – half of whom I hadn't heard from in ages because of the whole Alice thing – sending mass WhatsApp invites to New Year's celebrations. The old me would've been up for it, but the new Alex – wrecked after a night working 'supply as an HCA on A&E – couldn't think of anything worse. As I went to put my phone down, another notification had buzzed through. It was a text from Jonno:

We're in the Pig and Bucket. Come and find us when you've finished playing doctors and nurses. Fizz on ice.

Oh, piss off, I thought, and chucked the phone across the table. The joke was wearing a bit thin at this point. I've heard a million and one variations on the doctors and nurses theme, countless boring jokes about male nurses, and I still get the odd bemused message from former uni friends who'd heard through the grapevine I'd given up a perfectly good burgeoning law career to retrain as a nurse.

'Hi,' Emma had said, and I'd looked up. I had to admit she looked pretty bloody amazing. The cut of the dress emphasised the curve of her waist and cinched her breasts up so they were balanced, like two scoops of ice cream, spilling over the top of her dress. I looked away rapidly. Note to self: do not look in direction of chest. I stared down and picked at the label of my beer. She threw her keys on the table and sat on a chair, looking disconsolate.

'Bad night?' I asked.

'Shitty.' She screwed up her face. 'I hate New Year. Too much enforced jollity.'

'D'you want a beer? I think there's a couple left in the fridge.'

She nodded. 'Yes please.'

I got up, fetching one for her and another for me out of the fridge, and cracking them open.

She hooked a long strand of hair back behind her ear, and took a sip of beer from the bottle. 'I knew it would be a disaster. Work friends, and a load of people I didn't want to see. Well, one person, to be completely honest.' She grimaced again. 'My ex.'

God I could sympathise there. I'd been avoiding all social gatherings where there was a chance I'd bump into Alice for ages now. It made the whole division of friendships thing quite easy, mind you. Alice got pretty much everyone, and I got – well, most of them were work colleagues, so it wasn't a major deal. And I'd made a couple of good friends on the course, which really helped . . .

'Sorry, you were saying?' I said, realising I'd drifted into my own thoughts. 'So you work with him? That must be awkward.'

Emma pulled a face. 'Sort of. He's in the same building, and our companies work side by side, so he's always sort of – there. Which is how I ended up in a relationship with him. But he's still very married, despite his insistence that he was going to leave her.'

'Oh God, that old line.'

'Yeah. Exactly.' She fiddled with her keys, spinning each one round on the ring, before putting them carefully back on the table. 'Anyway, much as I am over him – and I am . . .'

As she trailed off, I raised my eyebrows, giving her a look. 'Really?'

'Totally. But you know what? Not the sort of over him that I want to spend my New Year's Eve watching him with his wife, drinking champagne and casting glances in my direction. I'm not some bit on the side, which is what I told him in the first place. Anyway.' She took another swig of beer, then got up, heading for the fridge. 'It's almost midnight. We can celebrate here, instead.'

She pulled out a bottle of champagne. I'd seen it in the fridge and wondered who owned it – my guess was right. Emma looked like the sort of person who'd drink posh champagne. Becky was a tequila girl, Rob would have to be around at some point to have left champagne in the fridge, and so far he hasn't been, and Jess hadn't moved in yet. The champagne was an expensive brand, the kind we used to open to celebrate successes in the office. Now I was on a student loan though, and living on my savings, it was beer all the way. Cheap beer, at that.

'Want some?'

I nodded. 'Yes please.'

She found two glasses and popped the cork. 'Let's put some music on. Alexa, play some New Year's music.'

'Here's a playlist for New Year's music,' said the speaker. Ed Sheeran started playing and we both shouted 'Alexa, stop!' at the same time, laughing.

'I'll find something on my phone,' Emma said.

A couple of glasses – and some debate over Emma's dodgy taste in music – later, we decided to go through to the sitting room to watch the New Year celebrations on television at midnight. As if by agreement, we both flopped down on the sofa. Emma kicked off her heels and curled up her legs underneath her. In the background, a band was playing music at Edinburgh Castle with a horde of familiar TV faces standing at the side of the screen, trying to look animated. They were clearly freezing cold.

'So what about you?' Emma said. 'I know you said you were living with someone before. Are *you* still friends?'

I gave a groan and stretched my arms out above my head until various joints creaked. I really needed to get to the gym. 'Not really,' I replied.

'Hard, isn't it? I don't know many people who stay friends with their ex.'

'Yeah.'

Emma poured another glass of champagne for us both. 'The thing is, Alice signed up for the lawyer boyfriend, lots of money, and a nice house.' I looked around at the tattered Seventies décor and raised my eyebrows at Emma. 'This isn't exactly her sort of thing. We had a place in Stoke Newington – a nice little flat. It was pretty much all mapped out – two-point-four children, dog, cat, move out to the suburbs eventually . . .'

'Ugh,' Emma said, making a face. 'That sounds like hell.'

'Everyone says that,' I said, spinning my glass round on my knee, slowly. 'Thing is, I think I'm a bit of a romantic at heart. I wanted the whole thing.'

'That's quite sweet,' Emma said. 'Even if it's my idea of hell. I don't even like being responsible for a potted plant.'

'Yeah, well, we were engaged and everything. Then we had some family stuff happen, and I realised that actually I didn't want to carry on doing law. I wanted to do something that made a difference. That's how I ended up getting into nursing.'

'That's fair enough.'

'Yeah. Not for Alice, it turned out. She'd had our future all mapped out, and my giving up the well-paid job with prospects for a career in a failing NHS wasn't on her to-do list.'

'So when you gave up on law, she gave up on you?'

'Yeah,' I said, and took a large swig of champagne. 'Pretty much.'

Emma reached over, putting a hand on my leg. 'I'm sorry. That's pretty brutal.'

'Thanks,' I said, and looked down at Emma's hand, which hovered there for a second. And I'd like to say that we carried on watching the television and then went to our separate beds after the bells struck midnight and that was that. But no. Turned out I was only human, after all, and that after a bottle of champagne and some sort of dodgy liqueur from the back of the kitchen cupboard, and some pretty direct flirting from Emma, my resolve to stay celibate and focus completely on my studies was – well, it wasn't as steely as all that. And afterwards, when I was lying on the bed watching her fastening her bra and slipping the impossibly tight red dress back on, Emma had turned to me and smiled.

'Nobody needs to know this ever happened,' she'd said.

'Not a soul,' I'd agreed. 'Becky would murder us, for one thing.'

'Nice though,' she'd said, and given a wicked little smile that had made me want to pull her back into bed.

Bloody hell.

And then last night it happened *again*.

I wipe the mirror in the bathroom and look at myself through the condensation. Still look like the same old me – bit knackered, perhaps, because I've been up shagging half the night – but no, definitely still the same old Alex. I raise my eyebrows at Mirror Me and suppress a snort of laughter. It's the most out-of-character thing I've ever done. I try and imagine the faces of Jack and Lucy when I tell them. Jack and Lucy are my two best friends back home in Canterbury (who conveniently got off with each other a couple of years back, meaning that now they live together and I can see both of them in one go when I go back to visit). They're always telling me to get on dating apps and have a rebound shag to get over Alice. Well, I guess I've done it. Didn't even have to download Tinder.

I wrap the towel round my waist and head back to my bedroom, opening the window even though it's freezing cold outside. It's ridiculously early in the morning and the house is almost completely silent, but I can hear noises, I think. Sounds like someone's moving boxes in the room next door. Jess? I check the calendar hanging on the wall. God, yes, it's the third. She must've arrived overnight – I put a hand over my mouth – God, I hope she didn't arrive when we were . . .

No. We'd have heard the door, wouldn't we? She must've arrived when I was in the shower.

I pull on jeans and a clean T-shirt, running my hand back through my hair to shove it into place. Even if Jess had heard, she wasn't likely to say anything. It didn't have to be a big deal. Even if I have to have a conversation with Becky about the whole no-couples thing . . . well, it's not like we're actually a couple.

This is all completely new ground for me, though, and it's weird. Jack and Lucy always took the piss out of me for being an old romantic, but the thing is, what happened with Alice really took the wind out of my sails. I loved her, and I thought we were going to do the whole married, house, kids, dogs thing – especially the dogs, I've always wanted a golden retriever – but it floored me completely when she told me it was over. I was a complete mess for ages, but I've got a grip now. I'm just not putting myself in that place again for a long time. Relationships are not for me.

I'm glad Jess is back. Now the house is full, it feels sort of . . . complete, somehow. I'm sure she said she's not starting work until the second week of January. Maybe I'll see if she fancies coming for a walk tomorrow, to find her feet a bit. It'll be nice to have a friend who's a girl, and not a girlfriend. I miss Lucy's point of view on things – since she and Jack got together they basically come as a package.

I lace up my boots and I think about Jess chopping limes and chatting to me in the kitchen. Grudgingly, I have to admit to myself that in another life, Jess would be completely my type. She's funny and she's interesting, and I love the fact that she's doing the same as me: taking the plunge to try something new and start life over again. It'd be good to have a partner in crime. It makes it seem less terrifying, somehow.

CHAPTER FIVE

Jess

10th January

'What's with you and the whole Instagram thing?' Alex asks.

He's walking behind me on a narrow pavement in Covent Garden when I stop dead. He almost crashes into the back of me. I turn around, before he's stepped back, and we're so close we're almost touching. I stumble backwards, knocking into the wooden shutter of the cheese shop.

'Sorry,' I say, but he's laughing.

'It's fine. I just . . . What're you even taking a photo of?'

I motion to the alleyway to our left. 'I love stuff like that. Little hidden doorways and things.'

'Right.'

'Let me just . . .' I fiddle with the phone then hit share. 'Sorry. Done now.'

'Shall we stop for lunch?' he asks.

'Yeah.' I point to the sign that beckons us through the little alleyway. 'There's a café upstairs there, in Neal's Yard.'

We climb the stairs, which are rainbowed with a million postcards and posters, advertising everything from toddler gymnastics to Chakra Rebalancing.

'D'you get your chakras rebalanced often?' Alex grins.

'Never. That's probably why I'm so clumsy.'

'Maybe they should start offering it on the NHS.'

The café's cramped and the staff seem slightly frazzled, which feels at odds with the whole hippy Zen vibe it's giving off from the signs outside. We find an empty table. The uneven walls are painted with thick white paint, and woven hangings are displayed on a rail with price tags underneath. I lean forward, thinking I must have read it wrong, but no.

'They want £120 for that?' I nudge Alex and his eyes widen in surprise. He passes me a menu. We both look at it in silence for a moment.

'Hi, people,' says a tall woman with her braids tied back in a thick ponytail. 'Do you need time to have a think, or are you ready to order?'

I catch Alex's eye and I can tell he's trying not to laugh, because the menu is – well, it's not Starbucks, that's for sure.

'Can we have a couple of moments?'

'Sure. I'll leave you some of this for now. It's rose-quartz-infused water.'

She puts a carafe down on the table. There's a pink crystal sitting at the bottom of it. We both contemplate it for a moment before Alex drops his head in his hands.

'If we weren't so bloody British, we'd get up and leave,' he says.

'I know.'

'Instead, we're going to have to have a rice milk latte and a—' he looks down at the menu and frowns '— spiralised courgette and carrot hummus open sandwich on pressed raw grain bread?'

'I dunno, I quite fancy the radish and sprout salad,' I say.

'I want a cinnamon and raisin bagel, and a large bucket of coffee.'

I groan at the thought of it. 'I wouldn't say no to a bacon roll.'

'Maybe we could get one on the way back.'

'Ready to order?' The woman has returned, and – being too polite to leave – we request our food, then sit back and look at the clientele. There's a woman with two scruffy-haired children who've been freed from their pushchair. They're climbing over the cushions on the bench to draw pictures with thick crayons.

'Cute.' Alex looks over at them.

'I bet they're called Hephzibah and Moon Unit, or something.' I take a look at them, trying not to catch their eye in case they come over and start making conversation. I find small children slightly alarming.

'No way.' Alex shakes his head. 'Myrtle and Theodore,

and they go to a Steiner school and her husband earns shitloads working as an investment banker.'

'Like the ones next door to us? You reckon?'

'Totally.'

We've seen the family from next door going in and out a few times. They've got two nannies, I think, and a gardener, and a fleet of cleaning people who come in every morning. The children go off to school wearing the kind of expensive-looking woollen coats and hats that suggest they're at a posh private school.

'They must think we're lowering the tone, don't you think?'

Alex grins. 'What, Becky and her random collection of low-rent waifs and strays?'

After the waitress brings our food, Alex takes a bite of his open-topped sandwich and makes a face. 'God, this is disgusting.'

'It is a bit weird,' I say, picking a radish off the top of mine and biting into it. It's got some sort of lime dressing on it. I steer the conversation back to Becky and the house. 'I don't think Becky knows what to do with the house, so it seemed like the easiest thing to do.'

'Have you looked at the price of houses on our street?' Alex raises an eyebrow.

I nod. 'Have you?'

'She's like – literally beyond your wildest dreams rich. She could sell that and give up work forever.' He sits back, giving up on the sandwich.

'Not if she wanted to live in London.' I carry on dissecting my food.

'True. Anyway we better not go putting ideas in her head when we've just signed a lease, or we'll be screwed. There's no way I could afford a place in central London on what I've got.'

'Me neither.'

We sit back in silence, watching the children as they try and climb out of their chairs and escape.

It's only been a week, but Alex and I have got into a bit of a routine with our Exploring London walks. He's had some time off, and it's been nice to wander about and find my bearings a bit. I still reckon I could get lost quite easily, but I'm beginning to join bits of the city up and make sense of it. My first day is next Monday – and I'm being extremely noble about the fact that there's *something* going on with him and Emma. Although I'm not sure what that something is – I haven't heard any more nocturnal happenings but I can't be sure. I'm just repressing all thoughts about how gorgeous he is.

He gets up to use the loo, climbing out of the tiny space in the corner where our table's situated. A woman with a baby in a backpack asks him to help reach the highchair that is hanging folded on the wall behind us, and I try very hard not to notice as he reaches up, showing a strip of slightly tanned skin and the edge of his boxers peeking out underneath his jeans. Okay, I've repressed *almost* all thoughts. I am human, after all, and living with the nicest man you could imagine who just happens to be sleeping – on the quiet – with one of your other housemates isn't quite as easy as you'd think. I grit my teeth and make a face, surprising the waitress, who looks at me with a confused expression.

-

.

.

-

.

'

CHAPTER SIX

Jess

14th January

The office of Elder Branch Publishing is smaller than I remember from my interview. Or maybe I just expanded it in my imagination in the six long weeks between being offered the job and waiting to start. Anyway, the nice thing is that it's as bookish as I remember. And when I walk in, an office full of heads shoot up, meerkat-style, and my face goes very red.

'Ah, Jessica,' Veronica greets me. Veronica is the publisher, which I've learned means she's basically where the buck stops. She's very nice, very posh, and very busy. I don't correct her and tell her it's Jess, because she's quite fierce and I'm extremely nervous.

'So, as you'll know, as Operations Manager you're responsible for keeping all the publications on track, but of course you got the job, so we can be certain that you're going to be absolutely wonderful. This is Sara. She'll show you the ropes.'

Sara gives me a tour of the office. She's tall and thin, in a flowery dress, and opaque mustard-yellow tights that match her cardigan. In fact everyone in the office seems to be wearing a variation on the same outfit. Most of them are in a meeting, but the handful I've met have that shiny, expensive-looking hair that comes from being well-nourished and brought up with lots of healthy outdoor activities. They've all got the same accent too – sort of home counties crossed with London – and I'm feeling distinctly suburban. Sara's hair is held back from her face with a Kirby grip, which she takes out and puts back in about five times in the process of our conversation.

'So, basically your job is just to make sure you keep all of us in line, hahaha,' she snorts, as if the idea is slightly unlikely.

'Not all of us are as disorganised as you,' says a voice from the other side of my desk. A head pops up. 'Hiya. I'm Jav.'

She's tall and slender in a pair of black trousers and a jade green tunic, her long black hair hanging down her back. Her desk is neatly stacked with books and thick printed manuscripts, a pencil case from The Strand bookstore in New York, and a reusable coffee cup. It looks exactly like you'd expect an editor's desk to look.

'Jess,' I reply, with a little wave.

'Jav likes to put us all to shame by terrifying her authors into delivering on time.'

Jav raises her eyes skyward. 'I just happen to be efficient, that's all.'

Unlike the rest of my colleagues, she's got an accent from somewhere up north – Manchester or somewhere around there – and I warm to her instantly. Not just because she's efficient, although I have to be honest and admit that's a bit of a plus. I've been used to working at my own pace in the past, and I'm a bit apprehensive about my work performance now hanging on whether a manuscript gets delivered on time or if a publishing schedule goes awry. I swallow and try and look as if I'm super confident.

Sara steps back and gives a ta-dah sort of wave in the direction of my desk. It's empty, with a desktop computer and a leftover stack of Post-it Notes sitting beside the keyboard. Someone's already left me three proof copies of books that aren't out until next summer. I look at the covers and can't help thinking how nice it would be to climb into one of them and—

'Right,' I say, tapping the top of my desktop monitor in what I hope is an authoritative manner, 'I better get to work.'

'I've left email logins on a Post-it Note – you can change your password and stuff, obviously, and there's a meeting about the Tiny Fish publicity campaign at half ten. You should pop in, meet the rest of the team.'

Jav pushes her chair sideways when Sara leaves, and swings herself round.

'Just shout if there's anything you need.' She tucks a stray lock of black hair back behind her ear. 'I know it's a bit scary on the first day, especially when you're not – well—' she lowers her voice '—one of the posh lot, but they're all very sweet really.'

'Oh God. How did it go?' Becky drops her bag beside me on the kitchen table with a crash. I'm sitting with my head in my hands, my hair hiding my face, so I can see why she's thinking the worst. I lift my face up to see her looking at me, head on one side, like a concerned sparrow.

'Oh, it was fine. I'm just so tired that I can't move. You know what it's like when you start a new job – you've got so much stuff to remember and your brain gets overloaded. I could literally fall asleep here.'

'That's not a good idea,' she says, briskly. 'We're supposed to be going to Pilates, remember?'

'Oh my God. I can't.'

'It'll be good for you.'

'I don't want to engage my core and strengthen my glutes. I want to lie on the sofa with a tub of Ben and Jerry's and watch crap on TV.'

'You can do that afterwards. It's not on until nine.'

'You know what I mean.'

She hooks me under the elbow and tugs me up to standing. 'Come on, I'm not going on my own. Last time I did that creepy Charles tried to hit on me afterwards.'

'FINE,' I say, yawning so hard my jaw cracks.

The thing about living in Notting Hill is that even the most basic gym class is super posh. There's a string of black Range Rovers parked outside the fitness studio, and inside everyone's Lululemoned from head to toe. I'm in a bog-standard pair of sports leggings from JD Sports and a vest top, so I hide at the back of the room so nobody notices me, taking a yoga mat and parking myself in the corner beside a young mum who has a sleeping baby in a carrier. Becky's standing at the door answering a last-minute call when the instructor walks in.

'Hello, everyone.' She's a cheerful looking Australian woman of about forty-five, with the figure of an eighteen-year-old. Her buttocks are so perky that they look like they need their own morning TV show. She tosses her water bottle to the side of the room and claps her hands. Her ponytail swings. Oh God, I think, this is shaping up to be a torture session.

'Now then,' she says, giving me a welcoming smile. 'We're going to shake things up slightly this evening, for those of you who like to hide in the corners. Pull your mats back a couple of feet.'

Everyone does as they're told. There's a very quiet murmur of dissent, but nobody's brave enough to speak up.

'Excellent. So the back row is now the front row, and the front row is the back.' She looks very pleased with herself.

I don't know who's more disappointed – the Lycra-clad goddesses who like to show off in front of everyone, or the scruffy reprobates like me who are now centre stage. I'm pretty certain my knickers have gone up my bum and now I can't hoick them back out.

I haven't been to a gym class since school, when Miss Bates the terrifying PE teacher used to make us do yoga with a side order of military-style barked instructions. Now I'm standing beside my mat wondering what exactly I'm expected to do.

We start off lying down, and it all seems very restful and soothing. But the next thing I know we're on our sides doing something with our legs that's making me want to cry. I'm not the only one. Just as we shift positions, the baby starts screaming at the top of his lungs, and there's a brief – but oh God, much appreciated – pause as his mother hisses an apology and gathers him up and exits, trailing muslin cloths and water bottles, her yoga mat unravelling behind her. I eye the clock. Another half an hour to go and then I can escape.

'Keep those heels together. We want to feel those glutes engaging,' she says, cheerfully.

My glutes feel like they've been set on fire and I don't think I'll ever be able to sit down again. This is torture.

It's possible it'll go down in history as the longest half hour of my life. I've seen Pilates classes before, and I always thought they looked pretty gentle – like exercise classes for people who can't be bothered getting all sweaty. Except now I'm lying face down on the floor with my arms by my sides, doing what looks like the tiniest little movement. I wait until the instructor has passed by me and flop my arms down onto the mat, and lie there quietly, like roadkill.

Next morning, I wake up with the alarm and sit up with a yelp of pain.

Last night, as we'd walked home Becky had said, cheerfully, 'You're not going to be able to walk tomorrow.'

Bloody *hell* she wasn't joking.

'You all right?'

I bump into Alex as he's coming out of the bathroom, wrapped in a grey dressing gown. He's towelling his hair and looking amused.

'No I am not all right. Becky took me to a torture chamber last night and now I can't actually walk, and I've got three meetings in a row this morning.'

'You need to come for a walk to loosen yourself up. You free on Friday afternoon?'

I nod. 'Ow.'

'It hurts to nod?'

Stupidly, I nod again. 'Apparently. Ow. Anyway, yes I am free. Well, I'm working, but we all get Friday afternoons off to work from home, so . . . as long as I catch up over the weekend, I think that's fair enough.'

Alex looks at me, one eyebrow cocked slightly.

I press my lips closed. God, I can't half go on. 'Yes.'

'Excellent. I'm free at one. Want to meet me here and we can go for a wander?'

CHAPTER SEVEN

Alex

18th January

I meet Jess after lunch. She's still in work clothes – a pair of dark grey trousers, black boots and a soft red jumper, which is an improvement on my work uniform. I've been living in scrubs for the last week on a placement in the paeds ward, and it wasn't until I got home last night that I realised I had a teddy bear sticker stuck to the side of my beard. I'd like to think nobody noticed, but knowing the staff of Paddington Ward, I suspect they thought it was amusing.

'You okay?'

'Yes,' she says, but it's in that sort of brittle, not very convincing kind of way.

'What's up?'

'Just one of those days. Loads of work stuff.'

'We don't have to do this if you'd rather get on?'

She shakes her head. 'No, I need the fresh air. Just that first week of work thing. I feel like I haven't a clue what I'm doing.'

We start walking.

'So how did you end up knowing your way round London so well?' Jess asks as she pulls her hat down a bit further on her head. It's weird that January's often colder than December – even though December is the month most associated with winter and snow. It feels a bit like it might snow now – the sky's a funny sort of yellow-grey colour.

'My dad worked here for years. He used to get the train up, and when I was old enough I'd come up with him in the holidays and just sort of wander around.'

Jess looks at me sideways like I'm a weirdo. 'On your own?'

I pull a face. 'Yeah.'

'That is a *bit* weird. What did you do?'

'I wanted to be an architect like him. So I'd wander about and look at stuff. I always had a Travelcard, so I could go wherever I wanted – within reason. Plus I wasn't a baby – I was fifteen, sixteen.' I tail off a bit. It does sound a bit weird, come to think of it. 'Anyway. The good thing is that I didn't become an architect, because it turns out I'm pretty hopeless at precision stuff.'

'That's good to know. I'll avoid you if you're wielding a scalpel in future.'

'You know what I mean. Architecture's all about the detail. I'm more slapdash and that'll do.'

She grins at me. 'All right. So how did you go from

wannabe architect to lawyer to student nurse?' she asks.

'Ah.' We pause and wait for the lights to change at a crossing. There's a coffee shop opposite. 'I'm dying for a coffee. Shall we get one to take out?'

'Sure.'

Two takeaway lattes later, we set off again. I'm explaining how I fell into studying law because it seemed like a sensible thing to do, and Jess is nodding vigorously.

'That's like me with the marketing job. I finished my degree and went back home to work out what to do, and I saw the advert and the next thing I knew I'd applied.'

'And then you got the job and the next thing you knew the rest of your life was all mapped out?'

She nods again. 'Exactly!'

'That's what happened to me. I thought I'd do law, then maybe do a postgrad in something else, do a job that made a difference. But I kind of got caught up in the whole job thing by mistake, and of course I'd met Alice by then . . .'

'Your girlfriend?'

'Ex.'

'Sorry. That's what I meant.'

'And it just all sort of slotted together. And it would've been fine, except then my dad got sick, and then he died.'

'Oh.' Jess puts a hand on my arm as we stop at another crossing. She squeezes it gently. 'I'm sorry.'

I shake my head. It's taken me time to be able to talk about it so calmly. There were times when someone being kind would bring tears springing to my eyes. Grief is weird like that. But now I feel like – well, I guess I've made my peace with it. And somehow, I feel like Dad would be quite impressed that I'd decided to do something I felt passionate about, just like he did.

'It's okay. But the thing was, watching him, it made me realise I'd always wanted to do something that was going to make a difference and sitting in an office doing corporate law shit wasn't going to do that. The nurses in the oncology unit – they were amazing when my dad was in their care.'

We've stopped now, and somehow we're sitting on a wooden bench that looks down Elgin Avenue. Buses trundle past and heave to a halt at the stop a few metres away, spilling out a sea of people who scatter in different directions in the late afternoon greyness. It's so cold I can see Jess's breath as she looks at me over the top of her coffee cup.

'So, that's what made you want to do it?' she asks.

'Yeah.' I take a sip of almost-cold coffee, make a face and lower it again. 'Only it turned out that unravelling the life I'd made wasn't as easy as all that.'

'Tell me about it. So, what happened?'

'Well, I got talking to one of the Macmillan nurses after Dad died when she was picking up some of the stuff we'd had at the house – equipment, and things like that. I thought she'd think I was crazy, but it turned out she'd only done her training a few years before herself – and she was almost forty.'

'So you jacked in your high-flying career and got a place at uni.'

'And now here I am. I mean, it wasn't that much of a high-flying career, to be fair. And I had some savings and some money that Dad left me, so I thought I might as well just go for it.'

'Exactly.' I notice Jess is sitting with her hands inside her sleeves. It's cold, and sitting still makes it seem even more so. 'Shall we keep going?' Jess stands up.

'Where are we going? The suspense is killing me,' Jess says.

We turn the corner and I nod my head towards the sign on the edge of the road. It's a second before she gets it.

'Abbey Road? Like the Beatles' Abbey Road?'

'That's the one.'

'I didn't even know it was a real thing.' She laughs.

'Ah, my dad would be turning in his grave at that.' I stop and point to the building opposite, and the famous doorway. 'He took me here when I was little. He was a massive Beatles fan.'

Jess has her phone out and she's taking a photo for Instagram (of course).

'Oh look, there's loads of pictures of a wall with writing on it somewhere round here.' She shows me her phone, and under #abbeyroad on Instagram, there they are. I spin round and point to the wall behind us. 'This one?'

'Oh, that's amazing.' She bends down and starts taking photographs. I watch her, thinking about the first time my dad brought me here. He was a massive music fan. Not just the Beatles. He loved all kinds of music. When he died, Mum passed his entire vinyl collection on to me. It's all still stacked on shelves back home in Kent, though – there's so much of it it'd take up half my room in Notting Hill, and Alice wasn't ever that keen on it. I dream of getting an old record player and having them all with me one day.

'It wasn't just the Beatles that recorded here,' I say.

'No?' Jess says, straightening up.

'Loads of others. Amy Winehouse, Oasis, Radiohead . . .'

'Ooh, let's cross over and have a look. We might see someone famous.'

We join a group of frozen-looking Japanese tourists who are taking photographs of the outside of the building. There's a buzz of excitement when the door opens, but we all give a deflated sigh when a middle-aged bloke with a bomber jacket walks out.

'You can take my photo if you like,' he says, chuckling as he strides off towards his car.

Jess heads off out when we get home. I'm at the too-tired-to-sleep stage, and end up sitting up watching crap on television until I doze off. It's half two in the morning when I wake up and stagger into the hallway to find Emma pulling off a pair of vertiginous heels and throwing them on the floor.

'Hi,' she says. 'Fancy meeting you here.' She arches an eyebrow, and – it's ridiculous – there's something about her complete lack of artifice and the fact that there are precisely no strings attached that make it just too easy.

CHAPTER EIGHT

Jess

4th February

'Hello, lovey.'

I'm having a bit of a wobble when Nanna Beth calls. It's nothing, really, but somehow she manages to pick that up in about two seconds flat. I sit on the edge of the bed and listen to her telling me how life is going in the sheltered accommodation.

'So Clara who lives in number twelve had a party to celebrate her eighty-fifth, and caused ructions because she had all the family round including the great-grand-children *on bicycles*.'

I raise my eyebrows. 'I thought rule number twenty-three subsection five or whatever it was said strictly no bikes?'

'Exactly.' I can picture her face and it makes my heart feel warm. Listening to her is almost as good as having one of her hugs. I must get down there soon.

'So anyway Fiona, the accommodation supervisor, was fine with it, and then there was a big fuss because that old trout next door complained.'

I giggle.

'So what's happening in the Big Smoke? Any exciting news?'

'Well,' I say, wriggling backwards on the bed and curling my feet underneath me, 'I told you last time that I finally met Rob. He's been giving us lessons in baking sourdough bread.'

'That's the chef one, am I right?'

'Yes.' I nod, even though she can't see me. 'We've got to feed this starter thing – it's basically like flour and water mixed into a paste – and then leave the bread dough to prove overnight. Only nobody fed the starter and the bread turned out more like a brick than anything else.'

'I'll give you my recipe,' Nanna says, comfortingly. 'It's none of that new-fangled sourdough stuff, just a good old-fashioned loaf.'

I think of Rob telling us how sourdough was the most ancient method of baking in his gruff Scottish accent, and decide I'll just leave that bit out. My foray into baking has given me a whole new level of respect for the people that run Le Pain Quotidien. Imagine making all those loaves every day? The responsibility must be terrifying.

'And what's happening with your mum?'

'Mum?' I realise with a start that I haven't heard from her in ages. I've always been a bit out of sight, out of mind, for Mum, particularly when she's busy. I think maybe it's rubbed off on me a bit. I really ought to call her.

'Haven't seen her for about a week,' Nanna Beth tells me. 'She was telling me all about this job she's found selling something online. She's caught up with some project or other. You know what she's like.'

I sigh. I do. She's forever finding money-making schemes that are going to solve all our problems – or just hers, nowadays. The trouble is that every one of them so far has involved her ploughing a load of money in *'as an investment'* and none of it ever seems to come back.

'Remember the lifestyle coaching or whatever it was?' Nanna chuckles.

'And the meditation teacher training?' I laugh, thinking about how many times my mother's been utterly convinced about something that was going to make her fortune. Six months sitting in a dusty church hall three nights a week soon put an end to that one, and she was on to the next thing. I bite my thumbnail.

'Oh, I forgot,' says Nanna Beth. 'She said she was going for a cabaret job on one of the cruise ships when I spoke to her last.'

'Did she?' I say, sitting up sharply. How the hell is she going to look out for Nanna if she's halfway round the world on the *Disney Princess* or whatever it is?

'Anyway, enough about that. I want to hear all about your exciting new job. How's it going? Any nice men on the scene?'

I suppress a sigh. Nanna Beth doesn't miss a trick.

91

'What's happening with that nice-sounding lad? The one who's been taking you out?'

I drop my voice slightly. 'Alex? There's nothing going on there. We're just friends.'

'Pfft,' she says.

'We are. Honestly. He's got something going on with one of the other girls in the house.'

'Hmm,' she sounds mildly disapproving. 'Sounds like a bit of a ladies' man.'

I choke back a giggle. Alex is the most unlikely ladies' man I've ever met. I think it's that – coupled with the fact that I met him once and basically fabricated an entire romance in my head because I've spent too long watching romantic movies – that makes the whole thing with him and Emma bearable. Plus from what he's said – not much, admittedly – I get the feeling that the break-up he had with his ex was pretty brutal.

'He's definitely not that.'

'Well you mind yourself, my love. After all that business with Neil, I don't want you rushing into something else too quickly.'

'There is no chance of that,' I say.

'Right then. I'm going to get off, because it's almost time for *Coronation Street* and I'm dying to know what happens to Steve.'

'I'll see you soon, Nanna.'

'That would be lovely. Lots of love to you.' She blows kisses down the phone and hangs up.

Afterwards, I curl up in bed and watch *La La Land*

on my iPad. I've bought some noise-cancelling headphones just in case of any incidents next door. I've literally no idea how much of a *thing* the whole thing is, but I'm not taking any chances.

Later that night, I'm tiptoeing downstairs to make a cup of hot chocolate because I can't sleep when I bump into Emma coming upstairs. She's wearing a dressing gown and holding a bottle of white wine and two glasses. She gives me a look I can't quite decipher – I'm not sure if she's feeling weird about me noticing the two glasses, or hoping I won't tell Becky there's something going on. I give a sort of sympathetic smile (I have no idea why).

When I make the hot chocolate, I add a large slug from the bottle of leftover spiced Christmas rum that's been sitting by the sink for weeks and head upstairs to climb into bed, putting my headphones firmly over my ears.

CHAPTER NINE

Jess

10th February

I've been living in Notting Hill for a month now, and Alex has been as good as his word. He's showing me his London, piece by piece, like a jigsaw, and I'm falling even more in love. With *London*, I should add, not with him. Definitely not with him. Not even a tiny little bit. Not even one atom of my romance-loving, musical-addicted, happy-ever-after body is longing to throw myself into his arms and say *pick me, you idiot*. Because that would be completely pointless and I am not a fool. He spins round again, thrusting his hands in the pockets of his jeans so I can see his bottom (which is an exceptionally nice specimen – just saying, purely objectively). Well, perhaps I am a little bit of a fool.

Because the thing is, I can't help thinking that if I hadn't gone on that bloody skiing holiday, which was admittedly lovely, perhaps Alex wouldn't have got off with the beautiful, effortlessly glamorous, high-flying Emma the night before I got back. And instead of lying with my head under two pillows gritting my teeth and trying not to listen to the sounds of them *definitely* not being a couple in the room next door, I could be in there. Literally.

As it is, I feel like a complete fool. And Alex hasn't a clue. He's so sweet. Whenever he's got time off, he's taking me on adventures around London, showing off his favourite places to me. And he loves this city so much that even if I didn't already, he would have converted me.

And he's got no idea I know something's going on with him and Emma. The weird thing is, they're perfectly civil to each other in the house the rest of the time, so it's like nothing's going on and it's all in my head. Except I'd have to be pretty screwed up to be imagining that.

'It's called fuckbuddies,' Gen said to me on the phone earlier in the week, as if she was explaining something very simple to a child of about four years old.

'I know what it *is*,' I said. 'I just didn't think it was actually a thing.'

'God Jess, you are so naïve sometimes. Of course it's a thing. Look at me and Marco.'

'Marco from the Ballet?'

'Yes.' I could picture her rolling her eyes.

'I thought you two were just friends.'

'With benefits,' Gen said, with a dirty sort of chuckle. 'When it suited me. Or him.'

'But what if it suited you and not him? How did you know when he'd be in the right mood? What happened if he turned up and you were like, "No thanks, I'm wearing a face mask and watching reruns of *Gilmore Girls*"?'

'Jess, you are illustrating precisely why you have never been, and probably never will be, the sort of person who has a friend with any sort of benefits.'

'I could,' I said, feeling a bit injured. 'If I wanted to. Which I don't.'

'Sure, Jess,' said Gen, laughing, but not unkindly. 'You're a total hearts and flowers romantic. And that's okay.'

After we'd ended the call, I looked at myself in the mirror. I tried a sexy sort of pout, and held my hair up off my face to try to imagine what it'd be like to be the sort of person – someone like Emma – who can just have sex with whoever she feels like and then get up the next morning and ask them to pass the cornflakes without feeling even the slightest bit awkward. I pulled a face at the thought, and let my hair drop back down to my shoulders. You know what, I said to myself, maybe it's okay if I'm just not that sort of person.

'And here we have the lesser-spotted tourist,' Alex says in a David Attenborough voice, turning around on his heel and walking backwards, facing me.

It's a Sunday afternoon and miraculously he's not working. A week has gone by and I've hardly seen Alex because he's been working nights and sleeping in the daytime. He's not just doing his placement, but he's doing some bank work as a healthcare assistant as well to earn a bit of extra money. He looks hollow-eyed with exhaustion.

Right on cue, he yawns widely. 'God, I'm sorry.'

'You should probably be asleep,' I point out, reasonably. 'Not wandering around showing me slightly interesting parts of London.'

'Yeah but I can't just work all day and sleep all night,' he says, then bursts out laughing realising his mistake.

'You could. Like the rest of the sane world. Only you've decided on a noble vocation where you get precisely no sleep and work ridiculous hours instead.'

He laughs, his bright eyes twinkling in a way that is disturbingly sexy, and I look down at the squashed, end-of-winter grass and scuff it with the toe of my boot. I know how it feels.

I look sideways at Alex as we're walking. He's checking his email on his phone and not really paying attention, so he doesn't notice. I'm trying to size him up and decide if he's *that sort of person*, or if he's just going along with it and half-hoping Emma might want to make something more permanent out of their arrangement. I can't tell.

I think I'm doing quite a good job of dealing with the fact that I can't actually get away from the one that got away (as I think of him, quietly, when nobody's looking) because he lives in the bedroom next to mine, and we've got a twelve-month bloody lease. Not that I'd want to move out, even if I could afford it. I love living there, and

I like him, and Becky, and – weird as this might sound, given their nocturnal habits – I like Emma, too. And Rob, even though I don't see him very often. We're a weird mix, but we work really well as housemates. I take a deep breath. I'll just have to focus all my romantic thoughts in the direction of Sophie and Rich's future wedding.

'Do you want to see something really interesting?' Alex says, out of the blue, as two small children zoom past on scooters, their mothers following close behind with tiny babies in prams. We've been walking along in a peaceable sort of silence for a while now.

'Really interesting?' I look at him sideways. 'You're not overselling this are you?'

He shakes his head and laughs. 'Yeah, all right. It's a bit interesting.'

'Oh go on then.'

'It's down here. Bit of a walk.'

'I'm not in any rush.'

'So this is what I was going to show you.' Alex steps aside and points between a gap in the railings.

'Oh my God, it's a miniature graveyard. You are seriously weird.' I lean in closer, peering at the little stone graves.

'It's a pet cemetery.'

'Yikes. Like the film?'

'I hope not.' He laughs. 'It's been closed to the public for years now – but there are about three hundred pets from the turn of the last century buried there.'

'That's creepy. Imagine if they all come to life and London's taken over by spooky little pet zombies.'

He shakes his head with a rueful smile. '*You* are seriously weird, Jess.'

Before long, we're meandering down the paths along the Serpentine. After a while we find a bench and sit down for a rest.

'It's funny,' I say, looking at the jumble of people I can see. 'In between the tourists, there are people just living their lives here. This is their park.'

He nods, thoughtfully. 'And of course—' he gets up, holding out a hand to help me up '—down that end, you can hang out and spot Kate Middleton and her kids – or the Duchess of Cambridge, I should say – sometimes.'

'Seriously?'

'Yeah. I guess she has to try and live a normal life some of the time.'

We start walking up towards home – my sense of direction is improving a bit now we're walking everywhere. It's funny, because when you don't live in London and you go everywhere by tube, the city feels completely different. It's actually not that big, when you start walking around.

'There,' Alex says, pointing to the huge, ornate building that is Kensington Palace. 'That's their house. Well, not all of it. There's loads of other random royals in there too. But they've got a little flat with about fifteen bedrooms down the side. I've seen her once, pushing a pushchair and walking a dog.'

'No way.' I realise I sound like an overawed tourist, but the idea of bumping into the royal family when I'm out for a stroll just seems completely bonkers.

'I don't think it happens that often, if you were planning on hanging out all day on the off chance.'

I give a little snort. 'As if,' I say. And then we keep walking, but my head swivels left and I have a little daydream about what I'd do if I bumped into the Duchess of Cambridge one sunny afternoon.

The trouble with me is I've always been a daydreamer. Always been a sucker for a romantic film, always loved a book with a good old-fashioned happy ever after ending. And now I'm working for a publisher that specialises in that sort of story and I'm as happy as a pig in – well, rose petals might be a nicer way of putting it. I had no idea that working for a publishing company meant I'd be given as many free books as I could get my hands on. The shelf in my room is groaning with advance reading copies – early editions of books, offered to reviewers, librarians and booksellers.

'Let's go back down this way. Fancy something to eat?'

My stomach growls in answer. 'Definitely.'

Crossing the road out of Hyde Park, we head down towards Portobello Road, and the smell hits us almost as we turn the corner onto the street. The fizz and spit of burgers being cooked mingles with the sweet scent of cinnamon buns from the bakery stall, and sour-spiced olives and paella in a huge frying pan.

'What d'you fancy?'

'Everything.' I laugh.

'Bockwurst, genuine German sausages, get your sausages here,' shouts a voice, and I turn to the right, seeing a market stallholder handing one over. 'Mustard and sauce over there, love,' he says to the woman, who gives a nod of thanks.

'What can I get you, love?' he asks as he turns to me.

We take our sausages and sit down on the stone wall outside the Electric Cinema. At last the beginnings of spring are showing themselves. There are crocuses peeping through the earth in wooden window boxes, and bright yellow daffodils standing proudly in the garden beside us. Portobello Road is a riot of noise and colour, alive with people and bustle and everything I love about London. I sit there with Alex by my side, and we eat our sausages, and we watch the world go by in a companionable silence.

'There's a place I'd like to show you,' Alex says, as we stand up after we've finished eating. He looks at me, his expression concerned. 'Unless you want to get back? We've been ages.'

I shake my head. What I want to say is that I'd be quite happy walking the streets of London every day with him, because I think he is lovely. What I do say is: 'No, I'm not in any rush to get back.' And off we go.

We walk to Little Venice, which looks exactly like you'd think from the name. It's like an oasis of calm in the middle of the city – canals lined with pubs and cafés, willow trees dipping their branches in the water, and colourful narrowboats moored by the canal-side.

'I've always wanted to live in one of those,' I say,

peering in the window. A small child presses her nose against the window from inside and I laugh.

'Me too,' says Alex. 'This is the café I wanted to show you.'

It's not posh. The curtains are faded gingham and outside there are a couple of rickety wooden tables and chairs.

'They do the best coffee – and breakfast – around here. I love it. And you can sit and watch the world go by.'

'Yes please.' I pull out a chair – it's freezing cold, but there are thick red fleece blankets hanging on the back. I wrap one around my knees and sit, watching. It reminds me more of Amsterdam than Venice, in a funny way.

I watch the sun streaking the sky pale coral pink and red as it begins to set. After a few minutes, Alex reappears with two flat whites, each with a pretty heart on the top. I pull my phone out and take a photo, adding it to my Instagram story.

'I like your Instagram.' Alex stirs sugar into his coffee, and the heart disappears from the froth. 'It's like you see all the good bits in London.'

'Thanks.' I sip my drink and look out at the people on the canal. The little girl we saw earlier has climbed out of the narrowboat now. She's wearing a thick padded coat and wellie boots, waiting for her dad to get her bike. She stamps her feet and catches my eye, jumping in a puddle and laughing. 'I like sharing the nice bits.'

'That's a good way of looking at life,' he says, smiling at me in a way that makes his eyes crinkle and my heart give a disobedient thud.

103

'It's partly a way of saving up memories, and it's also because I like sharing them with my Nanna Beth.'

'And your mum? Is she an Instagram addict as well?'

I shake my head, laughing. 'Definitely not. My mother only likes to do stuff when there's applause at the end of it. Put her on stage and she's quite happy. There's not enough feedback from online stuff.'

'She's an actress?'

I want to say no, she's a drama queen, but that's not really fair. I had a long, rambling voicemail from her earlier, complaining that she's had to go over and help Nanna Beth when she's got a performance tomorrow and she should be saving her voice. The performance Mum was talking about is the local theatre's rendition of *Chicago*, but nonetheless . . . apparently she's been working on it for weeks now.

'She's a part-time actress, yeah. Never quite made it to the West End, but she's done a few bits on television and stuff like that.'

'Wow. That's amazing.'

'She's hoping to get a job on one of the cruise ships, so she'll be away for ages.'

'That'll be weird for you,' Alex says, looking up at me through his dark fringe.

I shake my head. 'She was always away a lot when I was growing up.'

'With work?' He looks at me, head slightly to one side, his expression thoughtful.

'Um,' I frown a bit and fiddle with the wooden coffee

stirrer. It's not something I talk about very often, but there's something about Alex that makes me feel it's safe to open up. 'She wasn't great at the whole birthdays and Christmases thing, so my grandparents kind of picked up the slack there. And sometimes she had boyfriends who weren't that keen on children – well, on me – so I ended up spending more and more time with my grandparents, until it ended up being pretty much a permanent fixture.'

'Wow.' He sort of sits back a bit, looking at me. 'That must've been hard then. I mean, when your grandpa died, it was like losing a parent.'

I chew my lip and look across at where the little girl is playing. She and her dad are heading off down the canal-side now. She's meandering on her bike, unsteady on two wheels, and he's got his hand at the small of her back, protecting and guiding her. I blink hard, because for a strange half-second I feel tears stinging at my eyes.

'Yeah.' I look down at the table for a moment, gathering myself, then look up at Alex. He's got such a kind face. 'It was hard, because it was like we lost him twice – first when the dementia set in, and then again when he died.'

Alex nods. 'I get it. When my dad died I felt guilty because the first thing I felt was relief. He'd been sick for ages – and cancer just seemed to change him. He wasn't the same person at the end.'

'That's exactly it.' I let out a sigh. 'And so you decided to retrain as a nurse.'

He nods. 'I know everyone thinks it's insane. It's just – I saw the difference they made to Dad. To everyone in the ward. And I watched him fading away and I thought about all the stuff he'd done, and how he made a difference – the buildings he worked on are actual, concrete things. There's a children's hospice in Liverpool that he worked on, and they took the parents' and the children's views into account when they built it, because he said that mattered.' He looks away then for a moment, and I reach across the table, forgetting myself, and put a hand on his arm. He looks back and his eyes are shining with tears, which he wipes away with a sleeve, making a self-deprecating face. 'Sorry.'

'God, don't be. That's so lovely.'

'Yeah. I haven't ever really talked about that, you know?' He rubs his nose for a moment and then picks up the other wooden stirrer and starts snapping it into tiny pieces. 'Thing is I wanted to do something worthwhile. Corporate law wasn't it. I want to do something that I can be proud of, if . . .' He tails off.

'I get it.'

He looks at me then, holding my gaze for a second. My hand's still on his arm and I move it away, feeling suddenly shy.

He smiles and stands up, holding his hand out to me to pull me up to standing. 'I'm glad you do.'

We walk home together through the gathering dark of the February evening. There's still the tiniest hint of spring streaking across the sky as the night falls, and I feel happy. Properly, straightforwardly happy. It's a good feeling.

When we get back, the house is in uproar. Emma is standing on one of the kitchen chairs, holding a loaf of our home-made sourdough bread and swearing profusely.

'Um,' says Alex, looking at me and raising his eyebrows. 'Hi?'

'There's a – *thing* – eating my bread.'

I look at Alex and burst out laughing. 'You didn't take a bite after working a long shift yesterday?'

'Not guilty.'

'It's no' one of us,' says a gruff voice from downstairs. Rob emerges from the hall, brandishing two old-fashioned mousetraps. He's a short, bearded, red-haired man – older than the rest of us – probably in his forties. Rob looks and sounds so Scottish that I always expect him to be wearing a kilt. 'I think we've got a wee bit of a mouse problem.' He puts the mousetraps down on the table and holds his hand out to me. 'Hello, stranger,' he says, with a welcoming smile. 'Long time no see.'

'A mouse?' Nanna Beth gives a snort of laughter as I tell her the latest on what's been happening in the house. I'm curled up on the bed, a fleecy blanket over my knees because it's freezing cold and there's something wrong with the heating. It feels good to hear her voice, and I feel a wave of longing.

'You need to put some peanut butter on a trap. They can't resist it.'

'Then we'll have a squished mouse to deal with.' I shudder at the prospect.

'Oh for heaven's sake, girl. You're made of tougher stuff than that.'

I pull a face, but don't say anything.

'So you seem to be quite settled in with the housemates now.'

'I am. Work's a bit . . .' I try and think of the right word, but can't. 'It's all a bit new, that's all.'

It's like trying to stuff an octopus in a string bag; that's what it's like. When I was working at the marketing company, everything went according to plan – admittedly mainly because I was doing most of it. But here, now – well. I'm reliant on authors delivering manuscripts on time, editors getting their work done on time, the vagaries of cover designers and delivery dates and all sorts of things. It's like Jenga, only with books. If one thing goes wrong, the whole tower falls apart. This week an author decided the book she was working on wasn't right, and that she wanted to rewrite the whole thing. Trouble is, we've got production all set up and it's meant to be going to print in eight weeks. I go to bed worrying about printing schedules and wake up with my teeth gritted.

Nanna Beth makes a slight snorting noise. 'You sound a bit stressed out to me, my love. Maybe you need some sea air and some of my cherry scones.'

I sag slightly. The thought of both of those *and* a comforting hug from her makes me feel about ten years old again, and I ache with homesickness like I did at that age when we went on a school trip to Wales for a week.

'Oh God, I do. In fact, I'm going to come down and see you next weekend, if you're free.'

'Oh, that would be nice, lovey, but I'm going on a coach trip to Hastings.'

I sag a bit more.

'The weekend after, perhaps?' she says, cheerfully. 'I've got a chess competition, but that's only Saturday afternoon. You can have a nice bath or go for a walk along the prom with your mum.'

'You've got a better social life than me,' I say, and I'm not even joking. Since moving into the sheltered housing complex, she's been busier than I've ever known her. It makes me wonder if she's been storing all this social energy up for all the years she was married to Grandpa. And then it hits me – she's lonely.

'You're okay, though?' I ask, concerned.

'Me? Right as rain.'

'You're not – not missing Grandpa too much?'

The last couple of years when he was at home, and the dementia was making it harder and harder for him to manage, had been tough on her. I'd lived there, determined to help as much as I could, especially as Mum had – par for the course with her – checked out and gone travelling with a new boyfriend she'd met. She didn't really do responsibility. It's not that she didn't care, it's more that she – well, she's always been sort of focused on herself.

'No, lovey. I mean I miss him, of course, but he wouldn't have wanted to carry on like that. It's a blessing, in a horrible way.'

'I know.' I think of Grandpa before, when he was well, pottering around the garden in his slippers and a woolly jumper, dead-heading roses and sorting out the shed that was his pride and joy. I try not to think about him sitting, lost in a world of his own, staring into space for hours on end.

'Anyway, enough of that. What else is happening with you?' she asks.

I tell her a slightly filtered version of how it's really going at work, and how I managed to survive a meeting with a load of important people without screwing it up. I don't mention Alex, or how I'd taken to sleeping with earplugs in just in case I accidentally overhear him and Emma in the room next to mine, or how I'm grateful for the solid Victorian walls that muffle most of the noise even though they unfortunately make this place freezing cold on days like today.

And then I hang up, because she's got to get going to her chair yoga class, and I hug my knees and I smile to myself, because somehow, at twenty-nine and seventy-nine, the two of us are doing okay in our new lives.

CHAPTER TEN

Alex

14th February

Valentine's Day is *everywhere* this year, even more than usual. I can't decide if it's that confirmation bias thing, or if we're just going full on Hallmark, but it feels like the entire city of London is festooned with pink ribbons and covered in love hearts, and to be perfectly honest with you, it's a bit much. I've had a really shitty day, and I'm well and truly over all of it.

I pull my beanie hat down low over my head as I make my way up the station steps.

'Bunch of flowers for the girlfriend, love?' a woman outside Notting Hill Gate tube station asks. She's standing with two huge buckets of red roses and thrusts one in my direction. I shake my head.

'No thanks,' I say.

'Or boyfriend?' she calls, hopefully.

'Not that either,' I mutter, waiting for the lights to change, looking across the road where there's another stall drowning in a sea of red roses, teddy-bear-shaped balloons, bouquets of flowers, and ribbons tied to everything.

It was a genius idea of Becky's to turn the house into a sort of anti-Valentine celebration with plenty of wine, pizza, and a horror movie or two. Thank God I don't have to get up in the morning either. I've done a week of nights – again – and a weekend. Nobody told me nursing was going to be easy, but my God, I am so tired. And today was a really crappy day, too. We lost a patient, which happens, but this one came completely out of the blue. It's a million times harder when you're working on the paeds ward and it's a child. I shake my head and try and wipe the faces of her parents out of my head. Valentine's Day was always going to be synonymous with the most painful memory for them.

I stop at Tesco Express on the corner and pick up a bottle of red wine and some tubes of Pringles. All I want to do is get the 14th of February out of the way and forget Valentine's Day exists.

This morning I'd sat on the tube on the way into work, staring mindlessly at the adverts opposite, avoiding the gaze of the woman sitting across from me, thinking about last year. It was hard not to reflect on how different life had been. I'd taken Alice for a surprise dinner to Clos Maggiore in Covent Garden, and we'd both known why. Yeah, it was more than a little bit clichéd and cheesy, but I thought that was what romance was supposed to be about. We'd passed forkfuls of food to each other, a waiter had lit a candle between us and smiled knowingly, and the whole evening had gone exactly as planned. We'd shared a crème brûlée – two spoons and one bowl – not fighting over the last mouthful but me politely telling her she could have it even though it was my favourite. God, if that wasn't love, I don't know what is. I'd kill for a crème brûlée normally.

Everything, Alice had said afterwards, had been perfect. And then I'd got down on one knee on a tiny side street sprinkled with a million fairy lights (I'd even chosen the location, scouting it out beforehand) and asked her to marry me. She'd said yes before I'd even got the ring out of the box. And then I'd kissed her and she'd called her parents as we walked home, waking them from an early night in their neat Georgian house in Surrey. They'd been delighted, and feigned surprise. And if I'd climbed into bed that night with a vague sense of unease, well, I'd told myself it was probably indigestion. The cracks were there, spreading invisibly. I think I'd just hoped if I tried hard enough I could make it all okay again.

It had only been a few weeks after the proposal that I told Alice I'd been offered a place. God, she'd been so *disappointed* in me. It was the first time I'd seen that side of her. She'd been humouring me all along, hoping I'd get a grip and stop having some sort of third-of-life crisis.

'Can't you just do voluntary work or donate some money to charity?' she'd said, trying to brush it off.

'I can't – it's not that simple,' I'd replied.

'You don't have to make up for your dad dying by giving up your life and becoming a nurse,' she'd said, trying to keep her voice even. I remember spreading my hands out on the table, looking down at them, wondering if she just needed a chance to get her head around the idea and get used to it.

'It's not that. I want to do something that makes a difference. I want to work with people.'

'Why don't you train as a doctor then? At least that's . . .' She'd paused, and the words had hung, unspoken, in the air.

'I don't want to be a doctor, that's why.'

'But you'd get a half-decent salary, at least.' She'd barely been able to disguise how cross she was.

But the idea had been nagging away at me since those long weeks we spent in the hospital with Dad. It wouldn't leave me alone. I wanted to be a nurse. I was going to be a nurse. And if Alice couldn't get her head round it now, well, she'd get there in the end.

Weeks had passed, and Alice hadn't said anything about my plans; it's clear now she was hoping it would all go away. Occasionally she'd throw me the odd barbed comment about playing nurses, but other than that she carried on as normal. It was a bit weird, when I look back on it.

When it was clear the idea wasn't going away, particularly after I'd taken up the offer for the place on the course, she started throwing out every objection under the sun. A change in career would throw our perfectly ordered life into chaos, she'd said. She'd been making noises about having babies, and made it clear that there was no way that'd be happening if I was earning a nurse's salary. We wouldn't be able to carry on paying the rent on our pretty little place in Stoke Newington with me not earning. She became shrill and angry, yelling at me that I was putting her future in jeopardy just because I was having some sort of crisis. And the relationship that had seemed so solid had slowly but inexorably begun to show those tiny cracks, which soon turned into gaping huge chasms.

The one thing I know is that I didn't blame Alice. In a way, I almost felt that I'd lured her into getting engaged under false pretences. She'd bought into a lifestyle as well as a relationship, and then I'd decided – on what seemed to her like a whim – to take that lifestyle away.

I turn the corner onto Albany Road, still lost in my thoughts.

'Hi,' Becky says when she pulls the door open back at the house.

I've had all this stuff going through my head and I need to have a shower, gather my thoughts, try and wipe it all away. God I hate Valentine's Bloody Day.

I don't know why I find myself upstairs in my room, rummaging through balled-up socks and crumpled boxers, reaching right to the back until my hand finds the small, solid box. There it is – a tangible reminder of the life I left behind. And when I look up at my face reflected in the mirror I realise I look knackered. Also, I really need to get a haircut. I rub my face with both

·hands, before giving a huge yawn. What I really need is to get a decent night's sleep.

A couple of hours later, we're all sprawled on the sofas, so stuffed with Domino's pizza we can hardly move. Rob isn't there, of course – Valentine's Day being one of the big nights in the restaurant biz, with people like Alice and me last year keeping them in business.

'My God,' says Becky, rubbing her stomach as if she's six months pregnant. 'I swear I'm having a pizza baby.'

'I'm never eating pizza again.' Jess leans forward, taking a slice of Hawaiian from the cardboard box. 'After this bit, I mean. This is my last hurrah.'

'Pineapple on pizza is beyond disgusting,' says Emma, looking at Becky for back-up.

Jess sits back and takes an extra big mouthful to prove that she's wrong, making us all laugh. I watch as she curls her long legs underneath her, sitting tailor-style on the huge soft sofa cushions. And then – realising what I'm doing – I look away. She looks at the pizza, thoughtfully.

'Pineapple's the best bit.'

'You are so disgusting,' says Emma, walking across the room to get another bottle of red wine. 'Drink, anyone?'

'I'm with Jess. Team Pineapple forever.'

I take a piece of pizza in solidarity with Jess. Reaching across, she holds out her hand for a high five and then flashes me a beam of gratitude.

There's a general groan of disgust from the other two. Jess gives me a sideways look and a cheeky, conspiratorial grin, before taking the hairband from her wrist and – as

116

I've seen her do so many times before out of habit as we've been walking around London on our exploring trips – twists up her long, dark hair into a messy knot at the top of her head. I'd half expected to get back and find she wasn't here this evening, after what happened yesterday.

I'd got home from a long shift at the hospital, and found Jess sitting at the kitchen table with a couple of friends. They'd been screaming with laughter over photographs on Tinder, with – incongruously – a pile of open *Bride* magazines spread all over the table.

Jess had looked from me, to the table, to and back, to meet my look of confusion.

'Alex, this is my friend Gen I told you about, and this—' she motioned to both of them, but I'd already recognised them from Jess's descriptions '—this is Sophie.'

Sophie was blonde and very pretty, with her hair tied back from her face in a ponytail. I'm not sure how but she somehow managed to look as organised as Jess has told me she is. I think it was just because she seemed so neat. She looked like she'd never had a scruffy day in her life. Meanwhile, Gen was in a pair of rainbow-coloured trousers with a black vest top, and her wild red curls were pushed back from her face with a navy blue fisherman's cap. The look shouldn't have worked, but somehow it did. She looked exactly like you'd imagine someone in the theatre should look.

'We're trying to find a nice young chap for Jess,' Gen said, looking at me with huge, very direct blue eyes. She had a mischievous look on her face, as if she knew

117

something I didn't. It made me feel slightly unnerved. I went to the fridge, opened a bottle of orange juice, and poured myself a glass.

I looked down at the wedding magazines and then at Jess, who rolled her eyes.

'And you're moving straight from choosing someone on Tinder to planning the wedding?' I took a long drink of juice, then put the glass down on the kitchen counter.

'I'm not planning on marrying anyone right now,' Jess said, laughing. She gathered up the magazines and put them in a neat stack. 'These are for Soph. She *is* getting married.'

'And these two are terrified in case I'm going to force them to wear some sort of hideous meringue dress as bridesmaids,' Sophie said.

'Please, God, no,' said Gen, raising her eyes heavenward.

'He's quite nice,' Sophie said, leaning over Gen's shoulder and looking at her phone screen. 'Wonky nose, though.'

'Oh my God, this is hideous.' Jess hit the home button on the phone and the screen went blank.

I felt a bit weird. Maybe it was just the excess of female energy in the room or something, or the way Gen was looking at me as if she was sizing me up, but I didn't like the idea of Jess on Tinder. There are loads of really dodgy characters out there.

The truth was there's something inside me that feels slightly discomfited by the idea of Jess – London walking buddy, housemate, fan of midnight toast-and-Marmite snacks and chats over the kitchen table – dating anyone.

I have absolutely no right to feel like that for about eight million reasons. One, because I'd made an executive decision at the beginning of this year that I wasn't getting involved with anyone. And two, because of the whole Emma thing. Not that it's a thing, but it's basically my belt-and-braces guard against getting into a relationship with anyone else. I'm not the sort of person who'd mess around with more than one person at a time, even if it was all completely no strings attached. And it's the perfect solution to avoid me getting caught up in a relationship and messing up my nursing course and my – already pretty screwed up – heart.

I knew all of that made me a hypocrite and an idiot, so what I needed was to duck out of this situation ASAP. 'I'll leave you three to it,' I said, grabbing a can of Coke from the fridge so I wouldn't have to come in and interrupt them again later.

But now here we are, at the end of our alternative Valentine's evening. We've given up on the terrible horror film, which wasn't even scary, and ended up watching a really freaky episode of *The Haunting of Hill House* on Netflix, and chatting about ghost stories we've heard, trying to think of scarier and scarier ones until we're all completely spooked.

'I'm going to be too scared to fall asleep tonight, at this rate,' Jess says, getting up from the sofa. 'I'm going to bed before I completely terrify myself.'

'Yeah, me too,' I say, and stand up, picking up an empty pizza box. Jess stacks another two in my arms.

'Can you put them outside?' she says, pulling a face. 'There's no way I'm going out there in the dark now.'

'The man in black might get you,' says Emma, in a creepy voice.

'I'll do it, don't worry,' I say.

'Phew.' Jess mops her brow, then gives a wave from the sitting room door. 'Right, night all.'

I turn and say goodnight, and Emma flicks a glance over her shoulder. It's a split-second look, but I know what she's thinking. However, I'm stuffed with pizza and I've had way more wine than I should have. She raises her eyebrows slightly, and I give a slight shake of my head. I like Emma – she doesn't take life too seriously. She's got a body to die for and she's bloody hot in bed. And she knows what she wants. But the thing is, if I fuck this up I'll be out of a house, and that matters more than anything else.

I head out to put the boxes in the recycling and the howl of foxes somewhere nearby makes the hairs on the back of my neck stand on end.

When I go upstairs, the bathroom door's open, but the light's still on, so I push it open carefully. Jess is standing there, hair knotted off her face in a bun, carefully putting toothpaste on her toothbrush.

'Oh sorry, I'll come back in a sec,' I say.

Jess shakes her head. 'It's fine, I'm just brushing my teeth.'

She hands me the toothpaste and I pick up my brush, and somehow we're standing there side by side – me in my trackies and T-shirt, her in a pair of mismatched PJs – brushing our teeth. She waggles her eyebrows at me in the mirror, making me laugh, which is harder than you'd think when you've got a toothbrush in your mouth.

'Night then,' I say, once we've finished, and she's heading out to her bedroom. I contemplate a shower before bed, but decide I'll have one in the morning. I lie under the covers, thinking that I've made the right move in not sleeping with Emma tonight. I find myself wondering about Jess lying in the room next to mine, hoping she's not too freaked out by the ghost stories to sleep. I close my eyes and, exhausted after the impossibly long day I've had, I'm gone.

CHAPTER ELEVEN

Jess

12th March

'Welcome to my new house.'

Gen's standing on her bed. She reaches up and pushes the glitter ball that hangs from the ceiling so it twirls, casting squares of light that bounce and reflect off the walls, the furniture and us.

Gen's always lived in, well, unusual places. She spent a summer after university living·in a silent meditation retreat in Bali, sleeping in a hut and sweeping bugs off the floor before bed every night. The concept of the irrepressible Gen, the human embodiment of a can of Coke that's been shaken up then opened, keeping her mouth shut for a week at a time was pretty much unthinkable to me. But she said afterwards that she'd loved it, and that it had really helped her acting. That made sense. She's so dedicated to acting that she'd do pretty much anything if she thought it would make a difference – including, it would seem, saving money by sleeping in assorted battered-looking disused buildings to save money for more classes. Her large residence had been a mansion house – huge, grand and with a sweeping staircase that belonged on a movie set – that was waiting for redevelopment.

When she'd told Sophie and me that her new place was an ex-nightclub, I thought perhaps she'd be sleeping in a converted office or something, not on the dance floor.

Gen jumps down, and beckons me to follow her. 'I'll make us a coffee. Come this way.'

I climb wooden stairs lined with faded posters that have been plastered to the wall, their edges curled and peeling. Familiar faces look back at me, ghosts of the musical past. The place smells dark and cool and – if you inhale and close your eyes – you can almost imagine the thudding of the bass and the throngs of excited, wild-eyed clubbers ricocheting off each other on the dance floor, arms in the air.

'They've made a little kitchen for us, here – look.' Gen opens the door, proudly, and I walk inside what was clearly once the manager's office. It's got a brand-new IKEA unit, with a hob, a sink, and a fridge and washing machine. But it's clearly still a room that's pretending to be something it's not. Gen switches on the kettle.

Life as a live-in guardian isn't for the faint-hearted. The properties are vacant, so it can be a bit spooky and weird – basically, you're making sure the building isn't taken over by squatters. Gen heard about it from an actor friend while she was working on a play about a year ago. Before that, she'd done what most people do when they're trying to make their way in London – she'd lived in a tiny, cramped house-share, in a bedroom that was once a walk-in cupboard, with no window and a door she had to keep propped open at night so she didn't overheat or worse still suffocate. It was grim. Then she found herself looking up live-in guardians, and discovered that – as long as you didn't mind being relatively impermanent, and could cope with living pretty much anywhere in central London – you could get by paying about half what you'd normally pay for the area. It's still more than I'm paying Becky, but I'm in a very weird – totally miraculous – position.

'What d'you think?' Gen asks as she clatters spoons, spilling sugar and wiping it up, before handing me a coffee.

'It's . . . interesting,' I say.

'Cheap. And the other guy who is sharing it is pretty low-profile. Nice to know I'm not on my own here, though. We've had a couple of pissed people banging on the door in the middle of the night. I reckon they thought the club was still open. Ancient clubbing dinosaurs from another time . . .' She grins, sipping her coffee.

'I don't think I could cope with moving every few months, though.' I think about Albany Road and feel a wave of gratitude for Becky. She could have put that place on the market and sold it for millions. I still don't know what came over her when she decided to gather us lot together and let us stay there for a ridiculously low rent. As it is, my new publishing salary isn't stretching very far. By the time I've paid rent and my share of the bills, there's not an awful lot of money left. February wasn't so bad because it's a short month, but March has barely started and I'm already feeling the pinch a bit.

'I don't mind moving if it means I get to stay here. London's so bloody expensive.'

'We could move back to Bournemouth,' I say, waiting for her reaction.

'No chance in hell. I'd rather live on 20p noodles from Tesco for the rest of my life.'

'I think that's what's going to happen to me. Payday's only just gone, and I'm absolutely skint already.'

She looks at me, brows knitted together. 'I thought your snazzy job in publishing was paying really well?'

'Yeah.' I nod. 'In Bournemouth terms, maybe. Not so much in London.'

'It's fine as long as you don't want to go anywhere or do anything.' Gen lifts her mug up. 'Even a coffee's more expensive here. Not to mention drinks . . .'

'Yeah. I was invited on a night out to celebrate someone's leaving do the other day, but I turned it down when I looked up the menu. Cocktails were about £18 each.'

'Is everyone you work with loaded then?' Gen swivels herself round on the old black office chair, spinning herself like a child visiting a parent's workplace.

'I don't know. Maybe they've got private incomes or something. I reckon half of them are subsidised by parents, and the other half are like me. Jav didn't go on the night out, either.'

126

Jav and I have taken to going off to the café down the back street behind our office for lunch a couple of times a week. It's full of plaster-splattered workers from the building they're redeveloping round the corner, but they do a pretty decent soup and sandwich for the same price as a glass of freshly squeezed orange juice from the posh restaurant below our building.

Jav's nice, and I relate to her because she comes from a housing estate in Peterborough, and doesn't have parents in the business. There are an awful lot of people in the office who seem to have found their way into the job because of someone knowing someone. The MD of the company is so posh that when he talks I have to focus very hard to work out what he's actually saying. He doesn't just have a plum in his mouth – I reckon he's got several fruit trees.

'Jess?'

I shake my head. Gen's been talking and I've been lost in my thoughts.

'If you're struggling, maybe you should give notice at Becky's place and sign up to become a live-in guardian? I know you said the rent's cheap, but this is *really* cheap.'

I shake my head. I haven't actually told her how much I'm paying, because I feel a bit guilty that she's been struggling for ages to get by and then I just landed on my feet.

'I like it there. And the rent's not expensive. It's just I keep buying coffees and stuff and they're so bloody ridiculous. I was walking with Alex the other day in Bloomsbury and we went past a place that was charging £5.50 for a flat white.'

Gen whistles. 'That's ridiculous.'

'I know.'

'You need to get a flask,' she says. 'More to the point, what's with all the *walking with Alex* stuff?'

I make a face. 'Nothing. He's just showing me London.'

'Thought you said he came from Kent?'

'He does. He just used to spend a lot of time here as a teenager with his dad, and he's got a really good memory for places and stuff, and you know what I'm like with directions.'

'Completely, unimaginably hopeless?'

I nod. 'And it's really helping. I made it home on foot the other day without getting lost once. It's nice – like joining up a jigsaw puzzle. And that's why everyone wears trainers with their office stuff. I couldn't work it out at first.'

'Yep.' Gen waggles a foot. She's always in huge, chunky trainers. 'It's easier to walk most of the time instead of waiting for a bus or fighting your way through the tube. Nice that Alex is taking the time to show you round,' she says, giving me a sly, sideways look, one eyebrow crooked upwards. 'Out of the goodness of his heart?'

I feel my cheeks going slightly pink. 'There's nothing going on. He's completely wrapped up in work, and I get the feeling that whatever he's got going on with Emma is exactly what he wants – no complications.'

'What about Becky's no-relationships rule?'

'I don't think she knows there's anything going on.'

'Oh my God. So you're the keeper of the secret? Does he know you know?'

I pull an awkward face. 'Don't think so. Emma doesn't realise I saw her coming out of his room that morning, and there's nobody but me on our floor.'

'You should say something. Drop a little hint.'

'God, Gen, no. That would be awful.'

'Right. So you're just going to quietly carry on living with the man of your dreams while he's banging your flatmate on the QT and not say a word.'

'He is *not* the man of my dreams.'

'He so is. I've seen him. And I've seen the way you looked at each other. I reckon he's got the hots for you, too. Why else would he be spending his non-existent time trawling over London showing you how to get from A to B when Google Maps exists?'

'I can't work Google Maps, you know that,' I say, only half joking. Whichever way I start walking, I always end up going the wrong way. It happened the other day at work when I was supposed to pop out to a bookshop near the office. Fifteen minutes later, I'd walked in a circle and still hadn't found it. '

'That is *so* not my point, and you know it.'

Gen takes a sip of her coffee and narrows her eyes slightly, in that way she does when she's convinced she's right about something. I don't say anything.

There's a pause. I stand up and look around the little kitchen, and Gen spins round on the chair again. A couple of times she opens her mouth to speak, and then – uncharacteristically – closes it.

'Gen?' I sit back down, looking at her. 'What's up?'

129

She rubs her finger and thumb together. It's an anxious habit she's had as long as I've known her. Before a performance on stage, she stands in the wings doing it unthinkingly. I look down at her hand and up at her face. She realises what she's doing and lifts both hands up in a gesture of confusion.

'It's Soph. This wedding stuff. The baby stuff. All of it.'

Sophie's on the verge of something called the two-week wait. Apparently, it's something to do with waiting to see if her and Rich's attempts at getting pregnant have been successful. Our group chat has become a little bit . . . medical, these days.

'You mean you don't want to know how many times she and Rich have had sex?' I say.

Gen makes a slightly disgusted noise. 'No. I love her, but she's treating this exactly the same way she treated exams at school, and it's a bit TMI. And she's obsessing over wedding dresses and it's like there she is, on the verge of becoming a Proper Grown-Up. And I feel a bit shit. I'm living in—' she waves her arm, indicating the converted club manager's office that is her kitchen '—well, in this. Still hoping for my big break, still scrabbling to survive from one month to the next, still having to tap my parents for money when I'm skint and with credit cards up to my eyeballs.'

I totally get it. Admittedly I can't tap my mother for money, because she's always been skint and – oh God, I've just realised it's Mother's Day at the end of the month. I must check and see if it falls before payday. She's going to expect flowers, and wine. Mainly wine. I wonder if she'd mind if I skipped the flower bit.

I remember we're talking about Sophie. Now there's someone who likes things *just so*. Always has. If she has children, she's going to be calling Interflora to make sure they send reminders a week before every occasion.

'Soph's always been like that, though,' I say.

We both fall silent for a moment. I think of Sophie at primary school, her pencil case filled with neatly sharpened coloured pencils, ruler and strawberry-scented eraser, writing her name neatly at the top of her exercise book. Meanwhile, Gen and I would be scrabbling around at our desks, trying to find a pencil sharpener and rummaging in our bags for our crumpled, half-finished homework.

'She's just – naturally organised,' I conclude.

'It just feels like our ski trip was the last hurrah,' Gen says, looking a bit sad. 'I don't want to grow up.'

'Don't worry, Peter Pan.' I reach over and squeeze her hand. 'I'm always here to make you feel like a normal, functioning adult. I can't even manage to get relationships right.'

Speak of the devil, Sophie messages us a moment later, asking if we want to meet up on the South Bank for a drink later on – her treat.

⁑

'I need a bit of moral support,' she explains when we meet her a couple of hours later, shifting out of the way so the waiter can put our drinks down. 'Thanks,' she says, with a smile. The bar looks out over the Thames. We're protected from the still-cold spring weather by a wall of glass, but we can watch the people scurrying about like ants on the Embankment. I gaze out of the window for a moment, but Sophie gives a large sigh, drawing my attention back to her.

'What's up?' Gen puts her chin in her hand.

'Well, I'm not pregnant, that's what's up.'

I don't know a whole lot about trying to get pregnant. To be honest, I've spent the last decade trying to *avoid* it. The way we're taught at school, you'd think you just had to sit on the same sofa as a man to end up up the duff, so the idea that it's a bit of a challenge is news to me.

'You've had two goes,' says Gen, trying to be consoling. It's never been her strong point. 'I think it probably takes more than that. Look at all those people that have years of IVF.'

I spin my head round and give her A Look.

Sophie gives a wail. 'Oh my God, what if that happens to me?'

'I'm sure it won't,' I say, reassuringly. 'I think you probably just need to not stress about it. And have sex lots.'

'I have been. Rich says he's feeling a bit worn out. And I'm bloody exhausted. I fell asleep at work the other day.'

'That might be a sign you need to cool it a bit. Maybe

focus on the wedding stuff instead?' Gen flicks a glance in my direction. 'Have you got any ideas for our dresses yet?'

Sophie shakes her head. 'We haven't actually made it official yet.' She waves a naked left hand.

'You're not getting married?'

She shakes her head vigorously. 'Oh we are, it's just we haven't had the official Will You Marry Me bit.'

'Did you just instruct Rich he was getting married, Soph?' Gen gives her a look.

'I did not.' She looks offended. 'He did have *some* say in it.'

Gen gives a snort. The waiter arrives with a tray of drinks – gin and tonic for me, a beer for Gen, and a large vodka and tonic for Sophie.

'Cheers,' she says, clinking our glasses.

'What happened to not drinking?'

'Oh, bollocks to it. Just for tonight, anyway.' She takes a large swig and gives a happy sigh. 'God, that's good.'

A couple of drinks later and Sophie's feeling much better. She's visibly relaxed, and it reminds me that in amongst all the other stuff – finding my way through this new job, the house stuff (which is what I'm calling it and definitely not the Alex stuff) – it's so nice to have both my oldest friends living right here in the same city. I beam at them and they smile back.

'I love you two,' I say. 'And that's not the gin talking.'

We order another round of drinks. Thank goodness Sophie's paying, because this place is astronomically expensive.

'You should order the most tight-fitting, slinky, unforgiving wedding dress you can find,' I say, thoughtfully. 'I bet if you tempt fate you'll be preggers before you know it, and you'll have to have a bump-extension sewn in.'

'Or you can get a Meghan Markle style dress?' Gen's one hundred per cent Team Meghan and a bit obsessed. 'She looked like she'd left room for expansion in hers.'

'D'you think?' Sophie perks up a bit. I'm scrolling through Instagram to find photos of Meghan's dress, and before we know it, Sophie's writing lists and making plans and normal Sophie service is resumed. I catch Gen's eye over the top of Sophie's head as she scribbles down a list of wedding dress designers in her ever-present notebook, and we exchange grins. Friend duty complete.

CHAPTER TWELVE

Jess

30th March, Bournemouth

I'm on the train heading south to the seaside. It's Mother's Day on Sunday, so I'm staying with Mum and spending the day with Nanna Beth. It's only the second time I've been home since I moved – the last flying visit having to fit in around Nanna Beth's chess tournament. I hadn't factored in the cost of train journeys when I said I'd be back to visit as often as I could. But I speak to Nanna Beth on the phone all the time, and she's still swapping Instagram photos with me. She's developed a bit of a following: I showed her how to add hashtags to her posts, and it turns out there's a whole world of elderly people out there sharing their photos. Who knew? Jav keeps joking there's a book in it. She's following her, and now her grandma in Mumbai and Nanna Beth are Instagram friends too.

Nanna Beth's got a bit of an eye – I'm scrolling through her photos as we rumble out of the edges of London, past tired old buildings and graffiti-covered industrial units. The train stops and I snap a photo of a faded ghost sign and share it. Nanna B loves them.

The train pulls into Bournemouth and it feels like stepping into a pair of comfy old slippers after a long day in heels. I can smell the sea in the air and the sky stretches out huge in that way you only get at the seaside. I don't even have to think about where I'm going, which is such a relief after the constant map-checking that characterises my London life. I'm still trying to find my way around the city. But here – home – my feet carry me along the road towards the prom and I turn left at the end, crossing over to walk along the pavement beside the edge of the little stony cliff that drops down to the beach path. It takes half an hour, but I'm not in any rush. Every step I take, every breath of salty air I breathe in, I feel like I'm unwinding. I hadn't realised how much I missed being by the seaside.

I turn left and walk up the little street where Mum lives now. There's a row of doorbells, and her name's there, on a faded sticker. I push the buzzer and there's a pause before the front door clicks open automatically to allow me in.

'I could have been a mass murderer,' I say, as she opens the door to her flat and kisses me on the cheek. She's dyed her hair a dark burgundy-red and cut it into a jaw-length bob. It emphasises her high cheekbones and makes her look ridiculously young for her age.

136

'Sorry I can't stay. I have to rush. I've got rehearsal at twelve.'

Mum's opening words aren't the usual 'Darling! It's lovely to see you!' that a daughter might expect. It's just as well I'm used to her. But she's always been a bit – well, lacking in the traditional maternal side of things. She was amazing if I needed a costume in the school play, mind you. She bustles past, giving me a vague kiss on the cheek, and taking the flowers I'm holding.

'For me? You shouldn't have. Thanks, lovely.'

She sniffs them and tosses them aside on the table by the front door, and picks up her keys.

'Pop them in water for me, will you? I won't be back until after the performance because we've got loads to do to prep, but you'll be okay with Nanna Beth, won't you? There's probably something in the fridge for dinner if you have a look.'

And she's gone.

Growing up I got the distinct impression my mum would have been happier if she'd had Gen as a daughter. I was boring and bookish. Gen was like Mum – a rainbow of drama and glamour who made everyone look when she walked into the room. I didn't doubt for a second that she loved me, but she was always slightly disappointed that I wasn't as exciting as she'd hoped. She wanted a mini me, a second chance at fame. She was always desperate to hear how Gen was getting on.

'That could've been me, you know, if it hadn't been for parenthood getting in the way,' she'd say, unthinkingly. I guess I have learned some acting skills from her – the ability to remain impassive in situations like that, for one.

'Don't worry yourself, lovey,' Nanna Beth would always say. 'She doesn't realise what she's saying. She loves you very much.'

I look around the flat Mum's been renting since I've moved out. It's five floors up on a side road near the promenade, and the walls are painted a dull, uninspiring grey. She's covered them with posters from Vaudeville shows, huge colourful ones with high-kicking dancers festooned with feathers and glittering, tiny outfits. There are boxes stacked up against one wall.

I look at my reflection in the huge full-length mirror. I'm wearing a grey pinafore, a green cardigan and red shoes. I look about five. I can almost hear Becky's voice in my head, making a comment about the hidden psychological meaning behind the outfit I'm wearing. She's obsessed with power dressing and the effect of clothes at the moment, and I realise that dressing like a child on a trip home to see my mother is probably quite telling.

But I don't dwell on it, because she's disappeared for the day and I'm off to the sheltered housing place to see Nanna Beth. I run a brush over my hair and leave my overnight bag on the sofa. I'm about to head out the door when I think I'd probably better check there *is* something to eat in the fridge.

A dried-up lemon, an empty pack of low-fat butter substitute, a cracked, ancient piece of cheddar, and a bottle of Evian. I decide I'll pick something up on the way back.

I head out of Mum's flat and towards the seafront and the sheltered accommodation complex where Nanna Beth lives now. It gives me a pang when I walk past the street where her old house stands – there's a new family living there, all Grandpa's roses pulled up out of the front garden and a car parking spot tarmacked in their place. But my heart lifts when I see the brightly painted sign for Boscombe View. There's a couple of people in the garden, bickering happily over some wooden planters, holding a trowel each. It felt like the right place for Nanna as soon as we set eyes on it. I look across the car park, and she's standing at the window of her little apartment, waving through the glass.

'Darling,' Nanna Beth is at the door. She beckons me inside. Since I was there last, they've hung all her old pictures on the walls, and she's somehow managed to make the little sitting room feel completely like home. The green velvet sofa is up against the back wall, with the imitation painting of Constable's 'The Hay Wain' framed above it. The mantelpiece is crowded with photographs of me, Mum, Grandpa and Nanna Beth herself, and various great-aunts and second cousins I met as a child but don't really remember, but who are oddly familiar after years of their photos surrounding me.

'Sit down. You must be tired out after that journey,' Nanna Beth says.

I do as I'm told, and listen as she gently potters around

in the little kitchen at the end of the hall. I can hear the kettle going on and the sounds of her warming the teapot. The familiar clunk of the biscuit tin she's owned forever opening up, and the rustle of aluminium foil being taken off a plate of ham sandwiches she'll have made up earlier.

'Here we are,' she says as she returns with a tray.

We settle down with food and tea. It feels warm and safe, the way it always has. I look up at a photo of Grandpa in his gardening cardigan, a spade in his hand.

'He'd be proud of you, you know that.' Nanna follows my gaze. 'It takes a lot of courage to follow your dream, you know. So how's it going?'

I think for a moment. I've been in the job for over two months now, and I still feel like I'm finding my feet. 'Okay. Ish.'

'Bit of a change to working for Neil, I expect,' she says, with a chuckle. We'd met at work and sort of fallen together. There were definite pluses and minuses to working for your partner. I can't really think what the pluses were. The minuses were that when I found out he was sleeping with Claire from accounts, it was pretty hard to maintain a civil working environment. God, it doesn't matter how hard this new job is or how much of a learning curve I'm on (and right now it feels like I'm never going to get the hang of it) anything had to be better than working in that environment.

'It's so . . . fast.' I try and explain what it's like, but it's hard. 'And then so slow. It's like trying to herd cats, getting a book from start to finish.'

'Still enjoying it though? I bet you've got them all under control,' she says, and I think of Jav, who I'd left on Friday evening working on the final proofs of a book that was already a month late. It had to be finished quickly, because it was nominated for romance of the year in one of the glossy magazines, and the books editor had been on the phone asking hopefully if there were finished copies available. Jav had managed to stall her, and she'd messaged me at midnight to say she'd finally got things sorted out. Publishing is a lot like being a swan. You look very sleek and posh from the outside, but there's an awful lot of furious paddling going on underneath. And a lot of mud.

'I'm getting there,' I say, after a pause. She raises an eyebrow and looks at me over the top of her teacup.

'Rome wasn't built in a day. You've found a new house, and you're settling into a new life. Any other interesting news you want to share?'

'Becky's had a promotion. And Gen's up for a role in the new Cameron Mackintosh show at the Apollo. If she gets that, she's really going places.'

'Gen's going places, no matter what.' Nanna smiles fondly. She's always had a soft spot for Gen. I think she sees Mum in her.

'What's happening with Mum?' I ask. 'You know she's hopeless at keeping in touch.' The only thing I'd heard from her recently was that she didn't get the cruise ship work she'd been hoping for.

'Well, she's met some bloke from the theatre who's

doing some sort of pyramid selling thing, and she's convinced that she's going to make her fortune.'

'Again?' I say, realising that must be why the sitting room of Mum's flat was stacked with cardboard boxes.

'Again,' she says and our eyes meet. 'You know your mum; she's a sucker for a get-rich scheme and even more for a man with a good line of patter.'

I nod. Nanna settles back on her new chair – it's an upright one with an extending footrest, and sturdy arm supports. She puts a cushion on her lap and pats it. A moment later, as if summoned, Phoebe, her calico cat, appears. She hops onto Nanna's lap with a chirrup.

Nanna switches on the television. 'You don't mind if I just turn on the news? I want to see what's happening.'

She and Grandpa said this after every lunch. Sandwiches and soup at twelve-thirty, a sit-down, the news on, and one or other of them would doze off for quarter of an hour then act surprised, as if it didn't happen like clock-work every afternoon. It is nice that, even a year on from Grandpa's death, she is still doing the same little routines. It makes me feel safe, somehow. I eat another sandwich – they're sliced into little triangles, a throwback from when I was little and I used to ask for them that way in my packed lunch. Nanna watches the news, intently. She's always been fascinated by politics and mutters under her breath when a clip of Prime Minister's Questions appears on the screen. I suppress a smile, and drink my tea.

Sure enough, ten minutes later she's dozed off. I take

the plates and cups through to the tiny kitchen and wash them in the sink. She's already rinsed off the aluminium foil and left it to dry on the draining board – she's from the generation of make do and mend. I go back through to the sitting room and she's snoring gently. It's only then that I realise that she looks so much older, all of a sudden. But it can't have just happened. I suppose going away and coming back has brought it into relief. A knot of anxiety twists in my stomach at the thought of losing her and I hold on to the back of the sofa, gripping the edge of it with my fingers until my knuckles whiten.

'Dear me,' she says, waking with a start. 'I must have dropped off.'

I laugh, and the moment is broken.

'Let's go to the community centre,' she says, 'and I'll introduce you to Cyril, my new friend. He's setting up a mindfulness circle – used to be a bit of an old hippy, if you ask me. He's very nice.'

I look at her sideways. 'Oh yes?'

'Shush. He's just a friend. I'm far too old for that sort of thing.' She levers herself out of the armchair.

We walk to the community centre, which I recognise from Nanna's Instagram photographs. It's funny piecing it all together – makes me realise how much she must enjoy seeing the photos of my life in London. I resolve to take more. I've been slacking off a bit, because life seems to have been nothing but the commute to work, slaving over a hot desk all day, commuting home again, collapsing in front of Netflix, and then bed.

143

'This is Cyril,' Nanna Beth says, having taken me straight over to a man once we arrive at the centre.

I can see he was probably quite handsome in his day. He's got a kind face, and is dressed in a soft houndstooth checked shirt and a smart navy blue sweater.

'Ah, Jess, I've heard all about you. I'm a bit of a fan.'

'You are?' I say, surprised.

'I am. Anyone who brings a smile to Beth's face the way you do must be a pretty good sort, in my opinion.'

I look sideways at Nanna Beth and realise with amusement that she's gone a little bit pink. She ducks her head, laughing, and says, 'Oh, Cyril, you are a charmer.'

Cyril chuckles, sounding pleased with himself – but not in a smarmy way. It's nice for her to have something good in her life after all those years of looking after Grandpa with his dementia.

'I'm going to take Jess for a walk along the prom, and get an ice cream. You're never too old for an ice cream with your nanna, are you,' she says, squeezing my arm. I shake my head.

'Do you want to join us?'

'Ice cream, in March?' Cyril shakes his head and does a mock shiver. It's sunny outside, but there's still a definite chill in the air. But ice cream on the prom is our thing, and we've always done it no matter what the weather. 'Absolutely not. I'm sure you two girls have lots to catch up on, and I've got plenty to be going on with here.'

I swear if he could have had a cartoon twinkle in his eye, he would have. Nanna positively skips out of the

144

community centre on my arm. I can't help wondering if I'll be as sprightly as she is at seventy-nine.

It occurs to me as we're wandering along the prom with ice cream cones, admiring the massed plantings of daffodils in their huge pots by the shelters, that Nanna's got a more interesting love life going on than I do. Something Sophie said the other day comes back to me – she pointed out in the bar the other day that I needed to get back on the horse. I said I'd think about it. And as I stand in the queue waiting for ice creams, I do. Maybe I should take the plunge and try dating again. It can't do any harm, can it? We've got a half-populated Tinder profile sitting there. Maybe – ugh. I grimace. I can't face the dick pics and the endless stream of weirdos sending messages. I've heard so many horror stories.

'No nice young men on the scene?' Nanna asks, looking at me over her glasses. It's as if she can read my mind.

I shake my head.

'None.'

'The trouble with you, lovey, is you've got a streak of your mother in you.'

I step back, stunned. Mum and I couldn't *be* more different. 'Me? And Mum?'

'Both old romantics, the pair of you. She's always dreamed that someone's going to come and sweep her off her feet, take her away from all this. That's why she's addicted to the drama of being on stage. And you're the same in your own way – hooked on those romantic films.'

145

I look at her, feeling my brows gathering in a frown of confusion.

'I don't think I'm like Mum at all,' I say, then eat some more ice cream and think about what she's said. I like it better when Nanna and I talk about day-to-day stuff, when she doesn't make me confront unpleasant realities. Today it's as if someone's taken her filter off. Maybe it's an age thing.

'I *definitely* don't want someone to sweep me off my feet,' I say, firmly. 'I've seen more than enough of that with Mum. She's been swept off her feet by so many dodgy con artists that I'm surprised she even knows whether she's the right way up or not.'

'No, but you'd like a nice happy ever after, wouldn't you?'

I let my guard down a little at that. 'A bit,' I concede.

'What about that nice Alex boy, then? I can't help noticing you're spending a lot of time with him.'

'As *friends*, Nanna. That's all.'

She gives me an old-fashioned look. 'Just friends?'

'Definitely. It's nice to have someone showing me London – that's it.'

'Hrmm,' she says, and then changes the subject, in a way that makes it clear she doesn't believe me for a second.

CHAPTER THIRTEEN

Alex

31st March, London

'Stick the kettle on, Alex, I'm gasping for a cuppa.'

I hear Becky call, and the slam of the door, thud of her bag full of papers on the dresser, clatter of her keys landing in the dish she keeps beside the half-dead geranium that's keeling over on a stand in the hall.

Jess got back from a weekend in Bournemouth an hour or so ago. I was sleeping off a night shift when I heard her coming upstairs and the sound of the shower turning on. It's nice that she's back. I don't know why, but I like it when everyone's here. I fill the kettle and put it on to boil, absent-mindedly picking up some dishes from the draining board and stacking them on the shelf. The dishwasher's on the blink again – I got home at half ten this morning to find it had sicked up grey water all over the floor, and I stood for about five night-shift-fuzzy minutes trying to decide if the right thing to do would be to a) pretend I hadn't seen it and leave it for someone else to deal with or b) unload the half-washed dishes and stack them up by the sink. In the end, I'd given a fairly hefty sigh then got on with it. Meanwhile, someone else had clearly washed them and left them to dry – most likely Rob. He was a stickler for a tidy kitchen.

With the dishes sorted and the surfaces wiped, I sit down at the kitchen table with a couple of pieces of toast. I'm so tired I feel like I've got jet lag, only without the exotic holiday to show for it. And with tiredness comes all the feelings I try to keep squashed down with work and the gym and all the other stuff people do to get a handle on emotional crap. I feel a bit shit that I haven't been able to make it back down to Kent for Mother's Day today, because I worked a late shift yesterday and I've got an assignment due next week that I've barely started, so I blew way more money than I can afford sending Mum a massive bunch of flowers. And then I went for a run, even though I was completely knackered. It helped, a bit. Not as much as the delicious three hours of sleep I've just had, mind you.

The guilt's worse now that Dad's gone, of course. My big sister Mel's in finance, and she's working in New York on secondment, which is a pretty reasonable excuse not to be able to make it, but it feels a bit crap to be an hour away on the train and stuck here in London because I've got an assignment to get done and I've worked a weekend shift. It's weird. I knew that we'd be thrown straight into placements in our first year, but I thought there'd be a bit more time to – I dunno. Breathe, maybe?

Nursing's way more all-consuming than law. I can't help thinking of all the friends who took the piss when I told them I was leaving. They thought I couldn't hack the pace at work, but the irony is nursing is way more pressurised than anything I experienced in law. If I'm not writing essays or studying for never-ending maths tests for medication dosage formulas, I'm cramming in a couple of agency shifts to get a bit of extra money coming in. Thank God for Becky – if she hadn't offered me a room in this place, I'd have spent every last penny on rent before I'd reached the end of my first year. As it is, money's tight. Rob's promised to give us another lesson in baking our own bread one day this week – he's got a couple of days off, and nothing to do in them, he says – so perhaps I can save some money by making all my own sandwiches from scratch.

'Look what I've got.' Becky appears in the kitchen, wearing a fluffy cat onesie. I assume she's been upstairs to change in record time, rather than going to Costco wearing it.

Jess appears moments after. She looks tired as well – it's like we've all got sleeping sickness. She puts a hand to her mouth, suppressing a massive yawn.

'Cock Soup?' I say, peering at the sachet Becky's holding. She snorts with laughter.

'It was on special offer. I got loads of noodles, too. We can split the cost.'

149

'Soup, made from cocks,' I say slowly.

Becky starts laughing. 'I like a nice cock in my soup,' she manages.

I don't know why, but for some reason Becky goes into hysterics and it's contagious. It's a good five minutes before we stop laughing, and my stomach muscles are killing me.

'I am *not* eating that,' Jess says, wiping her eyes.

'It's good for you. Packed with—' Becky turns the pack over and scans the ingredients '—monosodium glutamate and chicken flavouring. Mmm.'

'I'd rather starve,' Jess says.

'You're going to have to, unless you've got any other plans for making the rest of your crappy paycheque stretch.' Becky throws her a packet.

'I bet it's not that bad. Try it. Delicious salty goodness.'

'Don't start that again.'

Emma comes in at that point. She's looking pissed off about something, and she doesn't stay in the kitchen long before heading upstairs telling us she's going to have a bath. I hang around, watching as Becky checks the kitchen cupboards for signs of the mouse, even though I know I should go upstairs and get to work on the assignment that's due next week. In the end, I compromise and get my laptop and my notes and take them into the sitting room where Rob's watching the Arsenal match.

'They're playing like shit, man,' he says, offering me a beer.

'I shouldn't, I've got work to do,' I say, shaking my

head, but he gives me a sceptical look and extends his arm a bit further, waggling the bottle under my nose.

'Go on, then. You've twisted my arm.'

Predictably I end up spending more time watching the match than I do on the assignment. Rob's easy company, which helps. He's not one of those blokes who watches the football and screams at the TV – probably because it's not his team playing (he's a Liverpool supporter), but also because he's pretty laid-back by nature, as I'm discovering now we're spending more time together. His odd hours and mine seem to overlap, so we're spending more time than I expected just hanging out, cooking and watching television.

'How's it going?' He indicates the printouts and the laptop, now sitting on the coffee table.

'Good,' I say.

'You're not missing the legal stuff?'

'God, no.' I shake my head vigorously.

'I reckon when you start a career as an adult, you've got more of an idea what you're getting yourself into,' he says, in his gruff Glaswegian burr. 'I used to work in construction management,' he continues.

'Really?' I ask, trying not to sound surprised. He doesn't really look the type.

'Aye. Gave it all up and went back to college when I was about the same age you are now. Everyone thought I was off my head.'

'And no regrets?'

He gives a deep laugh. 'I wouldnae mind doing a few

less split shifts, but they come wi' the job. I bet you'd no' say no to a nine to five nursing job if one came up when you graduated.'

'They're rarer than hen's teeth,' I say.

'Aye, exactly. But you wouldn't give it up, would you?'

I shake my head again. 'Definitely not.'

'Weird, isn't it? I guess that's why they talk about vocations. You must've been born to it and it just took a while to find out.'

I think about the nurses in the hospital when Dad was sick, and the palliative care nurses in the day hospice in his final days: their kindness and the way they always seemed to hold it together no matter what was going on.

I recall a recent shift when I'd had a really hard night working as an HCA on a geriatric ward, doing a bit of agency work, and I'd been covered from head to toe in – well, let's just say I pretty much had to hose myself down afterwards. One of the nurses had got wind of the fact that I was a career changer and she'd been pretty catty about it. I'd been given all the crappy jobs – literally – but there was no way I was being accused of being 'too posh to wash' by the others on shift. So, I rolled up my sleeves and got on with it. By the end of the evening, the entire ward had been given a personal hygiene wash – head to toe, and everything else in between – and the sarky nurse had buttoned it.

Rob's right. Placements are long, the essays are never-ending, but I still don't regret it one bit.

Becky pops her head round the door. She's all dressed up, and tells us she's off to meet some friends from work. The fact that it's a Sunday night means nothing to her – she's always up for a night out. I pick up my assignment and head upstairs, saying goodnight to Rob, quietly convinced that I've done the right thing. It's a good feeling.

CHAPTER FOURTEEN

Jess

6th April

'I've chosen a dress,' says Sophie, brandishing a magazine at us.

We're sitting in gorgeous yellow sunshine on the little balcony of Sophie and Rich's flat in East London, where you can almost see the canal if you lean over at a precarious angle and peer between the houses in front. There's just about enough room for the three of us, as long as we don't try and move too fast.

'I took your advice – can't remember which one of you said it, but I've gone for the slinkiest one I could find. If that doesn't get me pregnant, I don't know what will.'

'If you think that's what makes you pregnant, it's not surprising it's not happened yet,' says Gen, drily. She looks up at the magazine. 'Ooh, very nice.'

It's a gorgeous, dark cream dress and it will suit Sophie's slender figure perfectly. 'I love it,' I agree.

'Anyway,' Gen says, tapping on the table with her finger, as if calling us back to order, 'let's get back to the task in hand. Which is *get Jess a shag*, in case anyone's forgotten.'

'Excuse me,' I yelp. 'I want a date. I'm not after a one-night stand.'

Sophie leans over and looks at my phone screen, where we've finally uploaded a decent photo to my Tinder profile, and we're trying to work out what to put on my bio. We used Gen's one before to look through profiles, but now I've – well, they've – decided that I need to get out there.

'You should get a dog. I was running in the park the other morning and I saw loads of good-looking men with dogs,' says Sophie.

'Should you be running in your condition?' Gen looks at her thoughtfully, tapping a pen against her teeth.

'What condition?' I spin round to look at Sophie. 'Have I missed a memo?'

She shakes her head. 'Still in the waiting period. Or hopefully *not* period.'

'Yeah, but you might jog it out of place or something,' says Gen, waving an arm, vaguely.

'I can't put my life on hold because I'm trying to get pregnant,' says Sophie. 'Anyway I've got a good feeling about this month. I did a headstand after sex on day fourteen.'

I glance at Gen, who looks faintly disgusted.

'TMI,' we both say, in unison.

'Soz,' says Sophie, shrugging.

There's a For Sale sign hanging from the railings in front of us. When Soph decides she wants something, she doesn't hang about. She's decided she wants a wedding ring, two-point-four children, a dog, and a house in the suburbs. And by sheer force of nature (and a few headstands) she'll get it. She always does.

Rich pops out to the balcony to kiss Sophie goodbye.

'Just nipping up to the gym,' he says, dropping a kiss on the top of her head. 'See you two later.'

I flick a glance in Gen's direction, wondering if she's thinking what I'm thinking. I know way more about Rich's sex life than I feel is necessary. Meanwhile, my sex life is completely dead in the water, and I'm pretty sure that Alex and Emma hooked up again the other night. Not that I've a problem with that, of course, because we're *friends* and that's perfectly nice. But I did kind of hope maybe it had fizzled out.

The most logical conclusion is to do as the saying goes, and get over him by getting under someone else. Or on top of. I'm not fussy, really. So, I've done it. Committed to signing up for online dating, starting with Tinder, because it's free, and the idea of paying for online dating seems a bit – well, it doesn't really matter what it seems, the truth is I'm skint.

'Why don't you just put something nice in your bio: "likes long walks and lazy Sundays drinking coffee and reading the papers"?' Sophie suggests, as if it's that easy to bag a man.

'Yeah, that'll definitely do it,' Gen says, giving me a bug-eyed stare.

'What's wrong with that?' Sophie sounds slightly offended.

'It's just a bit – sad.'

'But it's true. She does like walks and Sundays and coffee and all that stuff. Don't you, Jess?' She looks to me for confirmation. I feel torn.

'I do,' I say, hesitantly. 'It's just a bit . . .'

'Clichéd,' says Gen, firmly.

'Oh.' Sophie sags a little bit in her chair.

'Oh God,' Gen looks slightly shame-faced. 'Hang on, you met Rich at uni. I was feeling guilty in case I'd exposed your secret Tinder technique.'

'Yes, we met in the debating club, remember?'

Gen and I exchange glances. Nope, don't remember that at all, but it couldn't be more Sophie if she tried.

I should channel her, I think, and then I'd meet someone nice. My thoughts float in the direction of Alex, and I realise that if I was Sophie I'd probably just channel my thoughts in the direction of him, and he'd realise that he was looking for a relationship after all, and definitely wasn't after a no-strings-attached shag-fest with Emma. I wrinkle my nose at the thought.

'You all right?' Gen looks at me with concern.

'I've heard some horror stories about Tinder,' I say quickly (it's the first thing that springs to mind, and it's true at least). 'What if I end up being chopped into pieces by an axe murderer?'

'That could happen any day of the week regardless of dating apps,' says Sophie, reassuringly. She even squeezes my arm to underline what she's saying, her face creased into a little frown of kindness.

'Right, well, that's comforting,' I say.

'They're more likely to be married players, looking for a bit on the side,' says Gen.

'Nice,' I say in despair.

'Well, they're not *all*. I mean there are *some* decent men left out there. There must be,' Gen adds.

I look down at my screen, feeling faintly sick at the thought of my photo being out there, and my face being swiped left (or was it right? God, I better find that out) on a whim.

'One of the girls at work was telling me that she got a match the other day,' I tell them. 'He was a really nice-looking guy, really good job working as an invest-ment banker, et cetera, et cetera, et cetera. Two messages in, the formalities over with, and he asked her what she was doing. "Just having a coffee and thinking about heading to the shops for a bit of a wander," she said. "What about you?"' I grimaced, thinking about poor Jav's face when she'd been telling us over lunch.

'And he replied: "Just cracking one off over your photograph".'

'Ugh.' Sophie's nose wrinkles in disgust. 'And that was supposed to be a come-on?'

'A come-over,' Gen said, also looking a bit queasy. 'This is why I intend to remain single forever. I'm not putting myself through all that crap.'

'Uh, thanks, Gen,' I say.

'Sorry.'

'I'm not sure I'm ready for this.' I pick up the phone. There's a photograph of a nice-looking man with dark, brown hair and green eyes looking back at me. 'Oh.'

Gen snatches the phone back. 'Exactly.' She swipes at the screen.

'Oh my God, did you swipe him away?'

'Nope.' Gen puts the phone back down on the table, looking triumphant. 'I just took your Tinder virginity.'

'Ewww,' I say, feeling slightly sick. The phone buzzes and I pick it up.

'Oh my God, he's replied.' Gen gives a squeak of glee and high-fives Sophie. 'Get in.'

I look up and catch a glimpse of my face in the mirror. It looks more horrified than excited, but they don't seem to have noticed that.

CHAPTER FIFTEEN

Jess

13th April

And so, that's how I end up standing – one week, and a lot of surprisingly saucy Tinder chat (which I have to confess I liked more than I expected, so maybe I'm not as much of a prude as I thought) later – by the bridge leading to a riverboat on the Thames, dressed in one of Sophie's mega-expensive dresses, sheltering under Rob's golf umbrella in the pouring rain. Theo, my date, has told me to meet him here instead of the bar we were meant to be at, because he's running late. I guess that's what happens when you work in the city and you're a high-flying investment banker type. I peer through the sheets of rain, trying to see if I can spot him through the crowds. There's a mixture of people dressed up and heading into the party boat, drenched tourists with raincoats, and pissed-off-looking commuters making their way back home.

He'd left it late to tell me about the change of plans. I'd stood in the bar looking around for him for a while, scanning the place in case he was one of those people who didn't look anything like his picture. But then a waiter had come up and asked if I wanted a table, so I'd said yes (because I'm a strong independent woman and I don't mind sitting alone at a table in a crowded bar drinking a glass of red wine that costs £15). But then the glass of wine – which I'd been eking out for as long as I could – ran out, and he still hadn't turned up. And just as I was paying the bill and thinking that literally everyone in the entire place knew that I'd been stood up (because who goes to a bar dressed in a peacock-blue body-con dress with expensive hair and ridiculous really-hard-to-walk-in shoes for a casual solo drink?) my phone buzzed. And it was Theo, full of apologies, asking me to jump in an Uber and telling me he'd sort it out when I got there.

As first dates go, this is pretty bloody spectacular. I'm his plus-one at a masquerade ball, and despite the rain and the wind and the feeling that I might actually freeze to death if he doesn't turn up soon, I'm so excited I could burst. And I can't wait to get my hands on him, if I'm honest. He's gorgeous, charming, has an amazing job in investment banking, and a pretty good line in chat. I think I might have struck lucky the first time. It has to happen to some people, doesn't it? I mean statistically speaking, for all those people kissing frogs there has to be a one-in-a-million chance that I'll be the one who ends up with the prince?

I wrap the long coat Sophie has lent me around my chest, trying to keep the rain out. Emma's been really sweet, and done my hair up in a gorgeous mass of curls and so many kirby grips I won't have a clue how to get it down tomorrow morning, but that's the last thing on my mind. I don't even care (well, all right, a tiny bit, but I'm going to let that go) that I'm pretty sure I heard her creeping out of Alex's room yesterday morning. It might've been my imagination, anyway.

Oh come on, come on . . . It's five past seven, and Theo said he'd be here at five to. I'm standing in the rain, watching as glowing couples and groups of chatting people make their way across the little bridge and onto the boat. The railings are strung with fairy lights, which are swaying in the wind, and for a second it's as if I'm looking at myself from the outside, and it feels like I'm at the start of a movie.

And then I spot him. Hmm. All right, he's shorter than I imagined, but definitely still cute. And he's meandering along, talking on the phone – probably some terribly busy and important investment banking call, which is why he isn't rushing, because otherwise he'd get out of breath – and as he sees me he raises an arm in greeting, and ends the call.

'Jess,' Theo says, kissing me on the mouth. He smells of whisky and I realise in a second that he's already more than a little bit drunk. His eyes are crossing slightly, and he's swaying – and not just because we're being buffeted by the wind. 'Sorry I'm a bit late, got caught up in a –

163

thing.' His jaw is stubbled and he looks hollow-eyed and exhausted. 'You look lovely.'

He starts walking up the gangway towards the boat, and I realise I'm still standing, half expecting him to take the arm of my now-sodden coat. I hurry after him.

'I'll take your coat, madam,' says a man in a white jacket as we step onto the riverboat. He hands us each a black mask. Mine is trimmed with tiny diamante sparkles, which glitter in the light. Theo's is plain black. He slips his on immediately and his eyes gleam out at me.

'The ladies are just over there, if you want to—' He gives me an up and down look, and I suddenly feel very not-London and a bit scruffy, then checks his phone. He catches a glimpse of someone over my shoulder and waves at them. 'You nip to the loo, and I'll get you a drink. Don't forget your mask.'

A second later, he's gone. I go to the bathroom and look at myself in the mirror, fixing my lipstick – which I've chewed off, biting my lip in anticipation and nerves waiting for him to arrive – and try to tame my hair, which has come loose in the wind and rain so that lots of dark tendrils are fluffing around the edges of my face. I hook the mask on and look at myself once more.

I feel excited, and glamorous, and I tell myself that this is all very romantic. Me, at a masked ball, in London, with an investment banker as my date. A slightly drunk one, but nonetheless.

I climb the stairs and realise that while I've been down there they've loosed the boat from its moorings, and we're sailing. The floor is swaying slightly beneath my feet.

The space is thronging with people, and I stand for a moment, trying to work out which one of the hundred or so men in black tie and a plain black mask is Theo.

'There you are,' he says, over my shoulder. I turn around and he's holding a bottle of expensive champagne with a glass already poured for me. He takes a slug from the bottle. 'Thought you'd gone overboard.'

'Thanks,' I say as I take the glass and sip it, looking around. The women are wearing vibrant-coloured dresses covered in sequins and sparkles. Sophie's clingy peacock dress, which had felt so expensive before I left, now makes me feel a little bit drab, like a moth in comparison to their iridescent, dazzling butterfly garb.

'Theo!' A woman in a very short purple dress trimmed with feathers grabs his arm and he turns, taking another drink from the bottle of champagne. 'There you are,' she says. 'And who is this?' She looks at me, expectantly.

'This is Jess,' Theo answers.

'Hello,' I say, wondering if I should extend my hand for her to shake, or clink glasses, or what the etiquette is in these situations. She gives me a faint half-smile and turns, noticing someone else in the crowd.

'Jack!'

'My boss,' says Theo. He reaches forward and fingers the sparkling strap of my dress. 'You look gorgeous.'

'Thanks.'

I think he must've had quite a lot to drink already. His

voice is slurred and thick. 'Just got to do a bit of mingling, that sort of thing. You'll be okay here for a moment, yeah?'

I stand beside the bar, holding my glass of champagne, and try to look like I'm just casually people-watching, in the manner of a person who is happy in their own company. After ten minutes, Theo reappears, looking suspiciously bright-eyed. 'Jess. Sorry. Want to come upstairs?' he says.

We climb up the narrow metal staircase and onto the covered deck. The rain and wind have dropped, and the air smells fresh and clean. London sparkles, the lights on the embankment glittering like strings of jewels. The London Eye glows in the darkening blue sky and the buildings are a rainbow of lights silhouetted against the night. I turn to murmur something about how pretty it is to Theo, and realise he's gone – again. This is not going according to plan, and I'm on a bloody boat.

Help, I message Gen and Sophie.

What's happened? Sophie replies, instantly. *Man overboard?*

I shift out of the way as a couple, clearly very drunk, rebound against me, giggling, then disappear behind a pillar.

No. Man AWOL.

There's a moment before Sophie replies.

Oh my God, he stood you up?

No, I tap into my phone, as another drunk man in a mask steps on my foot as he walks past. I glare at him, but I think he's probably too pissed to notice.

Worse. He's here, he's pissed, and I've lost him on a bloody boat.

I go back downstairs, feeling like a complete idiot. An hour later, I've learned more than I needed to know about investment banking from that bloke in the office who nobody wants to talk to (there's always one), who has cornered me and downloaded the contents of his brain onto me. Occasionally I see Theo, who's clearly forgotten I even exist, passing by, always with a bottle in hand, rapidly reaching the staggering stage of drunkenness.

I excuse myself, leaving the office bore talking to another victim who'd found themselves in the corner of doom. And when I come out of the loo, I see what has to be the perfect end to a perfect date. Theo is standing, one arm propping himself up against the wall, the other burrowing like a ferret inside the front of a woman's dress, with his tongue halfway down her throat. I contemplate getting a drink and pouring it over his head, but I can't be bothered climbing the stairs and going to the bar, so I leave him there, and chalk it up to experience.

I see I have a message: *How's it going?*

God, I love Sophie. I think she's feeling guilty that my first Tinder date has turned out to be such a nightmare.

Well, he's now getting off with someone else, and I'm trapped on the boat from hell.

Where are you?

I message her the location.

I'm somewhere near Vauxhall.

Leave it with me, she replies.

A few minutes later, she messages again. Bless her, she's looked up the boat, worked out where the next stop on the Thames is, and has booked me an Uber. I really do love her.

'All right?' says the Uber driver as I climb in, having finally escaped the boat.

'I've had better evenings,' I say, sitting back against the seat and shaking my head in despair.

I get home forty-five minutes later, having messaged thanks in about fifteen different languages to Sophie, and rummage in my bag for the keys to the front door. I'm just about to put the key in the lock when the door opens and I stagger forward slightly, straight into Alex.

'Whoops,' says Alex.

'Sorry,' I say, steadying myself against the door.

He raises an eyebrow and gives that lopsided smile that makes my knees – bloody disobedient knees, which I wish would learn to behave themselves – go a bit weak. 'Good night, was it?'

I splutter. 'Hardly.'

'You coming in, then?'

CHAPTER SIXTEEN

Alex

13th April

Normal people would probably take advantage of the first Saturday night off in what felt like forever to go out and get hammered. Normal people – I think, as I stretch luxuriously, revelling in the fact that I've got the entire sitting room to myself and the house is empty – don't work the sort of week I've just worked. I put my feet up on the coffee table and sink into the battered pink sofa. This is exactly what I need.

'There's been an explosion in the Heart Surgery ward,' says a voice, urgently. No, I have no idea why watching a hospital drama on a Saturday night is my idea of relaxation but it's the kind of mindless thing I need right now. It bears precisely no relation to my experiences so far of hospital life, but I quite like it for that. For one thing, they're always using their phones in the ward.

169

Everyone knows there's generally only one spot in the entire hospital where you can get 4G service, and it's usually down a corridor near a supplies cupboard. You can always find them if you're in a hospital – just look for the spot where a disparate collection of NHS Trust staff are hovering, fingers tapping furiously, catching up on group chats or making plans for the end of their shift. Take it from me. It's the most useful information I've learned so far.

So, the plan is this: Sunday off, after six days working on the trot. Lie-in, lazy, scrambled eggs and toast sort of morning, followed by a walk around Hyde Park with Jess. The blossom's gorgeous this time of year, and we can have a wander up to look at Buckingham Palace, maybe do the Royal Mews, and be tourists for the day. That's assuming she comes home, of course. When she'd headed out earlier she looked – well. I'd had a moment when I'd had to remind myself sharply that just because I was used to hanging out with her in jeans, a hoody and her Converse, didn't mean she couldn't scrub up and look frankly amazing for a date. I'd made a bit of a joke out of it, and to be honest I was still feeling a bit guilty that I hadn't been generous enough to just tell her how great she'd looked. Emma had done Jess's hair, and her eyes were huge and smoky with dark shadow all around them. She'd looked amazing.

Thinking of Emma reminds me of what had happened next. I had nipped upstairs to get my phone charger and overheard Emma talking on the phone, her door ajar.

'Yeah, I don't know what I'm doing now. I think this evening I'm having a night in.'

There was a pause, and Emma had laughed. 'I suppose, yes. Boyfriend . . . no.'

I knew I shouldn't be listening, but that didn't stop me. It was as if time stood still for a second.

A tinkly laugh. 'Yeah. Yes. You'll meet him eventually, I promise. I'm working on it. Playing it cool.'

I don't know what made me listen. Some sort of weird sixth sense she was talking about me – or us, not that there was an *us*. At least, I hadn't thought there was. We'd had several *this is nothing serious, definitely just a bit of fun* type conversations.

'Yeah, I'd love you to meet him. I might see if he fancies dinner next week – I mean that might be a bit soon, but—'

There was a silence and then Emma laughed, and I realised that no, hang on, she was clearly talking about someone else. She must've met someone. I puffed out a breath, which was half a sigh of relief and half – well, nobody wants to feel like they've just been given the silent heave-ho without even being consulted, do they? Emma said something else I couldn't catch, and then laughed again.

'Yes, he's cute. Used to be a lawyer. He's training to be a nurse.'

I looked down at the skin on my knuckles, which was turning white as I gripped the stair wall. Who was Emma talking to? And – God. I felt my face invert in a grimace.

171

The deal we'd both agreed was that it was nothing more than a friends with benefits sort of thing. Nobody getting too involved, nobody getting hurt.

I'd crept back downstairs, keen to make sure she didn't realise I'd overheard.

In the end, half an hour later, Emma had popped her head around the kitchen door and said she was off out for last-minute drinks with a friend, and that maybe she'd see me later, if I was still up.

We'd slept together for the first time on New Year's Eve, and now it's April. I suppose it was naïve of me to think something could stay so casual for that long. It's not Emma. She's lovely. But after Alice – no way. Signing up for my new career meant walking away from a relationship I thought was for life, and I'm not taking that sort of risk again, not now, with years of training to do. I'm just starting to feel that, actually, I'm okay on my own, and I'm getting over the whole Alice thing.

I let myself think about Alice, which is something I don't often do. I'm over her – but I don't want to leap into anything else and end up in the same place all over again. If Emma is starting to think there's something more to this, I'm going to have to knock it on the head, gently. But – I rub my face in confusion – how the hell do I do that without causing ructions in the house-share?

This is exactly what Becky had meant with her no-relationships rule. It wasn't the being in a relationship that was the problem, it's the end of them when it all gets messy. And Emma's the sort of girl who likes things done her way.

Just as the credits begin to roll on my overdramatic hospital drama, I hear a commotion at the door. I figure it's probably someone at the wrong house. I get to the door and pull it open and there's a moment when Jess sort of falls through and crashes against me with a little 'oomph' noise of surprise. Her hair is damp and curling round her face in little strands, and all the dark eye make-up she'd had on is smudged. She takes a step back. Her coat's splattered with huge raindrops.

'Good night, was it?' I can't help smiling at her. She looks so cross.

'Hardly.'

'You coming in then?' She wipes her feet on the mat. 'So the date didn't go well?'

'Not exactly. I'm bloody freezing. If this was an April shower, I don't like it.'

She steps past me and shrugs off her coat, revealing the bluey-green dress she's got on underneath. I avert my eyes, as if she's undressing, not pulling off a pair of black heeled boots. And then she's Jess-sized again, standing in a pair of black tights on the carpet.

'Want me to put the kettle on?' I ask when I notice she's shivering.

'Give it five minutes. I'm going to run up and get out of this—' she motions to the dress '—have a quick shower to defrost, and put on something that doesn't make me feel like I'm dressing up.'

173

While Jess changes, I put the kettle on for tea, then make toast, buttering it thickly and spreading it with her favourite marmalade. And then I put it all on a tray, and take it into the sitting room. A moment later, Jess reappears, looking more like her usual self in a pair of checked flannel pyjama bottoms, and a light grey teddy-bear fleece top. Her hair and make-up are still in place, so she looks incongruous – like an actress after a performance on the West End stage.

'Oh my God. I think I love you,' she says, seeing the tea and toast. 'You're a mind reader.'

I hand her a mug. 'I figured you might be cold even after the shower.'

I watch as she creates the little nest she always makes when she sits watching television, wrapping her fingers around the mug and curling up on the sofa like a cat. She pulls a fluffy blanket down and wraps it over her legs, building a cushion fort around her, and almost purrs with happiness.

Then she takes a sip of tea, and pulls a face of absolute horror.

'Are you all right?' I ask, thinking maybe I've put salt in her tea instead of sugar.

'I am never, ever going on a Tinder date again,' she says.

I'm not sure why I feel something that is suspiciously like relief. She's my friend, nothing more. And I need to get a grip. It's nothing to do with me what – or how – she dates.

'What happened?' I say, carefully.

'Oh God,' Jess says, then regales me with the tale of Theo turning up plastered, dumping her in a corner, then getting off with someone else – making me roar with laughter.

'I honestly think dating is some sort of torture,' I say.

'You're not joking.' Jess pulls the blanket up towards her nose and turns to face me, laughing. She wipes a smudge of black mascara stuff from underneath her eye.

'I bet you can't beat that, though?'

'Mine's quite tame compared to that,' I say. 'I went on a blind date organised by a friend from uni once, when I'd just started working at the law firm. We were working such long hours, it was impossible to meet anyone.'

'Go on. So what happened?' Jess shuffles slightly on the sofa, so a cushion drops onto the floor. I pick it up and hand it back, and she hugs it, looking at me expectantly.

'Well, you know how everyone always has the old made-up emergency call thing?'

'You mean when you tell your friends to ring up and invent a disaster so you can make a quick exit?'

I nod.

'I was sitting in a bar in Clerkenwell, waiting for this girl to turn up. She walked up to the window, looked in, spotted me, picked up her phone and pretended to take a call.'

'What happened then?'

'She never came back.'

'Oh, Alex, you poor thing.' Jess reaches out and pats

me on the thigh. 'I wouldn't have left you sitting there like a lemon, I promise.' Her eyes are soulful. 'So what did you do?'

'Waited an hour, ate my entire body weight in olives, then went home.'

'And she definitely wasn't coming back? It wasn't an actual emergency or anything?'

I shake my head. 'Apparently she took one look and decided *no thanks*.'

'Brutal.' Jess gives a low whistle.

'Yeah, not great for the self-esteem.'

'That's dating in London for you,' Jess says, picking up the remote control and fiddling with it. 'But then you met Alice, and it all worked out okay in the end.'

'Well, okay until she dumped me, yeah. I mean basically great, apart from the whole thanks but no thanks element.'

I look at her with a dubious expression and she claps a hand to her mouth, realising what she's said.

'Oh my God, Alex.' Jess is laughing in horror. 'I am so sorry.'

We end up staying up for hours, watching a rom com that Jess has found on Netflix, drinking gallons of tea and eating toast. At one point Emma comes home, looks into the sitting room and says hi. I feel like a bit of a shit because I give her a quick wave of hello and Jess carries on talking. I don't know what to do about the whole Emma thing, and I don't want to think about it this evening. I just shove it to the back of my mind, and decide I'll leave it there until tomorrow.

CHAPTER SEVENTEEN

Alex

28th April

A few weeks pass. I still haven't worked out what to do about the whole Emma situation. Right now I'm opting for the very mature, completely self-aware *ignore the whole thing and hope it'll go away* approach. Emma hasn't been around that much, which helps. I think she's got a lot on with work. I've got a mountain of assignments to do, and another placement coming up, so the days pretty much pass without me even being aware what's going on. I'm still finding time to take the odd walk with Jess, but she's got loads going on at work as well. It's like the nicer the weather gets, and the more we'd want to actually enjoy it, the less time there is for us to get outside, which is a shame because I've been thinking maybe I could ask Jess for some advice on what to do about Emma.

But not this weekend – because whatever the weather, we're all outside for the whole of Sunday. Well, me, Jess and Becky, anyway. Matt, one of my old friends from when I worked with Becky, has been living with stage four leukaemia for the last year, and a couple of friends are running the London Marathon to raise money for Cancer Research.

'All you have to do is stand by the side of the road in Shadwell at the official cheering point for a few hours and gee up the runners,' Becky said, when she roped the rest of the house in. Jess is well up for it. Turns out she watches the marathon every year, so being there for the actual thing is really exciting for her. I volunteered last year in the St John's Ambulance tent, so I'm slightly less excited and slightly more aware that getting from our side of London to Shadwell on Marathon day is a feat in itself.

'It's really good of you guys to come along,' says Harry, the charity stand organiser. We're spread out across three folding trestle tables, with boxes of bottled water, bowls of jelly babies and packs of energy gel all ready to go. Jess dances around, banging the inflatable noisemakers together, trying them out.

'You might want to save that for later,' says Harry, grinning. He's an old hand at this. He tells us he's been running the cheering station here for the last ten years, since he recovered from leukaemia himself.

'Least I could do,' he says, with a self-deprecating grin.

'Lazy bugger,' says a woman who introduces herself as Andrea, Harry's wife. 'You could at least run the bloody marathon like I did.'

She's dressed from head to toe in the charity colours, with a ridiculous inflatable hat on her head. She's short and round and clearly the power behind Harry. Throughout the morning, I watch him glancing to her for approval regularly. She teases him incessantly and he winds her up. They're obviously mad about each other.

There's a long, long gap after the first runners go through, shooting past in seconds, following their pace-makers, and the wheelchair athletes, who move so fast that Jess almost misses the whole pack because she's gone to the loo.

'So what happens now?' Jess sits down on a folding chair and shades her eyes, looking up at Andrea.

'We wait.' Andrea tapes down a sign that's come loose.

'Sounds a bit ominous.'

Andrea nods emphatically. 'Rained the morning I ran it. I got soaked at the start, then had to run the whole thing in a damp T-shirt. And I lost five toenails.'

'Yowch.' Jess pulls a face. 'How did that happen?'

'It's fairly standard – 26.2 miles is a long old way to run.'

'Can't believe you did it. That's amazing,' Jess says, looking incredibly impressed.

'I can't either. It was bloody knackering,' Andrea says, then gives a snort of laughter. 'But it seemed a hell of a lot easier than going through six rounds of chemo like he did.' She nods in the direction of Harry, who is tying balloons full of helium to the side of the charity banner.

'I love watching the Marathon,' Jess says. 'Especially that bit at the beginning where you see everyone's stories and it makes you cry.'

'Oh God,' Becky says as finally she appears. She's been staying with a friend in Poplar, so she's on foot, wearing a baseball cap and sunglasses to protect her eyes from the already-bright sunshine. She pinches a couple of jelly-babies. 'Has she told you about how she sits there every year to watch the runners, weeping and eating toast?'

'Shut up, you,' Jess says, going pink.

'True though,' Becky says. 'God I am so hungover. I need a saline drip. You haven't learned to do that yet, have you, Alex?'

'I don't have one handy, no,' I say. 'And I don't think the medical tent would be that impressed if you turned up and told them you needed rehydration.'

'I'm going to go and find some full-fat Coke then. I need to be in full-on cheering mode for the lads from work.'

I nip to the loo and when I get back I stand for a moment, watching Jess chatting to Becky. I've been trying to work out how to talk to her about the whole thing with Emma – I mean if we're friends, there's no reason why I shouldn't be telling her, but at the same time, it feels – awkward. I don't want to mention it in front of Becky though, because of her whole no relationships thing – not that it *is* a relationship. That's kind of the whole point.

'Ready?' Andrea turns to me, and the moment is lost. From then on we're caught in a strange mixture of cheering then waiting, waiting then cheering.

The Mass Race runners come through first – super fit amateur athletes who zoom past us wearing our charity colours, grabbing a drink and tossing it to one side before pelting on down the road in search of a personal best time.

'I'm waiting for the people in fancy dress.' Jess peers into the distance again. 'I can't believe the noise.'

'That's why I said earlier that you'd soon have enough of it.' Harry grins and rattles the noisemakers near her ear. She ducks away, laughing.

Becky isn't joking when she says Jess cries at the runners. When the charity runners start coming through with the names of the people they're running for and their photos printed on the backs of their T-shirts, Jess basically starts sobbing and doesn't stop. Becky teases her about it incessantly.

'Shut up,' Jess says, wiping her face with both hands. Any make-up she had on is long gone. She blows her nose on a spare bit of kitchen roll from Andrea's picnic bag. 'I can't help it. It's just so . . .' and she points to a woman who's half-walking, half-jogging with "This one's for you, Dad" on the back of her T-shirt. And just like that, my heart cracks and I feel tears streaming down my face, too. I wipe them away, ineffectually. Jess hands me one of her tissues, silently, and bumps the side of my arm with hers.

'I feel like *I've* run a marathon after all that,' Becky says, hours later, as we fold up the last of the tables and high-five the other supporters. She blows us a kiss and heads off before we do, because she's left her stuff at her friend's place.

The tractors and clearing-up lorries have passed by now, following a handful of stragglers – some who were walking, some clearly baking hot in heavy fancy dress costumes. It's a long way to go dressed as Big Bird on a sunny day. Still, Big Bird gave us a cheery wave.

'You can do it,' Jess shouted, clapping as the last few people made their way past. They had another five and a bit miles to go, and they looked completely wiped out. But they brightened when she cheered them. I picked up my noisemaker and gave them a rattle, and together we called out their names.

'Come on, Brian, you can do it!'

'Go on, Sarah!'

'Jamie! Not long to go now.'

Without thinking, I put an arm around Jess's shoulders as we cheered the couple who were shuffling along in a tandem bicycle costume and as they passed it turned into a funny, awkward sort of hug and I think Jess's tears must be contagious because I saw they were running for our charity and I thought of Matt sitting at home watching the television and I had to wipe the tears away from my face again.

'Gets to us all in the end,' said Harry, clapping me on

the back. He dropped an arm around my shoulder and squeezed me. 'Get yourselves off for a drink.'

Jess went to collect her rucksack and Harry gave me a look. 'Got a good one there, son.'

'Oh she's not my—' I began, but he'd turned away before I could finish the sentence.

CHAPTER EIGHTEEN

Jess

3rd May

I look up at the sky, cerulean blue and cloudless, and feel the heat of the sun on my face. It could be the middle of August, instead of May. A little practical voice pops up in my head, and points out that I should probably be wearing sunscreen. I stop for a second and rummage in my bag – I'm sure there's some in there somewhere.

'It's better in May, before the summer holiday tourists appear,' Alex says. We're in Regent's Park near the zoo. We haven't been out for a walk for a while, or really out together at all since the Marathon; I've been flat out with work, and Alex has started a placement in the geriatric ward. He's been doing nights, which seems to be when they all die, grimly enough, so I'm cautious about asking how it's going because every tale seems to start with 'we lost another one last night . . .' I don't know how he does it and stays cheerful. It's weird. I can't imagine what would make anyone want to be a nurse, but I'm very glad that whatever it is makes people do it.

'I'm so tired I could sleep for a week,' says Alex.

'We can lie on the grass for a bit. We don't have to walk ten miles a day if you don't want to.'

He stops and looks at the grass. Newly mown, it looks quite tempting.

'Just for a bit?'

'Just for a bit,' I agree.

We lie down on the grass, side by side, and look up at the sky.

'When I was little I used to lie on the beach with my grandpa and spot shapes in the clouds,' I said. I'd forgotten that until now, looking up at a vaguely snow-man-shaped cloud, hovering above us.

'*Do you want to build a snowman . . .*' sings Alex.

'You've spent too much time doing agency work on the kids' ward.'

'Tell me about it. I reckon I know the entire plot of *Frozen* inside out.'

'Does it even have a plot?' I ask.

He turns his head to look at me. 'Have a plot? I'll have you know there are academics right now arguing the toss over whether *Frozen* is a feminist tract or if it's inherently problematic because of its depiction of the trolls.'

'Seriously?'

He nods. 'Seriously.'

'I think I need to watch it and find out.'

'Deal.' He turns his head and looks back up at the sky. The air is heavy with the scent of candyfloss machines, bitter coffee, and the faint waft of something distinctly animal-ish from the zoo.

'Roaaaar!'

Something flies past our heads and I roll over onto my side just as Alex does, so we are looking straight at each other. His eyebrows gather in a frown, but he's laughing. He rolls over, and pushes himself up to standing.

'What the hell was that?' I scramble up, brushing newly cut grass off my legs.

'Low-flying zoo escapee?' he asks.

I point across the park. 'I think I've found the culprit.'

A small child is holding on to a remote control, trying inexpertly to fly a tiny plane, and making sound effects at the same time.

'Timmy, don't fly that so close to the people,' his mother shrieks as she runs toward him, grabbing the remote control, but it's too late. The plane, which zipped over our heads a second ago, has crashed straight into the newspaper an elderly and grumpy-looking man is reading, while sitting in a striped deckchair. He shuffles the paper and looks at us all over his glasses. Both Alex and I turn away, trying not to giggle.

'Let's get out of here before we get into trouble,' Alex says.

We walk along the edge of the zoo fence, looking up at the netting that hangs over the high rails, keeping us out and the animals in.

187

A giraffe peers over the fence at us, chewing thoughtfully.
'Oh look,' I point to her.

Alex looks up, shading his eyes. 'Hello, gorgeous.'

'She's lovely, isn't she?'

'Might be a he. I don't know how you tell with giraffes.'

'Sorry. Hello, gorgeous giraffe of indeterminate gender,' I say, laughing. Alex has his hands in the pockets of his jeans, and he gives me a gentle nudge with his shoulder.

'Fancy an ice cream?' he asks.

'God, yes.'

He points to the stall on the other side of the park. 'Race you.'

'What are you, five years old?' I ask, but he's already gone. I get there ages after him, realising as I stand with my hands on my knees and my lungs feeling like they're on fire that maybe it's time I got some proper exercise.

'Sorry,' Alex says, from above where I'm bent over. I take a breath in and unfurl myself, standing up to look him in the eye. He hands me an ice cream, swirled with raspberry sauce and covered in rainbow sprinkles.

'For this—' I take it from him and lick a trail of ice cream that's dripping down the side of the cone '—I will forgive you. This time.'

'How's your friend Gen getting on with her property guardian thing?'

'Oh—' I look up. He remembers so much detail. Alex pays attention to little things, I've noticed. He's the only one in the house who remembers how everyone takes their tea and coffee and doesn't have to ask. It's nice. 'I forgot I told you about that. She's fine, I think. A glitter ball in the bedroom is very much her style.'

'I wanted to ask your advice about something,' Alex says, as we start walking again. I look at him sideways. He's biting the edge of his ice cream cone, frowning in concentration as he twirls it round. I've never seen anyone eat an ice cream like that.

'Go on.' I scuff my toe on the gravel of the path. A flock of tourists fly past us on Boris Bikes, shrieking with laughter, and we jump out of the way.

'It's about Emma.'

Oh.

No.

My ice cream becomes very interesting and I look at it intently, hoping that I haven't gone red in the face. Alex stops, turning to look at me. I try to put it off, but I have to look him in the eye and I swallow as I do so. 'Emma?' I say, breezily. 'What about her?'

'Well, the thing is . . .' He tails off, biting his thumbnail and gazing into the middle distance, back towards the zoo animals. I see the tall shape of the giraffe reaching up to take a mouthful of leaves from one of the trees. A plane flies past, with an advert hanging from the back of it, old-fashioned style. Bees are humming, and children are shrieking, and gravel is scrunching, and I'm waiting for him to say something, and then it all comes out in a jumble of words.

'I don't know if you know . . .' He pushes a hand through his hair. 'I don't want it to be awkward.'

189

'It's fine,' I say, airily. 'I mean, I think everyone must have some idea, so it's not going to be a major deal. And I'm sure you'll be very happy. You make a nice couple.' I think I've done quite a good job of that. Might be better to stop talking now, mind you. I press my lips together before any more words escape.

He runs a hand through his hair again, making it stand on end. I half want to laugh, but I also want to burst into tears and shout *it's not fair* like a child and run away. I like him, and he likes me, and we get on and make each other laugh and I've never seen him and Emma laughing together, and why does it have to be the case that I'm always the—

'We're *not* together,' he says firmly. 'And I don't want us to be. That's the problem.'

'Ohhh.' I raise my eyebrows, trying to look sage, and knowledgeable, and definitely not relieved. I'm not sure how well I manage it.

'Thing is, she mentioned something about me on the phone to a friend the other week and I – God I feel really awkward saying this. I'm not being a massive ego on legs. I just got the feeling that she's wanting more than . . .'

He screws up his face and goes a bit pink in the cheeks, then bites his lip, waiting for me to say something.

'Oh, but Emma's lovely,' I say, magnanimously. I can afford to be nice now. God, am I a bitch? I make a mental note to ask Gen and Sophie if they think I am.

'She is. I don't want to screw things up,' Alex says.

'God, no.' I think of Albany Road and try to imagine

190

someone else moving into Alex's room. We've all become accustomed to each other, and anyway, I don't want Alex moving anywhere. Not if his relationship with Emma's definitely off the cards.

'I'm sure it'll be fine. Just explain to her you don't want to be caught up in anything serious just now, or something like that.'

He looks serious then for a moment. 'We *had* that conversation at the start. It was her idea, actually. Maybe I need to make sure she realises it now. I think it's time to just knock it on the head.'

'Yes,' I say. We start strolling along beside the lake, watching the swans and the ducks swimming along, enjoying the sunshine.

Ooh, I think, maybe this means there's a chance after all. Not now, of course. But this was already the start of a beautiful friendship . . . maybe it could lead to something more.

But then Alex drops the bombshell, and I remember that being a daydreaming romantic doesn't mean the world's going to fall into place just to suit me.

'Thing is,' Alex says, thoughtfully, 'I'm just not ready to be in a relationship with anyone.' He sighs. 'Oh, I don't know. I got a reminder email the other day about my upcoming wedding.'

I open my mouth and shut it again. I'm not sure what the correct response to that is.

I go with 'I'm sorry.'

'Oh, don't be,' he says, turning to look at me and

smiling so his lovely crinkly eyes twinkle in a way that makes my knees go a bit funny. 'I mean it was clearly not meant to be with me and Alice. She wanted the whole package. House, money, lawyer husband, kids . . .'

'She could have had the almost-package,' I point out.

'Alice wasn't really an almost sort of person. She's a bit like your Sophie.'

'Ah,' I say. It all falls into place a bit then, and I think that maybe it's time I got a grip and recognised that neither Alice nor Emma were anything like me, and therefore I am very definitely not Alex's type, and that I should move on, in a very grown-up and sensible manner. To hide my face, I pull out my phone and take a photograph of two swans resting by a bush, their long necks intertwined. Even they're paired off, I think, crossly.

Later I meet Sophie for an emergency dinner summit. I'm all ready to dump all my feelings of angst and woe on her, but as soon as I walk into the pasta restaurant we love, I see her sitting at the table with her chin in her hand, looking glum.

'You okay?' I shove my bag under the table and look at her intently.

She nods. She's got her pale blonde hair tied up in a sleek ponytail, and her clothes and make-up are immaculate, as always. If you didn't know her, you wouldn't have a clue anything was wrong. But I could see that something was troubling her.

'It's not Rich, is it?'

She shakes her head. A waiter appears and asks what we want to drink.

'I'll have a glass of the Montepulciano d'Abruzzo,' I say, handing him back the menu.

'Lemonade, please,' says Soph.

I raise my eyebrows.

'That's what's wrong.' Sophie gives a gusty sigh. 'I'm doing all the right things. I even did that bloody head-stand again in bed last month after we had sex, because I read a thing on Mumsnet that said it can help you get pregnant.'

'Oh my God. You're not?' I pick up the wrong end of the stick completely. 'Is that why you're drinking lemonade?'

Sophie pleats the tablecloth with her fingers and looks at me. For a moment, her habitual cool and measured manner are replaced with an expression of genuine concern.

'You know, I just thought maybe it'd save time if I got pregnant now, and we'd be married in autumn, and then I could take maternity leave in the next tax year.'

I realise my mistake and blush. She's not pregnant after all. 'Oh my God Soph, you can't organise your life like that. Babies don't just come on demand . . . I don't think.'

'It's not organising,' she says, sounding slightly cross. 'It's more like multi-tasking.'

The waiter reappears with our drinks, and she sticks a paper straw in hers, sucking it gloomily. 'It's the first thing in my life that hasn't been under my control.'

God, I think about my chaotic life. The weeks between one payday and the next. The fact I'm utterly besotted with a man who thinks I'm well and truly in the friend zone. The fact that it's been ages since I saw my mother who was last sighted stacking essential oil equipment on the kitchen table and announcing that it was going to make her a fortune, and that I'm living in a subsidised house-share and if Becky decided to pull the rug out from under me I'd be screwed. 'I don't think I have anything in my life that *is* under my control.'

Sophie smiles ruefully at this. 'I suppose I should get a grip and stop complaining, really, shouldn't I?'

I shake my head. 'It's not that easy, though, is it?' I say. 'It's weird. Remember when we were little kids, and we thought being grown up meant having all the answers? Now we're almost thirty, and I feel like I haven't a clue what I'm doing.'

'Me neither,' says Sophie. She pushes back her chair. 'I must just run to the loo. If he comes while I'm gone, tell him I want the carbonara with some green salad on the side. No dressing.'

I watch her making her way across the room. With her long ponytail of blonde hair, height and long, long legs, she's always attracted attention. The waiter watches her with unashamed admiration before coming over to our table when I meet his eye.

'Your friend, she is very beautiful lady.'

I agree.

Very beautiful, and a slightly painful, jab-in-the-ribs

reminder of just how far I have to go in my life to start to feel like a fully functioning adult. How many years will it be before I even begin thinking about having a baby? I try to imagine it – I haven't even really given it much thought, and yet I am turning thirty this year. God, if I had a baby at, say, thirty-seven – I start doing sums in my head, and rapidly extend them to my fingers – I'd be fifty-seven by the time it turned twenty. That sounded like a lifetime away.

I think when Gen and Soph and I were young, we'd all been quite certain that by this age we'd all be settled and happy. Domestic bliss felt like a lifetime away for me. I guess that's what happens when you start all over again at the age of almost thirty.

CHAPTER NINETEEN

Alex

10th May

I get on the train to Canterbury. Not sure why it feels like the right thing to do, but it's been nagging at me. I dunno, maybe I'm reading too much into it, but the last couple of times we've spoken on the phone Mum's sounded a bit fragile: keen to tell me how busy she is, and how much she's got on.

I stare out of the window as the train pulls away, watching the familiar landmarks. I've sat on this same train countless times. An older man in an expensive-looking suit clears his throat in the chair opposite and spreads his newspaper over the table, and I feel a stab of grief. Weird how it hits you. It's not the anniversaries or the birthdays, it's the way a stranger shakes their newspaper open, or a song on the radio at the nurses' station, that reminds you of what you've lost. I rub my face with both hands, screwing up my eyes and then opening them wide. I can't remember not being tired. Everything's just a blur of—

I wake up as we pull into the station at Canterbury, because someone knocks me on the shoulder with their bag as they're pulling it down from the racks overhead.

'Sorry, mate.'

'You've done me a favour,' I say gratefully. I stand up, blearily, and pull my ticket out of my pocket as I get off the train.

I see my mother before she sees me – she's sitting in the car, waiting in the pick-up area beside the car park.

'Hello, darling,' she says, and gives me a kiss on the cheek.

'Mum.'

'I thought we could get a bit of lunch before we head home – go to the Red Lion?' she says, and we pull out of the car park.

The pub's busy, despite it being a weekday. We squeeze into a table in the corner and scan the menus.

'I spoke to Gwen the other day,' my mum says, casually.

I sit up and put the menu down. Mum carries on looking through the lunch options, as if we didn't both know that she was going to have the same thing she always has when she comes here – ploughman's lunch, no pickled onion, and half a pint of shandy.

'What for?' I ask.

I feel weirdly uncomfortable about that. Alice's mum was nice enough, but the idea of her ringing is . . . weird.

Is it weird? Maybe it's perfectly normal for them to stay in touch.

'You were going to marry her,' Mum says, clearly reading my thoughts. 'They would have been family. I thought it was nice.'

I make a vague noise of agreement. The last time I'd seen Alice had been anything but nice; we'd had a massive argument, where she'd made it more than clear that I was throwing my life away, ruining hers, and giving up a good career to (and I quote) *piss about wiping people's backsides for the rest of my life.*

I go up to the bar and place our order. We chat about mundane things for a while, then when our food arrives, Mum launches into a long list of all the things she's doing to keep herself busy. She's got a pretty full-on job as a social worker for the local council, so I'm a bit worried she's filling every second with things to avoid dealing with how she's feeling.

'I'm not overstretching myself, darling,' she says, when I suggest she might need a bit more down time. She looks at me for a moment. 'Have you just done a module on grief, or something like that?'

My mouth twists into a smile despite myself. 'Yes, I might have – but that doesn't mean I'm not right.'

'Your dad's health took up a lot of my time for the two years before he died. I had to give up pretty much everything apart from work and hospital visits, and then caring for him, and taking him to and from the hospice . . .'

199

'I know.'

'I still don't see how all of that – that dreadful time – made you want to give up a perfectly good career.'

'You know this.' I try and keep my voice level. I feel like I've had this conversation a million times over and it's like every time I see her – or anyone else in the family – they listen, then hit the reset button in their minds as soon as they walk away. The only person who actually gets it is Mel, my sister, but she's in New York, working her arse off on a secondment. Which reminds me, I must give her a call. WhatsApp is all very well, but it'd be nice to get a shot of her calm, measured approach to life, just to remind me I'm not insane.

'You're a social worker,' I say as I butter a bread roll, then look at her. 'You chose a job where you see some of the worst things in our community and deal with them on a daily basis.'

'Yes, but I'm making a difference,' she says.

I push my chair back in surprise and look at her, both hands pressed against the edge of the table. 'And I'm not?'

'Dad still died, didn't he?'

'Not because of nurses. He didn't die because the nurses did something wrong.'

She shakes her head. 'I just don't understand how you'd want to spend your life in one of those places.' She shudders then, and her face drops. 'Hospitals. They're like a prison.'

'It's nothing like that. We make a difference. That's

why I do it – that's why I'm doing it. I can't believe you'd honestly think that.'

'I'm sorry, Alex,' she says. She dips her head for a moment and when she looks up at me there are tears shining in her eyes, threatening to spill over and trickle down her cheeks. 'I just – I go cold thinking about Dad in there. And the doctor telling us there was nothing they could do. And . . .'

The threatened tears leak out and she dabs at them with a paper napkin, unrolling a knife and fork to get to it, and leaving them lying askew on the table.

'It's not a bad job. We're not in the habit of killing people off.'

'It just makes me so sad to think of you spending every day somewhere so depressing.'

'It's not depressing,' I say.

I think of the orthopaedic ward where I'd been doing agency work the other day, where three elderly women – all broken hips – were exchanging stories on how they'd got their injuries. Margaret, aged ninety-one, had been halfway up a ladder redecorating her dining room when she'd lost her footing and fallen. They were full of life and laughter and they'd spent the entire day winding me up. I got the usual good-humoured male nurse jokes of course – if I had a tenner for every one of those, I'd be able to retire before I even graduated – but they were a lovely lot. And when a girl of about twenty had turned up – tearful and clearly in a lot of pain – with a badly broken leg from an ice-skating competition, they'd all

201

cheered her up, making jokes across the little four-person side ward. That sort of thing – that's what makes it worth it.

'Well,' says my mother, sounding a bit dubious. 'As long as you're happy.'

'I am,' I say.

She chats about her pottery class and the outdoor swimming club she's joined, and I listen and make the right noises. I think if I told her about Margaret and the girls in the orthopaedic ward, she'd probably get it, but I can't face it. I'm tired of trying to convince people that I've done the right thing when there are others out there who don't need to be told. Look at Jess. She understands. She gave up a good job and stability and all the rest of it to follow her dream of working in publishing. I shake my head and bring my focus back to what my mother's saying.

'She's okay then?' Mel's on the phone from New York as I'm sitting on the train back to London, later that evening. She's about to go into a lunchtime meeting when she takes my call, and I'm trying to keep my voice down and not be one of those wankers making a call at the top of my voice.

'Yeah, she's good. I think you'd say she's keeping busy.'

'Sounded a bit manic to me.'

'Nah,' I say back, even though it's exactly what I was worried about. 'She's fine. Just getting on with stuff.'

'How about you?' Mel asks.

'All right. Tired.' Always tired.'

'Quit moaning,' Mel says, laughing. 'You chose this. You could've been sitting at a desk between meetings with your feet up, looking out over Manhattan like I am.'

'No thanks,' I say honestly. I picture it and can't think of anything worse.

'How's the house working out? Still in the honeymoon period with your fellow residents?'

'Pretty much. Everyone's pretty easy-going so it's no stress.'

'And what's the deal with *Emma*?'

Gah, I wish I'd never mentioned it to her. Every time I speak to Mel she winds me up about my 'house romance'.

'Nothing. I need to knock it on the head properly. I've got way too much on to be getting caught up in relationship stuff.'

'I knew it,' she crows. 'You are *so* not the friends with benefits sort. You've always been way too straight.'

'I am not,' I protest, but I know she's right.

'You so are. That's how you ended up with Alice. If you hadn't taken an uncharacteristic left turn and given up your job you'd be well on the way to domestic bliss in Surrey.'

'Shut up,' I say, laughing.

'Got to go,' Mel says suddenly. 'I can see them heading into the meeting room. Message me and let me know what happens with the whole Emma thing. She might go psycho on you and screw up your domestic bliss.'

I put the phone down on the table in front of me and close my eyes. I think Mel's reading way too much into this.

I hope she is, anyway.

CHAPTER TWENTY

Jess

3rd June

'You know when you don't notice something's missing until you realise it's not there?'

There's a long pause while Gen takes in what I've just said.

'Right,' she says, slowly. 'You're going to have to run that by me again.'

'Sorry,' I say, tucking my phone between chin and shoulder as I rip open the post that's addressed to me. Junk mail, junk mail, credit card bill . . . 'I mean—' I pause for a second, making sure there's nobody else home, but the house is silent, and there's none of the usual detritus in the hall that tells me my housemates are back from work '—I think something's going on with Emma and Alex.'

There's a moment where Gen processes what I've just

said. 'What, like they've been secretly shagging for six months?'

'No,' I say. 'Not just that, I mean like there's a bit of a weird atmosphere. I think maybe he's already broken things off with her. He walked into the kitchen the other day and she walked out.'

'Maybe she'd finished in there and he was just walking in?' Gen asked.

'No, it's more than that. Maybe she's really upset with him, even though he said it was her idea for them to be casual.'

I shove the letters in the recycling bin. Then I bend over and fish out the credit card bill. Tempting as it would be to leave it there, I don't think it would do my credit rating any good.

'And the thing is – apart from that I haven't seen Emma around for ages.'

'Hmmm,' said Gen. 'But you don't see thingy – what's his name? The chef guy much either. And you don't think there's something going on with him.'

'He works split shifts. It's different.'

'You're very interested in what's going on with Alex for someone who's not interested in what's going on with Alex,' she says, in that very familiar, arch, Gen-like tone.

'I am not. I just happen to work in publishing, so I'm particularly interested in stories.'

'Yeah, whatever,' she says, and I can picture her smiling.

There's a clatter of keys in the lock and I look up. It's Becky, home uncharacteristically early from work.

206

'Better go,' I say to Gen. 'I'll message you later, okay?'

'Don't forget. I want updates on this non-existent drama.'

Moments later, with a dramatic sigh, Becky drops her bags on the floor and collapses on the stairs. 'God I'm so tired,' she says as she lays her head down for a second. 'There's no way I can make it up two flights. I'm just going to have to sleep here – ugh.'

'What is it?' I ask.

She lifts her head up again, making a disgusted face. 'We really need to sort out some sort of cleaning rota. These stairs are covered in fluff and random stuff.'

'I'll hoover them in a bit. Coffee?' I point to the kitchen. 'D'you want me to put the kettle on?'

She shakes her head. 'I'm trying to give up caffeine.'

'Are you insane? You work about twenty-three hours a day. You can't survive without caffeine.'

'How's the celery juice looking?'

'Beyond disgusting. I'll make you a peppermint tea.' I leave her lying there looking like a deflated jellyfish on the bottom stair and head into the kitchen to boil the kettle. The fridge absolutely honks. I grab the milk, close the door quickly, and make my coffee and pour water over Becky's expensive-looking peppermint tea bag.

'There's something dying in the fridge,' I say, going back to the hall and handing her a mug. She sniffs it and takes a huge sip, making ecstatic noises.

'It's Rob.'

'In the fridge?'

207

'No, it's Rob's stuff. He was given some enormously posh French cheeses from a salesman, and he's brought them home because – oh, something complicated. Anyway, they're in the fridge. He said he was bringing home some artisan bread and stuff and we could have it for dinner, if anyone was around.'

My stomach rumbles at the thought, and it would be nice to get to know Rob better. Six months into our lease and Rob's still a bit of a mystery. We sort of adjusted to him being here but not here pretty early on. When the rest of us are hanging out in the evenings, shovelling in Ben and Jerry's and watching Netflix movies, he's out doing chef things until midnight, by which time we're usually staggering off to bed. He lies on the sofa reading the sports pages (he's a massive football fan) and unwinding until about two a.m. Then when we get up, he's fast asleep downstairs in the cellar. It's a bit like living with a Hobbit, only one who's really good at cooking and occasionally brings home leftovers to die for.

And really stinking cheese.

I take a sip of my coffee, and—

'Ugh.' I look down at my mug realising I've handed Becky my coffee and I've got her peppermint and fennel stuff. It tastes like someone dipped a pair of used socks in muddy water.

'I wondered when you'd notice,' Becky says, holding the mug tightly in both hands.

'I've got your tea.'

'And I—' she takes another sip, eyes closed in bliss, a

beatific smile on her face '—have your delicious, sleep-depriving, adrenal whatsit-damaging, blood-pressure-raising coffee.'

I reach across, laughing. She's not letting go of that mug any time soon.

'Gerroff,' growls Becky. 'This is mine.'

I make another cup, and we flop on the sofas in the sitting room. We'd made all sorts of plans to sort the place out when we all first moved in, but somehow none. of us had done anything. It always felt a bit like sitting in your grandma's sitting room as a result. I notice that the potted plant on the windowsill is looking like it's in danger of dying of thirst.

'How's work? You must be feeling quite settled in now?' Becky asks as she flexes her foot against the arm of the sofa, leaning her head backwards. Something gives an alarming crack. 'God, I'm falling to pieces.'

'Was that you?' I say, alarmed. 'I thought it was the furniture.'

'No, definitely me. That's why I'm trying to do this healthy eating thing. This job is bloody exhausting. I'm not surprised Alex gave it up for an easy life working as a nurse.'

We both laugh.

'So go on then, spill the beans. Any exciting gossip from the glamorous world of publishing? I was expecting a lot more invites to posh book launches and meeting famous people.'

'Yeah, me too,' I say.

'Not enjoying it?'

'Oh, I am. I really like it. I mean it's way more pressurised than I expected – I think I was imagining us all drifting about reading books and discussing literature, and it's not like that at all, but – yeah.' I nod. 'I feel like I've found my feet a bit. It helps that a couple of new people have started, so I'm not the new girl any more. And Jav's lovely.'

'You should invite her round sometime. We could have a house party. A housewarming. My God, why haven't we had a proper housewarming?' Becky says.

'Because we're only ever all in the same place at once about twice a month, and that's usually a Saturday lunchtime?'

'Oh. Yeah. That.' Becky flips through the pages of one of Emma's magazines. She buys them all – *Vogue, Marie Claire, Tatler* . . .

'Look, there's a launch for Nigella Lawson's latest book. Why aren't you going to stuff like that?'

'Because I work for a tiny publisher who mostly does romance, and we don't do stuff like that.'

'You should. You'd get loads of publicity. And I'd get to meet—' she peers at the photographs on the social pages of *Tatler* '—Robert Pattinson. D'you think he sparkles in real life?'

'I do not. And your sad *Twilight* addiction needs to be addressed. I saw you'd been watching the whole series again on Netflix.'

'It's comfort watching. I'm mega stressed with work. There's a load of exams coming up.'

'More exams? I thought you were finished with all that.'

'No, these are different exams. Professional development stuff. It's never-ending.'

'Weird to think of Alex doing all that,' I say, casually.

Becky curls her feet up underneath her. 'Alex? He was really good. Got one of the best degrees in our year, I think. Everyone's still stunned he gave it up.'

'He seems to really like nursing though,' I say, and I wonder how he's getting on with his new placement. He's moved on to a new one now, working in a retirement home on Primrose Hill.

'You know he'd be getting married this weekend?'

'Oh of course,' I say, remembering Alex mentioning it the other week, but it hadn't really sunk in.

She reaches across to the coffee table and takes one of the chocolates that Rob left there last night with a Post-it Note saying *help yourself*. She indicates the box with her head. 'Want one?'

'No thanks,' I say, trying to imagine scruffy, laid-back Alex buttoned up in a suit and tie, watching the mythical Alice walk up the aisle towards him. 'What was she like?' I ask.

'Alice?' Becky chews for a moment, making exaggerated faces, then swallows and carries on. 'Sorry, toffee stuck in teeth. She was very nice. Bit posh, in that Home Counties long swishy hair way. Mummy and Daddy had two Labradors and she probably went to Pony Club.'

'Really? I can't imagine Alex with someone like that. He seems way too down to earth.'

'Yeah, but she wasn't stuck up. I mean she was nice. Just – well, I think that she'd pretty much planned out their future, and I don't think Alex buggering off to train as a nurse and earn approximately a quarter of what he was on as a corporate lawyer was on her wall planner.'

'Whatever happened to *for richer, for poorer*?' I ask.

Becky gives a snort of laughter. 'In London? Are you joking?'

I think about the amount of money she'd be getting if she rented this place out, or sold it.

'You're the one sitting on a gold mine,' I point out. 'I'm surprised you haven't got a string of handsome young gold-diggers beating a path to your door.'

'Nobody knows I own it, that's why,' she says.

'I've had so many people asking how I can afford to live in Notting Hill.'

'Yeah, me too.' She laughs. 'What do you tell them?'

'I say I'm staying with a family member.'

'Me too.'

'How's your mum?' I ask. 'Haven't heard anything about her for ages.'

'Oh, she's completely off-grid now. They've rigged up some machine on the island to make electricity by cycling on an exercise bike.'

'Talking of which,' I say, 'I must give you my share of the bill.'

'Yeah, we'll sort it out at the weekend,' Becky says. 'I was thinking – Alex is off this Saturday, which would have been the big day. D'you fancy coming with me and we'll take him out? Take his mind off things a bit? Emma's away this weekend and I think Rob's working, so it'd just be the three of us.'

My heart gives a little skip of happiness at the thought of spending the day with him, which is slightly pathetic. I really need to get a grip.

'I think that's a brilliant idea.'

CHAPTER TWENTY-ONE

Jess

8th June

'A boat?' Alex is standing in the kitchen in his socks and a crumpled, faded grey T-shirt. His jeans are slung low on his waist and when he clasps his hands together and raises them above his head in a stretch that turns into a yawn, I see a faint trail of dark hair that travels from his navel downwards to . . .

I look away and pick up a cloth, wiping the kitchen sink, which is already clean. 'Yeah,' I say, rinsing the cloth and folding it and hanging it up to dry on the tap. 'Me and you and Becky. Emma's away this weekend.'

'Come on,' Becky says, appearing in her dressing gown. 'It'll be fun.'

'It's all fun until someone drowns in a hideous boating accident,' says Alex, grimly. But his mouth lifts in a smile and he nods, slowly.

'All right. I think you two are insane. But all right.'

'Excellent,' says Becky, giving him a high five.

As he's leaving the kitchen he turns, a hand on the door, his early-morning hair rumpled. He scratches his beard and looks from Becky to me, a slow smile stretching across his face. 'Thanks, guys. I appreciate it.'

'I *told* you he'd think it was a good idea,' Becky says in a whisper, as we hear his feet on the last – squeaky – stair.

'What are you two brewing up?'

I look at Rob, who has walked into the room and headed straight for the fridge. 'Oh hello,' I say. 'It's the scarlet pimpernel.' Our anticipated cheese night didn't happen in the end, because Rob was called in to work to cover someone else's shift.

'One of these days I'm going to have a week off,' he says, in his deep Glasgow accent. 'And you'll be complaining ah'm under your feet.'

'I think it's a myth. You basically work 365 days a year as far as I can see,' teases Becky.

'I'll have you know I've got today off to make up for going in on Monday, and I've got no plans.'

'Ooh,' Becky says, glancing at me. 'Do you want some?'

'Depends what they are.' Rob grins. 'You're no' wanting me to do DIY or something like that?'

She beckons him over. Looking pleased to be included, he comes and sits down, and listens while we explain that we're on a mission to keep Alex's mind off what today should have been.

'I'd love that. And then mebbe when we get back I could make something nice for dinner. What about a curry? Alex likes curry, doesn't he?'

'Definitely.'

'Right. What time are we leaving?'

Becky looks at the clock. 'Oh God, not for ages yet. About half twelve?'

'Great.' Rob rubs his hands together. 'I'm away to the shop to get some bits and pieces for dinner. I'll make a feast that'll blow his socks off. He won't have a chance to think about whatshername when I'm done.'

In the time it takes me and Becky to get showered, find something to wear, and bumble around the house in a Saturday-morning sort of way, Rob has been out to the market on Portobello Road, picked up huge bagfuls of meat and the freshest of veg, and he's standing at the kitchen worktop chopping onions and garlic with lightning precision. Despite his huge hands, the knife moves so quickly I can't quite take it in.

'I thought you were making dinner later?' I pinch a piece of chopped red pepper.

'Aye,' he says, slapping my hand and laughing. 'I'm just leaving this lot to marinate for a few hours.'

I peer inside the fridge and it's stuffed full of various dishes, covered over with cling film, and smelling delicious already.

'Right.' He scrapes a heap of chopped-up stuff into a Pyrex dish, mixes it with what looks like some chunks of fish, and covers them over.

217

'Can I help?' I feel a bit useless standing there when the master is at work. He shakes his head.

'Nah, that's it all done.' He runs the tap and washes his hands, shoving the prep stuff in the dishwasher and turning it on. 'You guys ready?'

We walk down to Paddington where the boats are moored. There's a little queue – families and tourists all waiting to get on board their boats. Everyone seems to be feeling the same as we are – slightly nervous and a bit giggly. I'm trying very hard not to worry about all the six million things that could go wrong. I'm not really a boat person. I'm surprised to discover that Becky knows exactly what she's doing. She ushers us all onto a boat and we sit down. I'm peering around, looking for oars.

'It's electric,' she says, laughing. She sits down at the back, and expertly steers us away from Merchant Square and the throngs of tourists who are milling around. There are loads of boats on the water, and yet somehow Becky manages to smoothly dodge out of the way, and before we know it we're sailing along, the sun reflecting on the water. I'm glad I've brought my sunglasses. Alex is wearing his, too, and Rob – his pale freckled arms covered in sun cream – is wearing a baseball cap, and sitting at the steering end of the boat – I think it's the stern, or maybe it's the bow; one of those, anyway – with Becky. It's clear he's dying to have a turn.

I sit sideways on, my knees almost brushing against Alex's jeans. He's gazing out at the water, lost in thought.

'It's so quiet,' he says, after a while.

Rob and Becky are chatting away about cooking stuff. I'm watching the way the long arms of the weeping willow branches reach down, their leaves swishing gently in the breeze. Families with dogs and pushchairs are walking along the canal-side and I think about Sophie and her trying-to-get-pregnant headstand and it makes me laugh.

Alex pulls his glasses off and looks at me suspiciously, his mouth turning up in amusement. 'What's the joke?'

I put a hand up to my mouth, hiding my smile. 'Don't ask.'

'I'm glad we came out,' Alex says, nudging my knee gently with his. 'Thanks.'

'It was Becky's idea. She thought you might want to be distracted today, because . . .' I tail off, taking my sunglasses off, too, and chewing on the arm of them. I look at him and push my hair back from my face.

'I wanted to talk to you,' Alex begins, in a low voice, changing the subject. 'I'm really sorry if I put you on the spot the other week, asking you about Emma.'

'It's fine,' I say, putting my glasses back on and tucking my hair behind my ears.

'Look.' Alex points over my shoulder. 'There's our café.'

I turn, carefully (I don't want to fall out of the boat) and see we've reached Little Venice, and I can see the little pavement café where we stopped for coffee after our first walk together. It's become a bit of a routine for us now, to end there after our walks and have a flat white and a chocolate brownie. I try to ignore the way it makes my toes go all curly inside my Converse that he called it *our café*.

'Anyway,' he carries on, and I turn around to look at him again. 'I just wanted you to know that I really appreciated you listening. And I've broken things off – well, not that it was a thing, really, but you know what I mean – with Emma.' His voice is low.

'How did she take it?' I ask. No wonder the house has felt a bit weird.

'Fine.' He clears his throat. 'Well, fine-ish.'

'Is that why she's been a bit low-profile?'

He nods, and picks at a loose thread on his jeans, pulling it until it snaps and then twisting it absent-mindedly between his fingers. 'She went back to stay with her parents.'

'God.' I try and think when I saw her last. 'I knew she was going away but hadn't realised where to.'

'Yeah.'

A boat passes us, and we all laugh at two spaniels wearing doggy life jackets who are sitting on the table, their owners holding hands and steering the boat together.

'D'you want a go, Jess?' Becky motions to the tiller. Or is it the rudder? Whatever.

I shake my head. 'I think the fact I don't know if it's a tiller or a rudder is probably a good reason to stay where I am.'

'Alex?' Becky asks.

'Go on, then.' He grins at me and they perform a

slightly dodgy manoeuvre that makes the boat wobble alarmingly.

'Next stop—' he shades his eyes and peers ahead '—The Pirate Castle.'

'The Pirate Castle? As in an actual castle?' I ask.

'Nope.' He laughs. 'It's actually a charity that do stuff on boats with kids from disadvantaged backgrounds.'

'How do you know so much about it?' We sail past and there's a group of kids in life jackets climbing onto a boat.

'The company I used to work for did some fundraising for them.'

'So they weren't just about corporate greed?' I tease him.

'No, they did some good stuff.' He pushes his hair back from his face. 'I mean there was a fair old amount of corporate crap in there as well.'

I think about my ill-fated date with whatshisname, the investment banker. That was on a boat, too. I seem to be floating my way through my first year in London.

And then we're back at London Zoo, the enclosure a huge geometric shape that stretches high above the trees.

'D'you think we'll see our giraffe again?' Alex peers upwards.

A group of people sunbathing on the top of a houseboat raise their glasses to us as we pass them, and Becky takes out a pack of beers from the bag she'd stowed under the table.

'Cheers,' we say, clinking the necks of our bottles together.

We float on, lazily, up to Camden Lock, where there's a traffic jam of boats, and back round again, heading towards home. My stomach rumbles so loudly that it makes Alex laugh.

'Shall we go and get food after this?' he asks. He doesn't know that Rob's been hard at work all morning, creating a feast for us to have when we get back. I look at Rob, raising my eyebrows in query. He nods, subtly.

'Why don't you two go and get a snack when we drop this back at the pontoon, and Rob and I will head back?'

If I didn't know Becky better, I'd swear she was trying to put us in a situation where we were forced together, alone. But a) Becky's not a matchmaking sort (she's way too practical for that) and b) that's not what today is about. We're supposed to be taking Alex's mind off his not-wedding. And she's got absolutely no idea how I feel about him. I think I've done a pretty good job of hiding it. I hope I have, anyway.

We get off near Primrose Hill and meander back across the park, stopping to pick up sandwiches, which we eat, sitting on the grass, legs crossed, facing each other. The sun is still bursting out of the sky. It's the perfect day for a wedding, I think. Alex is quiet. I wonder if he's thinking the same thing. I lie back on the grass, looking up at the sky, soaking up the heat.

He lies down beside me, so close I can feel the fizz of my skin prickling at his proximity. My heart hasn't got the *there's nothing going on* memo and is currently banging very loudly in my ears.

'Weird, isn't it?' he says, still looking at the sky. He shades his eyes against the sun.

'What?'

He reaches out, so the side of his arm just brushes against mine. I feel a whole rainbow of butterflies burst into life in my stomach.

'What might have been. Near misses.'

I think he's talking about the wedding. He's definitely talking about the wedding. Isn't he?

I lie there, keeping very still.

And then he reaches out, and for a second his little finger touches mine. I can't work out if it's an accident or not. I don't pull my hand away. I just lie there, looking up at the clouds, wondering how the tiniest bit of physical contact can leave me feeling like someone shot a bolt of electricity from my head to my feet. I'm fizzing like I'd glow in the dark.

CHAPTER TWENTY-TWO

Alex

8th June

What the hell am I doing?

We walk back to Albany Road together in what I hope is a friendly sort of silence.

All I did is reach out and touch her finger, for God's sake. The voice in my head comes back with a fairly reasonable counter-argument.

You're single *for a reason*. You're not getting caught up in anything with Emma *for a reason*.

Two different reasons, I argue with myself.

It's surprisingly hard to conduct a balanced and reasonable argument with your own inner voice. The truth is I really like Jess. Like her enough that I'm not going to screw up a friendship, and enough that I'm not getting myself caught up in a relationship when I've got enough going on with work and study right now, and after what happened with Alice – well, I promised myself I wouldn't even go there until I finished my nursing course.

It's not the same with Emma, my unhelpful inner voice says.

Hang on, I think. Weren't you on the other side a minute ago?

It's complicated, says the inner voice.

I groan out loud.

'You okay?' Jess's voice makes me start. I'd half-forgotten she was there.

'Yeah, just thinking about work stuff.'

'I thought maybe it was, you know—' She hesitates for a bit. 'Alice. The wedding?'

I shake my head. 'No,' I say firmly. 'Definitely not that.'

We turn the corner and get onto Albany Road. One of the kids from the house two doors down has set up a lemonade stall. They've got a table out on the pavement, and a stack of paper cups. A sign says, *Lemonade £4 a cup.*

'Bloody hell,' I say under my breath to Jess. 'Definitely London prices.'

One of the children looks up at me. She's got light brown hair and very piercing bright blue eyes. 'The lemons are organic, and the sugar.'

'Of course they are,' says Jess, snorting with laughter. Only in Notting Hill. 'I'm really sorry, I haven't got any money on me.'

'That's okay,' says the smaller of the two children.

'We're going to make some more so you can come back later.'

When we're out of earshot and walking up the steps to our house, we both burst out laughing.

'Well, you've got to give it to them. They're enterprising.'

'Those kids' school fees probably cost more a term than I make in a year.' Jess giggles. 'Not surprised they're enterprising. Their dad'll own half the property in Notting Hill. He's a private landlord.'

We're still laughing when the front door opens. I thought Emma had gone home, but she's there, with a look on her face that I can't read. I open my mouth to say hello and then close it again.

Despite Emma's cool welcome, I can't help noticing that the house smells warm and fragrant with spices. There's a sizzling noise coming from the kitchen. And over that, I can hear the sound of Rob singing as he cooks something amazing.

I walk down the hall and into the kitchen.

'All right, you two?' Rob looks up, wooden spoon in hand, an apron tied round his waist. He looks in his element, and he's beaming happily, a bottle of white wine half drunk beside the hob.

The back door's open, and light from the little garden is spilling into the kitchen. I can see the overgrown vines hanging over the doorway, and the light dappling through the leaves. It looks pretty idyllic – the perfect day for a lazy, sunny afternoon in the garden. We've hardly used it so far – mainly because it's so overgrown that none of us know where to start.

'Gorgeous day, isn't it?' says Emma from behind us, in her smooth, deep voice. She's looking at me curiously. I step out of the way to let her and Jess through.

'We should have Pimm's on a day like this. I bet there's mint in the garden. Have you looked?' Jess says. She clearly hasn't picked up on the weird atmosphere.

Becky appears from the garden with a piece of leaf caught in her hair. And she's standing between the back door and the kitchen. 'Ah,' she says. 'I wondered when you two were going to get back.'

And then there's a rustle as someone moves one of the vines out of the way and a shape – silhouetted against the sunlight so it takes a moment for me to recognise it – stands for a moment in the doorway.

'I told you he wouldn't be long,' says Emma, in an artificially cheerful voice.

'Hello, Alex,' says Alice.

CHAPTER TWENTY-THREE

Jess

8th June

So this is a bit awkward. I flick a glance in Becky's direction and she manages to articulate, with widened eyes, a vague gesture with her hands, and a flare of her nostrils that no, she doesn't have a clue what's going on, either.

I watch Alex, trying to look as if I'm not watching him. He steps across the kitchen and puts a hand to Alice's waist, kissing her warmly on the cheek. Emma lifts an eyebrow almost imperceptibly.

'Jess, this is Alice,' says Alex.

And I reach out a hand – why on earth do I do that? It seems weirdly formal, but I don't know her well enough to kiss her and it feels like I have to do *something*. Alice takes it and we shake in greeting. Alex gives me an odd, sideways look.

'Very nice to meet you, Alice,' I say. 'I've heard a lot

about you,' I add. Becky, standing behind her, widens her eyes at that and gives me A Look.

'You have?' Alice tilts her head slightly, smiling. 'I hope it's not all bad.'

'Gosh, no,' I say, aware I'm digging myself into a hole. 'All very good in fact. Lovely.'

Becky's nostrils flare.

'Why don't I go to the shop and get some Pimm's? I was just saying it's the sort of afternoon you should be drinking Pimm's.'

I turn around and head for the door.

'I'll come with you,' says Becky, hotfooting it out of the kitchen.

'What the hell?' I say when we get outside.

'I have no idea. Literally none,' Becky replies. 'Has she come back to say she's made a terrible mistake and she wants him back?'

I almost say *'Bloody hell, I hope not'*, but manage to turn it into a cough and then a much more appropriate: 'Maybe she thought she should pay her respects, or something?'

'To their non-marriage?' Becky snorts with laughter again.

'I don't know. What kind of weirdo turns up on their not-wedding day and randomly appears from the garden in the middle of our Keep Alex's Mind Off Things mission? Is this the sort of thing she always does?'

'I dunno. I only met her a few times at work events. She always seemed quite nice, in a sort of horsey, Surrey,

I've-got-posh-parents sort of way. Bit like Alex used to be.'

'Did he?' I ask, surprised.

'God, yeah.'

I stop suddenly in the street and someone walking crashes into me from behind, swears, and then carries on, making a detour round me. I'm still not very good at the not-stopping-on-London-streets thing.

'Alex doesn't seem like a posh sort of person. He's . . .'

'He's lovely, yeah. But before his dad died he was much more like your stereotypical law type. Nice suit, pretty girlfriend, liked a night out at the Sloaney Pony.'

Despite having heard about the 'old Alex' a few times, I struggle to reconcile the laid-back, slightly scruffy, bearded, permanently exhausted Alex with the image she's creating.

'That's really weird. I can't imagine that at all.'

'I don't think Alice could imagine him the way he is now. She'd have that beard off him in about five seconds flat, for one thing.'

After picking up Pimm's, cucumber, a punnet of straw-berries and some lemonade, we head back to Albany Road.

'What d'you think's going on in there?' Becky nods towards our house as we approach.

'Have you got any change yet?' says the little girl from the lemonade stall.

'Sorry, no,' I say. 'Unless you take credit cards?'

She giggles. 'I did ask Daddy if he'd let us but he said no.'

'You'll have to catch me after payday, then,' I say, only half joking. I'm still lurching precariously from one month to the other. Becky's paid for the Pimm's, which is just as well because I've pretty much run out of money and there's still quite a lot of the month left. I clock the expensive-looking car parked opposite our house and wonder if it belongs to Alice.

'Is that . . .?'

Becky nods. 'Yep. You can see how downgrading to hoofing it on the tube on a student loan wasn't really her style.'

Inside, Rob's dishing up spiced chicken kebabs on a bed of colourful salad leaves. There's no sign of Emma, or Alex, or Alice, for that matter. I can't help feeling angry that we've arranged a day to take his mind off something and Alice has come along and put a massive spanner in the works.

'They're outside in the garden.' Rob nods his head towards the door.

'I'll make the Pimm's,' says Becky, quickly. 'You go and size up the atmosphere out there.'

Surprisingly, Emma's on her hands and knees, pulling up weeds from a flower border. She's gathered quite a pile, heaped up beside her.

'I didn't have you down as a gardener,' I say, nodding at the pair of battered-looking green gardening gloves she's wearing.

'They're not mine. Think they must've belonged to Becky's gran. But yeah, I love gardening. Used to help

j

my dad out at the allotment all the time. I still do, when I go home.'

Well, this day just gets weirder.

Meanwhile, Alex and Alice are sitting at a faded wooden picnic table. It's worn smooth and silver with age.

'Come and join us,' says Alex, patting the bench beside him. I slide myself into the narrow gap and sit down, not too close to him, and look at Alice. She seems perfectly composed, sitting with her hands folded neatly in front of her, a glass of Rob's wine half drunk on the table.

Well, I think. This is going to be a bit of an awkward afternoon.

'Pimm's, anyone?' says Becky, in a sing-song voice.

'God, yes,' I say, falling on a glass with as much enthusiasm as one of our marathon runners at the support table reaching for water. I take a slightly too-large sip and cough.

But of course, we're British, and what we do best is awkward, slightly stilted social gatherings. Rob insists there's more than enough food for everyone, so we spend a perfectly polite and charming evening around the battered old garden table celebrating Alex's not-wedding with the wife that never was.

CHAPTER TWENTY-FOUR

Jess

28th June

'It's lovely to hear you,' says Nanna. Her voice makes me smile as I walk along the narrow road towards Pimlico, where we're meeting for a wedding dress trying-on session. Gen's supposed to be meeting me at Starbucks, but she's texting a series of updates from the bus she's on, which seems to be stuck behind some sort of impromptu protest march. Her messages beep in my ear as I talk to Nanna and walk.

'So what's happening with you?'

'I'm off to play dressing up with the girls.'

'Ooh, lovely. Has she set a date?' Nanna loves a wedding – and a funeral. In fact she loves any sort of occasion where you can dress up and wear a nice hat. I step off the pavement to make way for a man carrying two buckets filled with flowers, then step back hastily as a black cab beeps loudly.

'No, she hasn't set a date – it's most un-Sophie-like. I'm not sure what she's doing.'

'That doesn't sound like her at all.'

'It's the baby stuff. I think she's all over the place, trying to plan something that can't be planned and it's making her computer brain malfunction.'

'Babies come when they're ready,' says Nanna Beth, soothingly.

'So everyone keeps telling her. She's threatened to behead the next person who tells her to relax.'

'It's not really Sophie's thing, is it?'

'Definitely not. Ooh, Nanna – I'd better go. Gen's just getting off the bus opposite. I can see her waving.'

'Give her my love, sweetheart.'

I blow a kiss down the phone and shove it back in my bag, waving to Gen. She's got a purple scarf wrapped around her hair and huge, ornate silver earrings that jangle and glitter in the light. I don't know how she does it – if I dressed like her, I'd look like I'd been raiding a dressing-up box.

'Hi,' Gen says, kissing me on the cheek and giving me a hug. 'Are you ready to be meringued?'

'There's no way she's going to put us in something hideous.'

'I don't care if she does as long as she hurries up and gets here. What kind of shop is by appointment only anyway?'

'A royal one?' Gen hops up and down. 'How the hell can it be this cold? It's nearly July.'

'It was sunny when I left the house this morning.'

'Well it's bloody well not now.' Gen starts doing actual star jumps in the middle of the pavement. A little girl walks past, holding on to her mother's hand, turning round to look as they walk away. Gen pokes her tongue out at her, making her giggle.

'Mummy, that lady has a shiny thing on her tongue,' I hear the girl saying in wonder as they turn the corner.

Right then – thankfully, because I'm beginning to think there's a danger we'll freeze to the spot – Sophie arrives. It's not like her to be late.

'Sorry,' she says, shoving her phone in her bag. She pulls her cardigan tightly round her chest against the cold. 'God it's cold round here in the shade, isn't it?'

'You're not bloody joking.'

She rings a bell and the door opens. I have to confess that I'm a sucker for a wedding dress shop. There's something about all that tulle and sparkly stuff. Even Gen gives a little *ooh* of surprise.

'This is lovely.'

'Welcome to Briarwood Bridal.' The woman who owns the shop is tall, with her hair cut in a severe black bob. She's dressed in the sort of angular, expensive-looking linen stuff that designers seem to favour.

'This place looks *seriously* expensive,' Gen whispers to me, as Sophie disappears with the woman into a back room.

'Can I get you two ladies a glass of Prosecco while you're waiting?'

I wasn't aware there was more waiting happening, but if there is, there might as well be Prosecco with it. I nod.

There's a lot of rustling and we've almost finished our Prosecco when the severe-looking woman calls us through. Sophie – who appears to be about a foot taller than normal – is standing in the middle of the room looking pleased with herself.

'What d'you think?'

She looks absolutely gorgeous. The dress looks even better on her than it did in the magazine, and it goes in and out in exactly the right places.

'If you're not pregnant by the time your wedding day comes, that dress ought to do it,' says Gen, giving a filthy wolf whistle that earns her an even filthier look from the owner of the bridal shop. I shoot Gen the sort of look that hopefully says *shut up*.

'Well,' says Gen, defensively. 'You are trying to get up the duff, aren't you?'

Sophie gives her a steely look and says nothing. She's so stressed out at the moment, even by Sophie standards.

'I thought we were here to try on bridesmaid dresses,' Gen says looking aggrieved.

'We're just going to take some measurements now, madam.' Bob-woman unrolls a measuring tape and approaches Gen. Gen, being an old hand at costume measurements for the stage, holds out a hand, palm flat in a STOP gesture. 'I can tell you mine right now,' she

238

says, parroting them off instantly. The woman inclines her head, looking slightly mollified. I lift my arms up as she measures my bust, waist and hips, feeling like I'm getting measured for school uniform. Sophie dismounts from the low stool she's been standing on and sashays off to get changed with the aid of the tea-making girl.

Afterwards we go to the cinema then for a drink. Sophie sneaks a look at her phone before, during and after the film to see if Rich has been in touch.

'Have you two had a fight or something?'

'He's just being an arse,' says Sophie. She plaits her long hair down one shoulder, which is what she's always done when she's feeling anxious, so I know there's something going on.

'What's up?' Gen cocks her head sideways. She might be loud and boisterous but she's a good person to have on your side. 'Do you need us to go and rough him up a bit?'

Sophie laughs. 'No. He's just – it's just – well, it's been seven months now and I'm still not pregnant.'

I look at Gen. I've never really contemplated that sort of thing, so I've no idea how long it normally takes. Like I said, we were brought up to believe getting pregnant happened the second you went anywhere *near* a male person. Maybe those sex education classes weren't completely accurate.

'Seven months isn't that long,' says Gen, kindly. 'I read somewhere it can take the average person twelve months to get pregnant. Plus, you're stressing about it, and the

239

wedding stuff, and work, and you've got the flat on the market. I mean basically all you need to do is have a bereavement and you've ticked off the four most stressful things a person can do.'

'I know.' Sophie sighs. 'I can't even get Rich to agree to a wedding date.'

Gen shoots me a sideways look. 'You don't mean . . .'

Sophie shakes her head. 'He's had this idea that he doesn't want a big fuss.'

I can feel my eyes widening into saucer shapes. Sophie's basically been planning her wedding since she was about nine.

'And how do you feel about that?'

I'm surprised when she shrugs. 'I dunno, actually. You know when you've always had your mind set on an idea, then someone comes along and says something and you realise that actually . . .' She tails off, taking a sip of her drink through a straw and gazing out of the window.

Gen glances over at me and subtly raises an eyebrow.

'Well, there's no need to think about any of that stuff right now.'

Sophie gives a gusty sigh. 'It's like telling someone not to think of a pink elephant,' she says. 'What's the first thing you think of?'

'All right. So we'll have to distract you. We just have to find you a project,' I say.

I go to the loo and when I get back I'm pleased to see Gen and Sophie are laughing about something and Sophie looks happier than she has done in ages. I head home once I finish my drink, because I've got plans to hang out with Becky tomorrow morning, and we agree to meet up for lunch on Wednesday.

Back at Albany Road, the house is surprisingly quiet. There's usually someone pootling around the kitchen making toast or curled up on the sofa watching television, but it's completely deserted. Alex's hoody is hanging on the end of the banister. It's weird that I have barely seen him since the day Alice turned up. Except I have to remind myself it is completely not-weird. Alex is just a friend. A housemate. But since his finger touched the side of mine, I've managed to reignite the world's biggest and most ridiculously unrequited crush. I need to get a grip. Plus he's probably back with Alice.

Alice, who seems perfectly nice. Alice who – as his ex-almost-wife – has rather more claim to him than I do as his housemate. And even Emma seems relatively unscathed – in fact, she was off on a date with a friend of a friend last night, as she confided when we met in the hall. It's ridiculous. I am ridiculous. This needs to stop.

CHAPTER TWENTY-FIVE

Jess

1st July

I wake up at half five in the morning for some reason, probably because the sun's shining through my curtains, spilling warm yellow light on my face. On a whim, I decide to go for a run. I throw on my ancient leggings and a T-shirt, and rummage under the bed until I find my trainers. They're a bit battered, but they'll do. I leave my phone behind, because I need to clear my head and stopping to check Instagram every five minutes isn't going to do that. I tie my hair up in a high ponytail that swishes as I walk.

I set off at a gentle jog from our place, feeling quite dynamic. That lasts until I hit the end of Albany Road, by which time my lungs feel like two exploding balloons in my chest. I stop for a moment, hands on my knees, doubled over and wheezing. God, I'm unfit.

But there's something quite nice about being out in London at this time of the morning with no phone and nothing to do but take in the sights. I run along towards Holland Park where the pavements widen and the houses are gleaming white, the railings shiny black and the cars outside are massive brand-new Range Rovers. It gets a bit easier, somehow, as I keep going. And then I circle back, heading up Portobello Road, which is a hive of activity already. The stallholders are clanking bits of metal and laughing as they assemble their stalls. Boxes of fruit and veg and huge buckets of flowers spill out everywhere, echoing the rainbow colours of the buildings, and I feel a lovely glow of happiness and love for this amazing place I get to call home. This must be the runner's high they talk about – or maybe I'm just delirious.

'Is this a mirage?' Rob says when he opens the door, before bursting out laughing.

'Shut up, you,' I say, collapsing in a heap on the bottom stair.

'I'm only kidding,' he says. 'D'you want a drink? Looks like you need one.'

I nod, gratefully. Once I've drunk an espresso and my breathing has returned to almost normal, I stand up and catch a glimpse of myself in the hall mirror. In my head I've looked cute and sporty, my hair swishing back and forth as I jog along the streets of Notting Hill. The reality is distinctly less glamorous. My ponytail has slipped to one side, my face is an alarming brick-red colour, and I have two half-moons of sweat under each arm.

'If you ever want a running partner,' Rob says, in his gruff Scottish voice, 'just ask. I did the marathon a couple of years ago.'

Still looking at myself in the mirror, I watch as my eyes widen in horror. I've managed to jog-walk about two miles and it's taken me ages. The idea of running twenty-six miles is completely insane. That's what public transport is for. Except there's a little voice in my head that points out that all the runners we cheered on in April must've started somewhere, and after all, I've told myself I'm going to make some changes in my life.

I peel off my horribly sweaty clothes and dump them in the laundry basket. After I've showered, I lie back on the bed, wrapped in a towel. I could sleep for a week, but I've got about twenty minutes before I need to get going if I'm going to get to work on time. Maybe I'll just have one more minute.

CHAPTER TWENTY-SIX

Jess

3rd July

'You?' Gen splutters, when I tell her and Sophie about my new running regime . . . of all of two days. Sophie, also laughing, pats her on the back. It's Wednesday lunchtime and we're sitting in a café in the city.

'Why not?'

'You're just not exactly – well, come on, Jess. The last time you ran anywhere was probably when you found out Tesco had reduced all the Christmas chocolate to half price last January.'

I'm slightly offended at just how funny Gen and Sophie find the idea of me running. 'I'm actually quite fit, I'll have you know,' I lie.

'Well,' Sophie says, looking at Gen then me. 'As you're on a mission to turn your life around, we've got a proposition for you.'

247

She's got that glint in her eye that I recognise, and I groan.

I'm about to be organised.

'So, Gen and I were talking about your lack of love life—'

I glare at Gen, who is trying to look angelic and chewing on the crust of her toasted sandwich. 'Sorry,' she mouths, pulling a face with her mouth still full. 'She needed a project.'

'I didn't mean *me*,' I say, scowling. But I can't deny it, Sophie's looking far more like her old self.

'You've tried one date. It was a disaster, but you can't just fall off the horse and stay there. You need to get back on.'

Sophie's tone is firm, like a primary school teacher encouraging a recalcitrant pupil to join in with a PE class.

'Honestly,' I say, trying to sound assertive, 'I'm fine. Loads of work stuff going on, lots of friends, I've got my running—' I've been twice, but that definitely counts '—and I really just don't want to . . .' I tail off.

'You don't want to end up stranded on a riverboat party cruise while some banking wanker gets off with someone else under your nose?' Gen looks at me, her huge blue eyes wide, eyebrows lifted.

'Exactly.'

'And that's why we've decided to stage an intervention.'

'I'm beginning to feel slightly nervous.'

Sophie shakes her head, and her pale blonde hair lifts

and settles back down, still perfectly neat. 'No need. We've found you The Perfect Man.'

'There's no such thing,' I say.

'Ah,' says Sophie, pulling her phone out of her bag, 'there is. Look.'

'I'm not signing up for online dating again. I had to delete Tinder – every time I looked at it there were dodgy messages from perverts, telling me what they'd like to do to me, or what they were doing to themselves, or worse. And the photographs?' I shudder dramatically.

'Will you stop talking for *one* second?' Sophie pushes her phone across to me and I pick it up.

There's a photograph on her screen. I zoom in on the picture so I can see it more clearly. It's a blond man with dark brown eyes. He's holding a bottle of beer and standing next to Sophie. They look a bit like a pair of Danish twins. Both tall, healthy-looking, blond, and with impossibly good teeth. Weirdly, he reminds me a bit of the man I saw in the hailstorm that day before Christmas. Only presumably Sophie isn't trying to set me up with someone who already has a boyfriend.

'Who's that?' I ask.

'James.' Sophie takes the phone away, looking slightly smug. I reach across, grabbing it back and zooming in on the photo again. He looks nice. Friendly.

'Is he gay?' I ask.

'I beg your pardon?' Sophie takes the phone back, laughing. 'Thought you weren't interested.'

'I'm not,' I say. He does look quite nice though. 'What's the catch?'

'No catch,' says Gen. She's doodling absent-mindedly on the expensive-looking menu, drawing groups of tiny little daisies. A waitress comes past and swipes it from her hands, giving her a disapproving look.

'Would you like anything else?' she says to Gen, who's already wolfed down her sandwich.

'I'd like another coffee, please – decaf, thanks.' Sophie smiles up at her.

'I'll have a diet Coke, thanks,' says Gen.

I look out of the window and watch as a couple of tourists wander by, hand-in-hand. It's weird, but recently everywhere I've looked people seem to be loved up and I've felt like a spare part, sitting in cafés watching the world go by and with a vague sense that my life is going by too, and if I don't do anything about it, I'm going to wake up one morning and find I'm forty-five, still single, and still wondering what I'm going to be when I grow up. I square my shoulders and turn back to look at Sophie.

'So what's the deal with James?'

'He works in the marketing department with me. Really lovely. Single – no skeletons in the closet. As soon as he was transferred in last month I thought he'd be perfect for you.'

'Okay,' I say, feeling bold. 'Where do I sign?'

Sophie blushes slightly and looks sideways at Gen.

'Ah. Well,' she says, pulling a face, 'I have to confess

250

I sort of organised a blind date for the two of you for next Friday.'

'You did *what?*' I reel backwards, my head banging off the window. 'Ouch.'

'That's what she meant by an intervention,' Gen says, wryly. She shifts over slightly as the waitress returns with our order.

'What if I'd said no?' I ask.

'But you didn't, did you?' Sophie looks very pleased with herself.

'A blind date, though?' I grimace.

'Don't knock it,' says Sophie. 'Worked for Harry and Meghan, didn't it?'

I roll my eyes. She's got a point though, I guess.

'Fine,' I say, and they high-five and say *yes* in unison.

CHAPTER TWENTY-SEVEN

Alex

.

5th July

'Bloody hell,' my sister says.

Mel's just flown in from New York. She's here for four days for a series of meetings. I've come out of a two-hour lecture, brain reeling with stuff I need to learn for an exam next week, and she's waiting for me outside the university entrance.

'Hello to you too.'

'I don't have time for niceties. I'm too busy and important for stuff like that.' She waggles an expensive-looking briefcase at me. 'Got a meeting at four. You're lucky I can fit you in.'

'Thanks,' I say, shaking my head and laughing.

I'd mentioned I'd seen Alice, and of course she wants to know all the details, so I tell her the sorry story over lunch at a café nearby.

'And she turned up completely out of the blue?' Mel asks. 'You didn't have even an inkling she was planning it?'

'Not a clue. I got back from a day out with friends, and we walked into Albany Road, and there she was.'

'Bloody hell,' Mel says again. She's not exactly helping.

'I was hoping you might have some sort of wise counsel. I can say "bloody hell" myself.'

'All right. So, let me get this straight. She turns up, plonks herself down on a garden bench, and tells you she's made a terrible mistake and wants to start things up again?'

'Pretty much, yeah.'

'And? Were you tempted?'

I shake my head. 'Not even a bit.'

'God, poor Alice. What a nightmare.'

'Yeah.'

'What d'you think brought it on?'

'Oh God, loads of things. Well, she started off just casually saying she'd been thinking that maybe she hadn't been fair.'

Mel gives a thoughtful nod. 'Reasonable point.'

'She wanted us to go out for dinner. All I could think was that I had a shitload of coursework to do before Monday morning, and Rob had cooked a meal for everyone and I didn't want to be rude to a mate.'

'Romance isn't dead then,' says Mel, drily.

'Look I didn't plan any of this. Anyway she insisted we go out the next day and said she'd pay. Then we had dinner and talked.'

254

'How did it go?'

I shrug. 'Not great. I mean for one thing, when she said she'd pay, she clearly didn't actually expect me to go through with that. We had a bit of a silent standoff when the bill arrived.'

'What did you do?' Mel asks.

'I paid.'

'Alex, you've got sod-all money. I bet it wasn't Pizza Hut either.'

Alice always did have expensive tastes. A bottle of red and two courses in the Grapevine in Holland Park cost me the best part of two weeks' food budget.

'I felt like it was the least I could do,' I say.

'She turned up on your doorstep.'

'Yeah, I know, but . . .'

'So what did she say? I bet she hates the beard, right?'

I laugh. 'She did make a comment, yeah.'

'And I'm guessing she's still not over the whole lawyer to nurse thing?'

I shake my head. 'Nope. I mean, she knew it was coming. It's not like I went to work one day with a briefcase and wearing a suit and turned up the next morning dressed in scrubs and carrying a thermometer. Anyway,' I say, fiddling with the edge of my plate, 'She came back, said she missed me, said we could make a go of things.'

Mel makes a dubious noise.

'I didn't want to make her feel bad.'

'Oh my God, so you decided to just flannel her with a load of "it's not you it's me" bullshit?'

'No.' God, sometimes talking to my sister is painful. She's hit the mark.

'Anyway, she went back home to her parents' place that night. She wanted to go for a walk the next day, so we did. I talked about work, and she tried to understand what I loved about it.'

There was a point when we were wandering along through Covent Garden when it felt like Alice was really listening. But it came back round to money, and how I was willing to give up everything that mattered just for the sake of a job, and that's when I realised that we're just fundamentally different in the way we see life.

'And then what happened? I'm dying to know,' Mel says, and I shoot her a sideways look because I can't work out if she's being sarcastic.

'So where have you left things?'

I rub my jaw. It was weird. When Alice had ended things, I'd been pretty crushed. It felt like the one person who was supposed to get me, and understand why I wanted to do something that would make a difference, just didn't. I'd been pretty devastated by it. And then she came back and I felt – nothing.

'I think she wanted to give me another chance to change my mind,' I say.

'About her or about the job?'

'Both. I think she was hoping I'd got the whole thing out of my system and maybe I'd just realise I'd made a terrible mistake. She did use the words "life crisis" several times.'

'To be fair,' Mel says, wiping coffee off her upper lip. 'We've all used those words. Normal people don't bin off a perfectly good law career to spend their lives wip—'

'Fuck's sake, Mel. For the millionth time.'

'All right, don't get touchy,' she says. 'I know you don't just wipe people's arses.'

I let out a sigh of irritation.

'So, how *did* you leave it?'

'I saw her before I got on the train down here. We had coffee at the station – she was off to a meeting – and we pretty much said our goodbyes.'

'What d'you think triggered her change of heart?'

'The wedding date thing, I reckon.'

'So what happens now?' Mel checks the time on the wall clock. 'And make it the short version. I've got about fifteen minutes left before I have to scarper.'

'Nothing. I get on with work, and get these assignments done.' I point to the folders on the table beside us.

CHAPTER TWENTY-EIGHT

Jess

5th July

James is – exactly as Sophie said – absolutely charming, and even better-looking in the flesh. I get to Polpo five minutes late, hoping desperately that he's the sort of person who turns up early, and that I'm not going to be sitting there looking tragic for half an hour and nursing a drink while the bar staff look at me with knowing glances. And I'm in luck.

'Hi,' he says, standing up as I arrive. He leans across, putting a hand on my arm, and kisses me on the cheek. He smells of something spicy and woody and sort of lemony. It's nice.

We order a bottle of red and look at the menu. The waiters are just the right level of helpful and take our order of a few sharing plates. For some reason, I don't feel nervous or butterflies-ish, and we chat about work, and Soph – laughing about the fact that she's such a super-organised perfectionist – and he tells me about growing up in Yorkshire. He's got a lovely accent.

'Here we are,' says the waiter, bringing a tray of assorted dishes and setting them on the table in front of us. It looks amazing.

'I don't know where to start,' James says, picking up the bottle and pouring some more into our glasses.

'These are amazing.' I pass him a tiny little piece of sausage wrapped in pieces of dried tomato.

'Try this.' He offers a little arancini ball, and our fingers touch as he passes it to me before I put it in my mouth. It's weird. I don't feel that nervous buzz I've experienced with Alex, but it's nice being with him. It's easy, and relaxed.

When I go to the bathroom, I check my messages and both Gen and Sophie have been in touch, dying to know how I'm getting on.

I like him, I say, standing by the mirrors.

EXCELLENT news, Sophie types. I bet she's planning a new side hustle as a dating service as we speak.

'We've finished this wine, somehow,' James says when I return, lifting up the bottle and shaking it from side to side. We've eaten all the food, too.

'We could get cocktails,' I say, spying a list on a board by the bar. 'Unless you want to get back?'

He shakes his head and looks at me directly with his nice, kind brown eyes. 'I'm not in any rush, are you?'

'Not at all.' I smile at him, and we order two negronis.

And then we drink another three, and as I stand up from the table – he's paid the bill, and refused to take my share – I realise I feel more than a little bit fuzzy round the edges. Outside it's not quite dark, the sky hazed a pale-around-the-edges blue, the moon a perfect half-circle.

'Thanks for a lovely night,' I say.

'D'you want to call a cab?' James looks down the street, scanning for black cabs.

'I'll just get the bus.'

He offers to walk me to the bus stop. We wander along, side by side, arms occasionally brushing. It's still warm, the heat of the day radiating from the pavement and the walls of the buildings.

'I love London at this time of night,' he says.

'I love London full stop.'

'I think when you're not from here, you really appreciate what an amazing place it is to live.'

I nod. 'I've been exploring since I moved here at the beginning of the year,' I say. I don't mention that I've been covering the city on foot with the housemate I have a crush on. It's been a while since we've been for a walk together – he's been doing loads of agency work, and – I shake my head, realising that I shouldn't be thinking about him when I'm on a real-life actual date with a handsome Yorkshireman. 'And there's so much to discover,' I say, sounding like a tour guide. 'History everywhere.'

'That's exactly how I feel,' James says. We reach my stop and I see the bus is approaching.

'Right, well, I better get going. I've had a really good night,' James says.

'Me too,' I say, again. I'm not actually sure how you do this whole dating thing. It's been so long that I'm completely out of practice.

'Do you – I mean would you—' He starts, then clears his throat. 'Would you like to go out again? With me, I mean?'

And something about the awkwardness of the situation makes us both laugh. I nod. 'Yes, please,' I say. 'I'd like that a lot.'

'I'll message you,' he says.

My bus arrives, and I climb on. When I get to my seat and look back, I see he's still standing there, waiting until I leave to make sure I'm on board safely.

CHAPTER TWENTY-NINE

Alex

1st August

I've had a couple of weeks back home hanging out with Lucy and Sam (who are so loved up, I can't decide if it's inspiring or nauseating, or possibly a bit of both) and I've gone straight back into two back-to-back weeks of night shifts, so I'm feeling a bit like Albany Road's nothing more than a place to sleep before I stagger out of bed and back to work again. I feel like the living dead, but I'll give hospital work this – it never stops being interesting. I'm doing agency work to get some money in the bank before the next semester starts. St Thomas's Hospital is huge and confusing, and I've got lost about five times already. The weird thing is I know that another few shifts and I'll have the entire place mapped in my head, permanently. I don't know how it works, but it does.

'Hello, darlin',' says a voice from the waiting area. I give a vague smile but don't engage. I've got a load of overnight reports to hand over, and if I don't get them in before the shift changes I'm going to end up hovering around for an hour like I did yesterday.

'I said "hello",' says the voice, again. It belongs to a woman wearing a hospital gown and a pair of tired-looking fleece-lined slippers. Her mouse-brown hair is suspiciously flat on one side, as if she's just got out of bed.

'Where have you come from?' I ask. We've got a wanderer, I suspect. I check her arm. 'You didn't have an ID band on, did you?'

'Took it off,' she says. 'They make me itch.'

I can't help smiling. She's feisty, I'll give her that. But we're in a hospital the size of a small village, and I've got a lost soul to sort out.

'So where did you come from – can you remember?' I ask.

'Not sure,' she said, and gives a cackle of laughter. 'These places all look the same. Don't you agree?'

I look at the chairs, the neutral walls, and the posters urging us to wash our hands and use hand gel between patients and I think that I could be pretty much anywhere in any London hospital.

'Yes, they are all much of a muchness, aren't they?'

'Are you a doctor?' she asks.

'Nurse.' I frown and peer down the corridor, trying to see if I can spot anyone. Can't leave her sitting alone when she's clearly vulnerable, but at the same time, I'm going to get a bollocking if I go AWOL with these reports.

'Nurse?' She clicked her tongue. 'Male nurses. Well I never.' She looks pleased at this. I smile politely.

'Excuse me,' I say when I see a pink-clad Healthcare Assistant appear from inside some double doors. 'I've got a patient here, and—'

'She's not one of ours, I don't think,' says the HCA.

'She's AWOL, I think.'

'Wait there two secs,' the HCA says, and disappears, returning a few seconds later with a hospital-issue wheelchair. 'I bet we can relocate her.'

Before long, we've traced her back to the ward she'd come from. She's not that old – pain can disorient you – and I watch as she's installed safely back in her bed. She hadn't gone far.

'Turned left at the loos instead of right. Happens all the time,' says the ward sister, wearily. 'We've got massive signs, but nobody ever looks at them.'

I head back down the never-ending corridors, but the patient's face stays with me for the rest of the shift, in that way people do, sometimes, even though we're supposed to retain professional detachment at all times. I remember it being mentioned in one of the first classes we had – that we had to find our own way of distancing ourselves. It's not that easy, though – especially when you see someone like her, wandering, alone – I don't know why it got to me. Maybe just that moment of realising that the old cliché about life being short really is true?

Back home, hours later, dead on my feet and bleary-eyed, I'm in the kitchen ripping off the plastic on a microwave meal for two, tipping it onto a plate, when Rob comes in with a couple of dirty mugs.

'That crap's no good for you, man,' he says. He shoves the mugs in the dishwasher and turns to look at me. 'You need some decent food inside you when you're working those long shifts. Believe me, I know.'

'It's better than Becky's Cock Soup,' I say.

There are still about fifteen packets of the stuff in the cupboard. It's become a standing joke. We've tried adding vegetables, throwing in noodles, even mixing it with a tin of sweetcorn. It's still absolutely disgusting, but come the week before payday, we're not too proud to give it another go.

The microwave curry tastes pretty grim. The chicken's somehow spongy and rubbery, and the rice has dried up in parts and is rock hard. But I'm exhausted and starving hungry and there's nothing else to eat, so it'll have to do. Once I've had a sleep I'll nip out and get some shopping.

'You working tonight?' I say, looking at Rob.

'Night off. Thought I might go and see that new Marvel film at the cinema if you fancy it.'

'I'd love to, but I can guarantee you that within five minutes of the opening credits, I'd be fast asleep. I feel like I haven't stopped for days.'

'I've been meaning to ask what the story is. You sort things out with that Alice lassie?' He grins. 'Wee bit awkward getting home to find your ex standing in the kitchen.'

'Just a bit.' I nod. 'Anyway, I've cleared the air with her, at least.'

'So you're just friends now?' Rob asks.

'Well, as much as you can ever be. Civil, I think, is probably as good as we're going to get. She's still not over me giving up law for nursing, no matter how much she's tried to convince herself it didn't matter.'

'Aye,' says Rob, sagely. 'Not easy to get your head round something like that. My ex-wife couldn't cope with my long hours working in the restaurant. Not many can. It's a killer, but I couldn't give it up.'

'Did she give you an ultimatum?' I ask, looking up with interest. I had no idea he'd been married. I don't know much about him at all, really. Rob doesn't talk about himself much, although I've found him chatting away to Becky a few times in the kitchen when I've got in from work. But Becky's like that – she could strike up a conversation in a room full of statues. Probably has, knowing her.

'No, but if she had . . . I cannae tell you which I'd have chosen. I bloody love my job. I spent years working in construction, and paid a fortune to retrain. You've got to follow your heart, haven't you?'

These words, coming from the stocky, gruff Scotsman make me smile. He's right, though.

Of course, what I've not mentioned to him, or to Becky, or to anyone – and I'm not sure why – is that it turns out that after we split, Alice had had a semi-serious fling with Paul, who I used to work with. I think it was them splitting up that was the catalyst for her getting back in touch. It's weird because he was one of the ones from the office who'd sort of kept in touch – for a bit, at least. We'd been out for drinks a few times since leaving, and yet he'd never mentioned it. Not that I'm in any position to comment, given what happened with Emma.

God, relationships are complicated. I head upstairs, pull the curtains, and climb under the covers. Sleeping after night shifts is a killer in the summer. It's so hot that I've got to leave the window open, but there's music blaring and car horns beeping and kids off school yelling at each other in the gardens, and there's no way I can possibly sleep with all that going on . . .

Weird thing is it's not Emma or Alice who get caught up in my daytime dreams when I'm tangled in the sheets, dozing, trying to catch up after night shifts. It's Jess. My subconscious is an awkward bugger.

When it becomes clear I'm not falling asleep any time soon, I shove off the sheet and climb out of bed, heading for the kitchen. I need caffeine, and fast.

Talking of the devil, Jess appears in the kitchen, her nose smattered with new freckles from the August sun outside, her hair in long waves around her shoulders. She's wearing a pretty flower-patterned sundress and flip-flops, her sunglasses balanced on the top of her head. She's standing in the doorway as a reminder that no, I wasn't imagining it. It is her I've been dreaming about. God, my subconscious needs to get a grip. A second later, the universe throws an ice-cold bucket of water over my subconscious when Jess steps further into the room followed by a tall, fair-haired, Scandinavian-looking bloke.

'Oh! Alex.' She goes a bit pink. 'This is James.'

I've only been gone a couple of weeks. Where the hell has this James sprung from? I realise I'm probably staring and extend a hand. James shakes it – firmly.

'Hi. I'm Alex, Jess's housemate.' Obviously I'm her housemate – that's why I'm standing here with bare feet and wearing track pants and a T-shirt.

'Ah, right,' he says, looking pleased he knows which one I am. 'You're the walking one.'

'That's right.' Jess beams.

I make polite small talk for a few more moments, then make my excuses. I pull the door of my bedroom closed and look out of the window at Albany Road and the sea of houses that stretches out as far as I can see. My stomach contracts with something I really don't want to acknowledge. I can't be jealous because Jess has met someone. We're friends, that's all. Yes, we flirted that first night in December when we met, and yes, we'd become friends as we walked miles together over the city. That's perfectly normal.

I think for a second about that briefest of touches, lying on the grass, staring up at the sky. I really need to get a grip. It was nothing. There's a soft thud as Jess's bedroom door closes, and I grimace. I'm not staying around to find out what will happen next. I grab a towel and head for the shower, determined to stand under needles of burning hot water until I've cleared my head, and then for as long as I can. Hopefully that way I can avoid whatever's going on in the room next door.

CHAPTER THIRTY

Jess

10th September

There's the first hint of autumn in the air as we walk to Sophie and Rich's place for dinner. A light breeze blows, and a few yellow-brown leaves eddy and swirl on the street as we get off the tube. They feel at odds with the warm weather. London seems to hold on to summer longer than other places, making more of the season. The shop windows, though, are already full of mannequins wearing long winter coats, wrapped in hats and scarves. It'll be Hallowe'en next, and then Guy Fawkes Night, and—

'You look like you're miles away,' says James, swinging my hand as we wait at the traffic lights. 'What are you thinking about?'

'Oh, Christmas, and stuff like that,' I say, shaking myself back to reality. 'Just daydreaming.'

James squeezes my hand and smiles at me. 'You're organised.'

I run my thumb over the top of his hand, and hope my face doesn't give things away. I wasn't thinking about Christmas. I was thinking about Alex and Alice, and what might be going on with them, and wondering why I was thinking about it when I was holding hands with a perfectly nice man.

Before long, we're standing outside Sophie's place waiting for her to open the door. James leans over and drops a kiss on the top of my head. 'You smell lovely,' he says, inhaling the scent of expensive Aveda shampoo that I've splurged on.

'Aww, look at you two,' Sophie says as she opens the door and catches him with his face buried in my hair. 'You have to admit,' she says, almost unbelievably smugly, taking our coats, 'I'm pretty shit-hot at matchmaking.'

James looks at me and rolls his eyes. He's used to Sophie, working with her in the office every day. And of course, I've known her forever. She likes nothing more than being proved right, and James and I seem to make the perfect couple. Everyone says so, after all.

'Come through, you guys,' says Rich, drying his hands on a tea towel and slinging it over his shoulder. 'I've just put the starters in. It won't be long.'

The sitting room is spotlessly tidy, of course. Sophie's hung a huge spider plant in one corner and it trails down, skimming the edges of the bookcase where all her books are neatly ordered by colour. The whole house looks like something from an interiors magazine. I make a mental note to snap a photo of the little grouping of cacti and old Observer's Books spotter's guides she has sitting on a side table for Instagram. Nanna Beth would love that.

'Hi, you two,' Gen says as we enter. Gen has brought along an actor friend called Malcolm. He's tall, willowy, and despite the late-summer sun, wearing a trilby and a floaty long raincoat. He has a drooping, strangely clown-like face and reminds me of a bloodhound.

Gen has a habit – I think it's an acting thing – of taking on the mannerisms and personality of the person she's seeing. So tonight she's dressed in similarly floppy clothes, with two long scarves hanging around her neck. She's sitting on the sofa beside Malcolm, draping her legs over his, and fiddling with one of his long, Byronic curls. He doesn't seem to say much.

'Did you get that report done, Soph?' James asks as he takes my coat and hangs it up. It's all very comfort-able, in a strange sort of way. Because James knows Sophie from work, we don't have the usual 'introducing a new boyfriend to your mates and hoping he'll get on with them' thing. Sophie approves of James completely, and of course Rich – silent and easy-going, currently doing something with the starter in the kitchen – is happy to go along with whatever Sophie thinks.

'Yeah. I had to stay behind for three hours, but it's been put to bed.'

'How's work, Jess? Are you still enjoying it?' Gen

stretches, raising her arms up in the air and balling her fists.

I nod, and take a seat next to James on a sofa. It's been a steep learning curve for the last nine months and I'm exhausted. I need a proper holiday. James made some vague noises about going away somewhere next year, and the idea of us having a next year together – well, it felt quite nice.

'Drink?' Sophie leans down between mine and James's shoulders, beaming contentedly. She loves playing hostess.

'I'd love a beer, please,' says James.

'Can I have one too?'

'Coming up.'

Malcolm gives a huge yawn, echoing Gen's a moment ago, stretching his arms up in the air. His huge clown-like face elongates and his eyes close. I look at James sideways. I get the feeling that perhaps this is all a little bit too tame and suburban for Malcolm. I sit back in the chair and take the beer Sophie hands me, looking around. It's weird to think that nine months ago we were sitting looking at the mountains on our ski trip, talking about how things might change over the next year. And now, here's Gen with Malcolm and me with James. It's all very neat and lovely. I shift a little on the sofa and James turns, giving me a look of concern.

'You all right, hon?'

I freeze slightly. He's never used that term with me before and I'd be quite happy if he never did so again. I am not a 'hon'.

Gen notices and snorts with laughter. 'You're going to have to break the spell, James, or she'll be frozen in that position of abject horror all night.'

'What did I do?' James looks genuinely anguished. His brow furrows and he runs a hand through his thick blond thatch of hair.

'I'm just not a very "hon" sort of person.'

'She's more of a darling, aren't you, darling?' Gen grins.

'What about poppet?' Malcolm raises his chin slightly and looks at me thoughtfully. 'You're quite posh. You seem a bit of a poppet to me.'

'Posh? Jess?' Sophie says.

'Excuse me,' I say, 'I am sitting right here.'

'Poshly.' Gen reaches for a crisp.

'I didn't say I was posh, Malcolm said I was posh.'

'James is posh,' Gen says, decisively. 'I bet your parents sent you to boarding school and you have an Aga and all that stuff.'

'My God,' he says, but he's laughing. He puts his hands up. 'Guilty as charged. Yes, my parents have an Aga. No, I didn't go to boarding school.'

'And did they call you poppet or hon?'

'Neither. Always James.'

'Exactly.' Gen looks pleased with herself.

'I'm just not a cute names sort of person, that's all,' I say.

With all that out of the way, we have dinner – prawn curry and a million side dishes, all prepared by Rich, who is a brilliant cook – and spend the rest of the night talking about the plot of a film we've all watched on Netflix. By the time we get home, I'm so full of curry and wine I feel like I have to be rolled upstairs to bed.

CHAPTER THIRTY-ONE

Jess

11th September

The next morning, so early that the birds are only just starting to stir and the streets are quiet and empty, I kiss James goodbye on the doorstep. I don't remember him getting into bed after he jumped in the shower when we got home. I think I was so full of food I basically passed out.

'I'll see you later,' he says, curling a hand into my hair and pressing a final kiss on my forehead.

He's reliable, he's handsome, he's solvent, and he calls when he says he will. My God, he reminds me of that Taylor Swift song. And my friends love him. I think of Alex for a second and then shake my head.

He's basically the perfect boyfriend. I watch him striding down Albany Road, turning to wave goodbye before he disappears out of view.

I turn around and head back upstairs. There's a moment when I pause outside my bedroom, one hand on the door, and I look across at Alex's door. I wonder if he's asleep, or if he's lying staring at the ceiling like I used to when he was sharing a bed with Emma. I shake myself. Of course he's not.

Alex

I put a hand up to lift my phone and check the time. A groan of exhaustion escapes almost unbidden. It's half five. I'd been woken in the middle of the night by the thud of Jess's bedroom door closing, and the sound of soft laughter, followed by silence. So I'd put a pillow over my head, determined to block out the sound – and the idea – of Jess in bed with James.

I roll over and stare at the ceiling, hands behind my head. James is a nice enough bloke, as far as I can see. Easy-going, stable, a proper grown-up – all the usual stuff. We've exchanged pleasantries in the kitchen a couple of times over the past few weeks since Jess started seeing him, and I think I've done a pretty good job of hiding how I feel. Feeling *anything* wasn't on my list of things to achieve this year. I'm not quite sure how Jess snuck in under the radar, but I have, in fact, decided the best way to deal with it is to just face up to their relationship head on (because Jess is a friend, and therefore I am – like a good friend – very happy that she has met someone nice), so I've suggested to Jess that she bring

James on one of our London walks. We're going to head up to Hampstead at the weekend and take a wander round. We'll have something to talk about, a set route, and an end point at the pub, where I can have a pint with them, then leave them to it and head back home to my room.

And then I'll have a cold shower or punch a pillow or something like that. Yep, completely sorted. Everything is under control.

CHAPTER THIRTY-TWO

Alex

15th September

All we have to do is take a walk around Hampstead. Normally, we would set off from home, jumping on the bus or the tube as necessary, grabbing a coffee on the way, and then walking, soaking up the atmosphere. But this time, with James joining us, Jess has switched things around. I think she's probably feeling a bit edgy about it. Maybe I'm reading too much into it. Anyway, she's suggested we meet at Kenwood House instead, and set off from there.

'You off out?' Emma says when we meet in the hall as I come downstairs.

I nod. 'You look nice. Off somewhere interesting?'

Emma flips her long dark hair over her shoulders and smiles. She knows she looks good. I like her for that. 'A third date, actually.'

'Nice.' Is this awkward? I wonder. But, you know what? I think maybe it's okay.

'Yeah.' She looks at me for half a moment with an odd expression on her face, and then she grins. 'He's a lawyer, funnily enough.'

She's dressed beautifully as ever, her hair hanging in a shiny curtain down her back. There's a rumble of music from downstairs – Rob must've woken up from his post-work sleep, and be getting ready to head off to the restaurant. I pick up the pile of letters and rifle through them, checking none are for me – which thankfully they're not, as all I seem to get is junk mail and credit card bills – and stack them neatly on the dresser in the hall.

'Anyway,' she starts, pausing to run lipstick around her lips, looking at me in the mirror in the hall. I look, back at her reflection for a second.

'You all right?' I ask.

She nods. 'You?'

I nod as well. It's the nearest we're going to get to a *well that was nice while it lasted, but that's it* conversation.

She picks up her keys and puts them in her expensive-looking red leather bag. 'I better get going. We're having lunch at the Granary this afternoon.'

She slings her bag over her shoulder, opens the door, and heads down the stairs and onto the street.

I sit on the overground train heading towards Stratford, head against the window, staring out but not really taking in what I'm seeing. It's only when the woman sitting opposite drops her bag on my foot that I glance up, realising I've almost missed my stop.

'Sorry, excuse me,' I say, climbing out of the seat and heading for the exit. I check my watch – I don't want to get there early and be hovering outside Kenwood House like a loser. I nip into the bakery beside the station and get a sandwich and a can of Coke, and eat them sitting at the entrance to the Heath, before setting off through the trees.

It feels like everyone in London's here today – dogs on extendable leads getting tangled round each other, and little kids on training bikes being chased downhill by exasperated-looking parents. I march up towards Kenwood House – I haven't been there for ages, and it was one of the places I'd planned to show Jess on our walks. I just hadn't banked on James being there, too. It comes into sight – huge and magnificent at the crest of the hill – and I wonder what it'd be like to live in a place like that. Mind you, I bet people think that about our place. I've had more than my fair share of raised eyebrows at college when I've told them I live on Albany Road. I wonder how long it'll be before Becky sells the place? I can't imagine her keeping it as a house-share when it's worth millions.

I walk around the edge of the house to the place where we've arranged to meet, and—

'Alex, there you are.'

Jess is tying her shoelace. She looks up and beams at me and I feel something in my stomach give a sort of flip. I can't help it – I grin back. Realising James is

283

standing just to one side of her, I reach out a hand and shake his hand in greeting.

'Hi,' I say.

'This is gorgeous,' says James. 'I've never been here before.'

'Pretty nice, isn't it? There's a gallery inside,' I say, realising as I do that James is the sort of person who'll probably want to go in. I've nothing against art per se, but the prospect of wandering around a stately home looking at paintings doesn't exactly fill me with joy.

'And a collection of shoe buckles,' says Jess. 'I've googled. Anyway, shall we walk?'

'Let's go,' James says, heartily. I realise this is probably as awkward for him as it is for me.

We set off through the gardens of the house. Jess stops to take a photograph of the Henry Moore sculpture, (because in Jess's world if you haven't Instagrammed it, did it really happen?) and while she's standing with her phone, trying to get the perfect angle, James and I are left standing side by side, making conversation.

'So I gather you two have been walking miles all over London?' James says, looking at me intently. He's very . . . solid. Golden. Like – oh my God, he's like a Golden Retriever. Sort of healthy and sturdy and reliable. I have no idea why that just popped into my head, and now it won't go away. The irony is that Jess would normally find that kind of comment funny, but under the circumstances . . .

'Well,' I begin, sounding very serious because I'm trying

284

not to think about James as a Golden Retriever in a suit and tie, 'it started because Jess didn't know her way around.'

'And Alex knows it really well because he spent loads of time here when his dad used to come up here for work.' Jess appears beside us and finishes my sentence, looking at me sideways and smiling. She hooks a strand of hair behind her ear. She's wearing a jumper and a dress that is patterned all over with tiny little rosebuds, and the necklace she told me her Nanna Beth gave her as a good luck charm before she moved up here. I blink hard and look away, wondering if I've been staring.

'And Alex just seems to know loads of history about the places we've been,' she continues, as if I haven't just been gazing at her for what felt like ages. Maybe it was only a couple of seconds. Maybe – no, definitely – I need to get a grip.

'That's only because I'm a complete geek, with a weird memory for random stuff,' I add.

'It's not random. If it wasn't for you, I'd never have discovered the delight that is the Hyde Park pet cemetery.' She laughs.

'I thought you'd like it here because of the whole *Notting Hill* thing.' I wave an arm down in the direction of the sweep of grass where a scene from the movie was shot.

'Ahh,' sighs Jess, happily. 'If only a young Hugh Grant would materialise in front of us right now.'

'What would you do?' I raise an eyebrow.

'Go scarlet in the face and hide behind a tree, of

285

course. I mean in my fantasy world I'd introduce myself and he'd fall madly in love with me, but—'

James clears his throat. 'I was thinking we could walk down to the Pergola – there's a lovely view over the city from there.'

Jess shoots me a quick look. I make a face. I'm not sure her Richard Curtis movie daydreams are really James's thing. He's going to need to get used to them, mind you. It's a standing joke in the house that every time we turn on Netflix in the sitting room we're asked if we want to carry on watching one of them. She's completely addicted.

'That sounds good, doesn't it, Alex?'

I nod. And we start walking – James slightly in front, because he's got a printed-out map, even though it's not exactly difficult to find, and if we keep walking in a straight line we'll get there. I don't say anything. Jess hovers somewhere between the two of us. This is – awkward. I feel like the third wheel on a date, only a date that isn't even going all that well. 'Um,' I start to say, trying to think of something intelligent and interesting to say that'll get James talking – and then a gust of wind blows a kid's plastic kite right through the middle of the three of us and we duck out of the way. James grabs it and walks over to the little boy and his parents, bending down to his level to hand it over. He smiles and shows James a handful of pebbles he's collected and stuffed in his pockets. The parents get involved, and I watch as he chats to them, probably about the weather and other suitable topics, and when he stands up and dusts down his trousers he looks across at us and smiles, and the little boy does, too.

'Well, he's good with children,' I say, with an eyebrow raised.

'Shut it, you.' Jess shoves me with an elbow.

'I'm just saying. Good marriage material, and all that.' Why on earth did I say that? Why am I trying to push her into his arms? Oh, God. I give myself a shake.

'Well, don't,' she says, looking a bit cross.

'Talking of children,' I say, 'what's happening with Sophie?'

'Nothing,' says Jess. She gives me a look that quite clearly says '*Stop talking*'. I turn around to see that James has rejoined us. At first I can't figure out what Jess is worried about, then I realise, shit. Shit. James works with Sophie and he probably overheard me.

'What's happening with Sophie?' James repeats.

'Just a party she's organising for her niece. I was helping her make plans.' Jess covers up quickly. I don't think James even thinks about it, mind you. He's looking at the map, brow furrowed. I lean across and show him where we are, pointing in the direction of the Pergola.

'There's a road in the way,' says James.

'Yeah, we just have to cross there and walk down a bit past the Spaniards – it's an old pub, been there since the sixteenth century – and then we're back on the heath again.

Jess is trailing behind, looking more at her phone than the scenery. I try and think of something to say to James, but somehow he reminds me so much of the life I left behind that I find it really weird. I hadn't really noticed

287

that I'd changed – I mean, I know Alice talked about it, but I still felt like the old Alex, on the whole. But here's James, talking about someone at work who'd just bought a house in the Highlands and a trip to Goa he was planning for Christmas, and it all feels like a world I used to know, but it's so far removed from my own life that I can hardly recognise it.

We're distracted – thankfully – by a group of Basset Hounds that are lumbering along just in front of their owners. They flock around our legs, long tails wagging, noses sniffing in case we've got any spare dog treats hanging around. It breaks the ice a bit, which is just as well because this walk feels like it's going to last a lifetime.

And then Jess's phone rings. 'Gen! Hi! Oh how funny, I was just thinking about you.'

James fiddles with the sleeve of his shirt, adjusting the buttons. I lean back against a wall, pushing my sunglasses up my nose so I can watch Jess without being seen. I am almost one hundred per cent certain that Gen's call was a set-up. Jess's tone is just a little bit too perky for it to be realistic.

Jess hangs up, sticking her phone back in the pocket of her jeans.

'Gen's just around the corner in the Spaniards having drinks, isn't that amazing?'

'Really?' James looks surprised. 'What's she doing up here? This isn't her neck of the woods, is it?'

'Oh,' Jess says, airily. 'Perhaps she just fancied a change?'

I tip my sunglasses down a fraction with a finger, looking

at Jess over the top of the lenses. She catches my gaze for the briefest of moments. Her eyes dart away from mine, and her mouth twitches in the way it does whenever she's trying not to laugh. I look the other way and smile.

Outside in the beer garden of the Spaniards, Gen's sitting at a wooden table with a tall, rather pissed-off-looking man in a long, drooping sort of coat that matches his long, drooping hair and face – like one of the Basset Hounds we've just seen. The other tables are full of tourists, cameras hanging round their necks and guide books and maps spread out between their drinks.

'Alex!' Gen stands up and kisses me on the cheek. She smells of apple shampoo and chewing gum. Her red curls are a wild halo around her face. 'Fancy meeting you here.'

'Fancy,' I say, drily. 'Shall I get us some drinks?'

'I'll get them,' says James, taking his wallet out of his pocket. 'What do you guys want?'

Gen and her lugubrious-looking boyfriend ponder for a moment, which gives me time to make a rapid escape plan.

I pull my phone out of my pocket, scrolling down the screen and frowning in an exaggerated manner, before firing off a rapid text.

'Alex? Drink?' James looks over at me. He's so solid and wholesome. All he needs is a tail to wag and he'd be off.

I shake my head sorrowfully. 'Sorry, guys, something's come up.' I wave the phone as evidence. 'Just had a message. I've got to get across town. Work stuff.'

Jess gives me a very sharp look. I look back, my expression one of injured innocence, and raise a hand in farewell, vaulting over the wooden fence of the beer garden, striding off in the direction of the tube.

Jess

I don't for one second believe that Alex had something come up at work. For one thing, he's not working today. For another, he was clearly finding it as excruciatingly awkward as I was. Introducing boyfriends to existing friends is bloody hard work. Even more so when the existing friend is – well, I'm not even going to go there. James is lovely, and charming, and when I get back from the loo he's sitting chatting quite happily to Gen and her boyfriend. There, you see. Perfect boyfriend material. And objectively speaking, he's good-looking too, in a sort of posh boy way. I mean not that I'm being objective. I should be being subjective. But – oh, you know what I mean. It's just . . .

I can't help wondering if the emergency text – if there even was one – has something to do with the whole Alice thing. He hasn't said anything more about it but I wonder if she's still on the scene, somehow. And then I have to remind myself that it's nothing to do with me, because I'm with James, and Alex can do what he wants. He's a friend, that's all. And there's no reason at all why a friend wouldn't send a text to ask if everything's okay, is there?

CHAPTER THIRTY-THREE

Jess

2nd October

'We've got a meeting at half eleven.' Camilla, operations director, pops her head over my desk. The open-plan office is buzzing with noise and industry because one of the biggest publishing trade fairs – Frankfurt – is coming up, and we have several big books going on sale. I've been so wrapped up in work that I haven't seen James all week, and we're supposed to be going to the cinema straight after work tonight. I secretly wonder if he'd notice if I just had a two-hour nap instead of watching the film. Even though I got home late from work and planned to go straight to bed, everyone in the house stayed up last night in the kitchen playing a killer game of cards, sharing a bottle – well, several – of wine and ordering pizza at midnight. I've had maybe four hours sleep, everything aches, and my head feels like someone's used it as a punchbag. When my phone buzzes on my desk, I pick it up, fully expecting it to be James, but it's my mother.

Nanna Beth not so well. Call me.

It feels like my stomach has just dropped through the floor. I put the phone back on the desk face down so I don't have to see the message, and stand up automatically, pushing my chair back. My hands are on the desk, my knuckles stark white. I take a shaky breath.

'Jess,' says a voice behind me kindly. 'You okay?'

I turn around, still holding on to the desk. It's Camilla.

'You look like you've seen a ghost. Are you feeling okay?'

'Just had a message to say my Nanna Beth isn't feeling well.' I look at the photo montage of the two of us on my desk. Pictures of me when I was a tiny baby perched on her knee, another of us arm in arm when I was ten and got a pair of roller skates for Christmas. There's a photo of her standing at Cardiff Uni the day I graduated, with Becky grinning in the background. I feel a bit sick and sit back down in the chair.

'Let me get you a glass of water,' says Camilla.

I look at the clock. It's twenty past eleven. Almost time for our meeting.

'Here you are.' She hands me the water, and – oddly – a tissue. 'Now, what can we do?'

I shake my head. 'We've got a meeting at half past.'

'You don't need to be in a meeting,' Camilla says, gently. 'Do you need to go home and see her?'

I turn the phone over and press the home button, looking again at the stark words lit up against a background of me, Gen and Sophie in ski clothes, laughing in the snow at New Year. I feel sick with guilt that I've moved to London and haven't been to visit Nanna Beth as often as I should have.

'I think maybe I do.'

'Okay. Leave it with me. We can give you some leave. Now why don't you get home and sort things out, pack a bag, and get on the train down to – where is it?'

'Bournemouth,' I say, my voice sounding strange and faint and far away.

As soon as I get off the train I'm aware of the sea not far off. There's something in the air – an openness in the big sky that stretches out over our heads – and of course the ozone smell of the beach. I jump in a taxi, and head straight to the hospital with my overnight bag over my shoulder.

Going home for a few days because Nanna Beth isn't well, I've texted Becky. Her reply – I check the clock, realising she's probably just finished work – flashes up as I'm sitting in the taxi.

You poor chick. Send her my love. Keep me posted.

I will, I reply.

When I get to the hospital I stand for a moment, not sure where to go. It crosses my mind – irrationally – that if Alex was here, he'd know. I head for the reception desk at A&E and they tell me she's been triaged and is in a cubicle. I follow the receptionist's instructions and make

293

my way through the swinging doors into a corridor throning with people. There's a young woman sitting on a plastic chair, a drip hanging from her arm. A youngish couple are sitting looking pale-faced and worried, holding a baby. I hear my mother before I see her.

'This is ridiculous,' she's saying. 'We've been here eight hours and she hasn't been admitted to a ward. How much longer do you think it'll be?'

A small woman in a pink hospital tunic, her braids tied back from her face with a wide band, looks at me as I peer around the curtain. She scribbles something on a clipboard and replaces it at the end of the bed, smiling at Nanna Beth before she slips out of the door.

'Hello, duck,' says Nanna Beth, faintly. Her skin is bluish pale and her eyes have bruised shadows underneath. 'Your mother is causing a fuss.'

I lean over the bed, putting my hand on hers, feeling the papery, whisper-thin skin and squeezing her hand gently. I kiss her cheek and smell the familiar scent of Nivea face cream and Elnett hairspray. I lift my head.

'Honestly,' my mother is saying, looking irritated, 'this is absolutely ridiculous. Hello, darling.' She leans across and gives me a peck on the cheek.

'Now you're here, Jess, I'm just going to go outside and make a couple of calls. I'm supposed to be performing this evening.'

'That's fine,' I say, exchanging glances with Nanna. She's well enough to roll her eyes, so I think that maybe things aren't as bad as they seem.

Mum slips out of the cubicle and I sit down on the chair next to Nanna Beth's bed, still holding her hand.

'So what's been going on?'

'Oh, it's something to do with my heart.'

I look at her, alarmed.

'Nothing to worry about. A bit of angina, something like that.'

'They wouldn't have rushed you in here if it wasn't something to worry about.'

She tuts. 'I just need a bit of medicine and I'll be right as rain. Now, I want you to tell me all about what's been going on since I saw you last. How's that nice Alex doing?'

We talk about what I've been getting up to in London, and after a while, Nanna's eyes close and she drifts off to sleep. I take my phone out of my bag. I'm not sure you're even supposed to use them in hospitals, but I check to see if I have any messages. The first one reads:

Any news? Thinking of you. Xx

Of course, James has been in touch already. I messaged him from the train, telling him what was going on.

Hey, says a WhatsApp from Alex. I watch as the dots form on the screen, suggesting he's typing another message. They disappear, and then reappear. And then the rest of the message comes through. *Becky told me what's going on. Hope your Nanna Beth's okay – from what you've said, she's a trooper. Let me know if there's anything I can do? X*

I smile.

A nurse appears.

'Hello, Mrs Collins,' she says, gently. Nanna's eyes flicker open. 'We've found a bed for you upstairs, so we're just sorting out some paperwork and we're going to get you admitted. Are you the next of kin?' she says, turning to me. Mum's still on the phone somewhere, so I nod. 'Yes. I'm her granddaughter.'

'Okay, well, you can go with her up to ward 12. Do you know if your grandma has a bag with her? There's a WRVS shop down by reception if you need to pick up a toothbrush and a flannel and that sort of thing.'

I point to the flowery bag that's sitting under my chair. I wonder whether it was Mum or the staff at the sheltered accommodation who packed it. Hopefully not Mum, or half the stuff Nanna needs will be missing. 'Yes, she's got a bag. I'll check it when we get upstairs.'

It's another hour before a porter comes and helps Nanna into a wheelchair. Mum has come back and told me she hasn't been able to get the understudy to take over in her play. She looks pale and anxious, her lipstick chewed off and her hair's sticking up at the back. I reach across and smooth it and she jumps.

'Sorry.' She puts a hand to her hair.

'It was sticking up.' I chew my lip. There's a clattering in the background somewhere as if someone's dropped something. I glance at Mum and she shakes her head slightly as if to say not to worry.

Mum hastily says goodbye and leaves for the theatre.

'You're a good girl,' says Nanna Beth, faintly. She looks small in her nightie and dressing gown – as if she's shrunk in the last few months.

'Come on then, love,' says the porter cheerfully. 'We'll have you upstairs in no time.'

Ward 12 is a small room with six beds in it. All but one of them are occupied, and it must be visiting time because almost all of them have family members sitting around. There are get well cards and balloons and boxes of chocolates sitting on top of the side tables, and a low murmur of conversation. A nurse arrives and helps Nanna out of her chair and into bed while the porter wheels the chair away.

'You're in the best ward,' the nurse says in a warm, deep voice that sounds like honey. Nanna, who can't resist a good-looking man, beams up at him as she allows him to tuck the sheets around her waist and plump up pillows behind her back. 'We'll take good care of you here, don't you worry.'

I watch as he walks away, whistling. It makes me think of Alex, and how he must be with the patients on his ward. He's working on orthopaedics right now, he told me the other day, and it's basically nothing but elderly people with broken hips. Oh and one mother of four with a broken ankle. She did it playing roller derby, apparently, and she said she was quite enjoying the peace and quiet.

Nanna Beth has closed her eyes again.

I take the opportunity to message Alex back.

She's in a ward. Mum's gone to the theatre.

A moment later, Alex replies.

You must be exhausted. Where are you sleeping?

Mum's place, I suppose. x

His answer flashes straight back.

When I said let me know if there's anything I can do, I meant it. x

Alex has heard enough stories about my childhood as we've walked around London to know exactly why the prospect of staying with Mum doesn't exactly fill me with joy. I spent most of my life growing up at Nanna and Granddad's little house, because Mum was almost never around. If she wasn't off with one boyfriend or another, she was on some hare-brained money-making scheme. She'd only been seventeen when I was born, and she'd been happy to let my grandparents bring me up.

'Hello, lovey,' says a different nurse, walking into the room. 'Just going to take some observations.' She picks up a clipboard and writes something down, taking Nanna's pulse and blood pressure.

'It's all go here,' Nanna says, faintly.

'Do you know what's happening?' I ask. 'How long will she be in?' I feel a bit stranded, waiting for something to happen.

'We've got Beth on some medication, which should lower her blood pressure. The doctor will be here tomorrow morning and do her rounds. She'll take it from there.'

'What about tonight?' I look at the clock. It's already half seven.

'Well, visiting hours are over at seven forty-five,' the nurse says, checking her watch, 'but you can come back tomorrow.'

I feel a wave of anxiety wash over me. 'What if Nanna needs me?'

'Don't you worry,' Nanna Beth says, reaching her hand over and squeezing mine, gently. 'I'm in the right place. You get back to your Mum's place and I'll see you tomorrow morning. And don't you worry about the cat – she's being looked after.'

I feel weird leaving her there. She looks small and faded and old against the bright white sheets, and my stomach contracts in fear at the smells and sounds of the hospital as I make my way down flights of stairs to the entrance. I can't bear the thought of losing her.

My mother's sent a text, at least, telling me that she's going to be at the performance until eleven, and that the key is under the stone cat on the front step. She's moved again, to a flat in a scruffy-looking part of town, and I have to check the map on my phone to make sure I'm on the right street. I climb yet more stairs – she's on the third floor, overlooking rooftops and a distant view of the sea. I peer out of the window in the sitting room, looking at the dark autumn sky. Winter is creeping in. I shiver, wrapping my arms around myself. There's a gas heater and I switch it on, clicking the button five times before it sparks into life.

I wander around the empty flat, noticing bits and pieces that Mum has brought with her from one house to the next. A green china mermaid, a painting of a naked woman gazing out of a window. Battered old tea, coffee and sugar canisters. I fill the kettle and switch it on, checking in the fridge for milk. Amazingly, there is some, and when I sniff it, it's even fresh.

I make a cup of tea, rummage around in the cupboard in her room to find a blanket, and curl up on the sofa to watch television, and worry about Nanna.

James texts to ask how it's going. I reply vaguely, explaining that Nanna's fine, Mum's off at a performance, and everything will hopefully become clearer in the morning. He's all for coming down tonight, but the thought of trying to negotiate Mum meeting him, and dealing with everything that's going on – I'm just too tired, and I can't face it. But as I put the phone down and my stomach growls – making me realise I haven't eaten since this morning – I can feel fear curling into the room like overnight mist from the sea. I don't want Nanna to die. I've already lost Grandpa.

My phone buzzes again.

You surviving?

It's Alex. I reply straight away.

I've left her in a ward full of old people, I type. *And I'm worried I'm going to lose her. I've hardly got any family.*

She'll be okay. His message comes through quickly. *You're made of pretty strong stuff. You've always said that comes from your Nanna Beth. What have they said?*

They've given her some medication and the doctor will be there tomorrow.

Are you going to be there?

Should I be?

Definitely. Get there for visiting hours – I had a look for you, they start at ten. The doctors won't do their rounds until after then, so you can just tell them you want to be in on the conversation. Get your nanna to say she wants you there.

I breathe a sigh of relief. It's nice to have someone onside who knows what they're talking about, and it occurs to me that Alex has such a kind, reassuring manner that he must make a really good nurse.

I will, I write. And then add, *Thanks – I really appreciate it. Xxx*

That's what friends are for, he replies. Another text appears a second later. It's just one single x.

CHAPTER THIRTY-FOUR

Jess

3rd October, Bournemouth

I'm woken by the phone the next morning at seven-thirty. I must've fallen asleep on the spare-room bed in my clothes – I'm still covered over by the blanket, my head awkwardly positioned on a velvet cushion. I grab my mobile, answering before I've even had time to register who's calling.

'Jess,' says Sophie, sounding breathless. 'Sorry to ring you so early but I'm in back-to-back meetings all day and I wanted to know what was happening with Nanna B.'

Sophie's known Nanna almost all her life, too.

'I'll know more once I've been into hospital.'

'Message me,' she says, urgently. 'I'll keep James updated. Is he coming down?'

I feel my face gathering in a frown. 'Coming down where?'

'Bournemouth. Don't you think it might be an idea to have him there for moral support?'

'I dunno.' I lift the covers and swing my legs out of bed, feeling the soft rug that used to be in my childhood bedroom beneath my bare feet. 'He said something last night about coming down, but I feel like it's just another thing to have to deal with. Plus – you know – family stuff, is complicated,' I say, lamely.

'And James is your boyfriend. If something like this happened, Rich would be there for me.'

'Yeah but you and Rich live together. You're like a proper couple.

Sophie speaks very slowly and clearly, as if she's talking to someone who finds it difficult to understand basic concepts, 'Yes, and stuff like this is what brings you together. I bet James would want to come down and keep you company.'

'And meet Mum?'

Sophie makes a noise between a groan and a snort. 'Mmm, yeah, well, there is that – that's the downside.'

'Tell me about it.' I rub sleep out of my eyes, and my jaw cracks as a huge yawn escapes my mouth.

'Well, he's going to have to meet her sometime,' Sophie says, reasonably. 'No time like the present, and all that.'

'I'll see,' I say, non-committally, and we say goodbye and hang up.

Later that morning, sitting by Nanna's bed waiting for the doctor to do her rounds I get a message from James.

Spoke to Soph at work. I'm going to come down tomorrow. No arguments.

I type *No, please don't* then look at it for a moment. Am I being unfair? He wants to be there for support. That's what relationships are supposed to be about, aren't they? I delete the words and look at the blinking cursor.

Bloody Sophie. I know she thinks she's doing the right thing, but – I give an exasperated sigh. It's just – it's not the right time. I can hear her saying brightly, 'There's never a right time, Jess,' and I feel slightly murderous. I'm still looking at the phone, contemplating my reply to James when the doctor appears.

The doctor makes us all feel better. I hadn't realised that I was basically holding my breath, but as she explains that Nanna's blood pressure has been up and they're giving her pills to keep it under control, but they're going to monitor her for a few days, I feel my shoulders dropping in relief. It's going to be a few days though, before they let her go back to the sheltered accommodation. She's not that happy about that.

'I bet that Maureen steals my favourite chair by the window in the lounge,' she says, crossly.

'There must be other seats, Mum,' says my mother, opening some get-well cards and placing them on the bedside table. I notice she doesn't read them. Later, I'll take each one and read the messages out to Nanna, who likes to keep tabs on stuff like that.

I go down to the WRVS café with Mum to have some lunch. The visiting hours are fairly relaxed, but we're expected to make ourselves scarce at lunchtime. The hospital's too far out of town to make it worth going in, so instead we sit and eat pale ham sandwiches and drink dark tannin-infused tea, and watch the other relatives as they do the same.

You'd love it here, I write to Alex. *It's people-watching heaven.*

Exactly why I love this job, he replies, five minutes later. *Hope it's going okay. Did she have a good night?*

Really good, I reply. *In fact, she's already started flirting with the male nurse,* I joke, thinking of the nurse from the night before.

Oh yeah, that happens to me all the time.

I bet it does, I type without thinking. Then I blush slightly, because the thought of Alex in his work clothes and the idea of him turning up at my bedside pops into my head and even though nobody else knows what I'm thinking, I feel like – God, what am I *doing?*

'Is that James you're texting?' Mum asks, looking at me with interest.

I'm caught between trying to explain the situation with Alex, and having her not believe for one second we're just friends, or telling a small white lie. I decide to settle for the easy option, and say it's James.

CHAPTER THIRTY-FIVE

Jess

4th October, Bournemouth

Nanna's clearly feeling better the next afternoon, because she's asked me to bring in her favourite red lipstick and a comb.

She puts on a crochet bedjacket, neatens her hair and puts lipstick on, so she looks much more like herself. We're talking about the other patients on her ward when I hear Mum. She's out in the corridor talking to the good-looking male nurse – she gives the tinkling laugh I recognise as her in flirt mode.

'Well this *is* a surprise,' she says, as she re-enters the little ward, pausing for a moment in the doorway as if she's waiting for applause. She gives a little flourish of her hands as James – looking slightly uncomfortable – steps into the room behind her.

'So I found this young man in the corridor, looking

for you.' She raises an approving eyebrow and gives a wide smile. 'Jess, you didn't tell me how *handsome* he was. James, this is my mother, Beth.'

I stand up, and Mum – apparently oblivious to the fact that we're in a hospital ward and not the foyer of a theatre after curtain fall – gives the whole room the benefit of her widest smile. She always perks up when there's a good-looking man around.

'Hi,' says James, leaning over to give me a kiss, which lands on my temple. He looks slightly wide-eyed, as if he hadn't quite been expecting the full Mum treatment. Nobody usually is. She gestures to the chair on the other side of Nanna Beth's bed, her armful of bangles jingling. 'James, do have a sit-down. You must be tired after working this morning and then driving down all this way. Was the traffic awful?'

'Not too bad.'

'Hello, James,' says Nanna Beth. She smooths down the white cotton sheet over her lap and looks at me for a moment. It's a look that says *well, you kept this one quiet.*

'I thought I'd better come and see if there was anything I could do,' says James. He's still in a suit, the top button of his shirt undone and his tie off. He looks pretty good, actually. I notice the granddaughter of the woman opposite eyeing him up and I feel a little surge of pride that I have a handsome boyfriend in a suit and a whole life in London and all that stuff. I catch his eye and he gives me a quick smile, before turning to Nanna Beth.

'So how are you feeling? I'm sorry we're meeting in these circumstances.'

'Not too bad,' she says. She definitely looks brighter. Mum's looking perky, as well. I – on the other hand – haven't had a second to brush my hair, am wearing no make-up, and the same top I've had on for the last three days because I forgot to pack anything besides pyjamas, knickers, and a toothbrush.

Half an hour later, when James has left the ward to go and get some bits and pieces from the shop (on a mission that was clearly made up by Mum, just so she could pass verdict), I sit on the side of Nanna's bed biting my thumbnail and listening to the two of them talking.

'He's very nice,' Mum says, looking as pleased with herself as if she'd selected James herself. She takes a little compact mirror out of her bag and applies some more fuchsia lipstick, then fluffs up her hair.

'Charming,' agrees Nanna. 'And so kind and helpful. Nice of him to go to the shop, wasn't it, Jess, darling?'

I bite the inside of my cheek, not quite sure why their praise of James makes me feel uncomfortable. In the end, I wander out into the corridor to go to the loo, and to see if I can catch him when he returns. But someone's using the bathroom, and I have to wait, standing reading NHS posters about hand washing and patient care policies, until I eventually get in.

When I look at myself in the mirror I realise I look even worse than I thought. I run water over my hands and comb them through my hair, turning my head upside down and shaking it to try and make it look less lank. The trouble with the new Dyson hand driers is you can't exactly stick your head under one and wake your hair up. I settle for washing my face and drying it with a green hospital-issue paper towel, and rubbing my teeth – which feel grotty – with another one. When I come back out I can hear Mum laughing before I see her, so it's no surprise to discover that James is in there, standing at the end of Nanna's bed, holding a bottle of lemon barley water and some sandwiches from the hospital shop.

'Oh, and I brought you these,' James says. He hands Mum a box of chocolates, and Nanna a crossword book. How on earth has he worked out that she loves them in that short space of time? It must be a lucky guess. Mum is over-the-top delighted and Nanna claps her hands.

'Thank goodness. I'm bored out of my mind already, stuck in here.' She chuckles and he pulls a pen out of his jacket pocket.

'He's thought of everything, Jess.' Nanna Beth beams at me. 'You've chosen well there.'

He's nice to my mother; he's charming to my grand-mother. Even the grumpy nurse in charge has found him an extra chair so nobody has to perch on the end of the bed. He's a massive hit with both generations. He's basically the perfect boyfriend. So why, I ask myself, as I surreptitiously turn my phone over to check for messages, am I looking to see if Alex has been in touch?

CHAPTER THIRTY-SIX

Jess

5th October, Bournemouth

I've been thinking, Alex has typed, *that you and me should go on another exploring trip when you get back.*

We're sitting on the sofa at Mum's place the next morning. We've slept in the little spare room bed, crammed together like sardines in a tin, and I'm exhausted and dreaming of my own bed. James is sipping a mug of coffee and reading the local newspaper, his long legs concertinaed in the tiny space. He looks a bit like someone's tried to put a giant in a doll's house. I watch him for a moment, looking out of the corner of my eye. He thinks I'm replying to work emails. I *am* replying to work emails. I just happen to be looking at a message from Alex and trying to work out why – when I have a handsome, eligible, kind, et cetera, et cetera, et cetera boyfriend sitting here in my mum's house – I'm more excited by the prospect of walking around London in the October drizzle than I am about being here.

I decide that maybe I'm just being fickle. But – I turn the phone over in my hands, pondering – I do like our wanders. And Alex makes me laugh. And it's important to have male friends when you're in a relationship.

I'd like that.

There's a pause when I see the dots on the screen, indicating he's writing something, and then they disappear. I wait a moment, but nothing comes.

? I type, waiting for his response.

Just, maybe we should skip inviting anyone else this time?

My insides give a disobedient little fizz, as if I've had a tiny electric shock. I'm not doing anything wrong, I tell myself, and I can feel the corners of my lips tugging upwards in a secret little smile as I tap out a reply.

Definitely.

And then I put the phone down on the table and turn towards James. He puts down the paper and gazes at me with his huge, soft brown eyes.

'You okay?'

I nod.

'And you're going to cope—' he pauses, glancing in the direction of Mum's bedroom, where she's still sleeping '—when I go back tonight?'

'Definitely.'

As if he's summoned her, Mum appears from the

bedroom, wrapped in a purple satin dressing gown. She rubs her face, and gives a huge, over-exaggerated yawn.

'Morning, James,' she says. She can't see my face, and I give him A Look – nostrils flaring and eyes wide. Mum has always been very much male focused, and with James around I've been relegated to a sort of incidental character, a bit-part player without a speaking part.

'Do we have anything for breakfast?' She opens the kitchen cupboard and closes it again, making a little noise of disappointment. It's as if she's forgotten that we're her guests, and she's the one responsible for catering.

'I noticed there was a deli on the corner when I moved the car last night. I thought I'd pop over and get us some pastries,' says James, unfolding himself and standing up, towering over me as I sit on the low, uncomfortable sofa.

'Oh, you are an angel,' Mum says, beaming at him. 'Isn't he a doll, Jess?'

'Absolutely,' I say, deadpan. James flashes me a look. He thinks I'm too hard on her. I haven't told him that much about growing up with her around – or rather, growing up at Nanna and Grandpa's house with Mum not around. It's weird that I've shared so much of this with Alex, but I think there's something about walking that makes it easier to talk about stuff. Anyway, I think he's got a more realistic view of what life with my mother was like.

'I'll be back in a couple of minutes,' James says, picking up the keys. 'I'll let myself back in.'

'He's *very* nice,' Mum says, for the fiftieth time,

313

watching as I put on the kettle and wipe up the kitchen surface from the night before. She'd clearly come in from a performance and made tea and a vodka and orange (or two) and the worktop is covered with a sticky layer of crumbs and juice that has dried into a rough layer.

'He is,' I agree, scrubbing at a particularly sticky bit.

'You should take a leaf out of Sophie's book,' she continues.

'Mum,' I begin, warningly. I know where this is going, because I've been hearing it since I was eight years old. I adore Soph, but my mother has been using her as a poster girl for as long as I can remember. Childishly, I want to point out that Sophie's in the midst of some sort of super early life crisis, because she and Rich still can't agree on what they want their wedding to be, so they've reached stalemate. But I don't say anything.

'I'm just saying,' she says, pouting slightly, her tone bruised. 'You're always looking for something to be offended by. Sophie's got a good job, nice house, she's trying for a baby – you're not getting any younger, Jess.'

'I'm not even thirty.' I'm trying to keep my tone level. How can she be so different to Nanna Beth?

'And he's a good-looking young man. *Very* good-looking,' she purrs, in a way that makes me feel slightly uncomfortable.

'This is 2019. I don't have to snare a man before it's too late. I'm not going to be on the shelf if I'm still single when I turn thirty. I've just started a brand-new job.'

'Well yes of course,' she says, shaking her head as if

I'm the one being unreasonable. 'I'm just saying, if I were you I'd put a ring on it before it's too late.'

She gives a little shimmy, and heads for the bathroom, humming Beyoncé. I stand there, open-mouthed, fuming.

When James walks in a few moments later, I'm still recovering.

He puts the paper bags full of pastries down on the table and turns to me, smiling with his lovely white perfect teeth. I go over and kiss him, taking him by surprise.

'What was that for?' He takes me by the shoulders and steps back, looking at me as if he's taking me in. I look back at him. He is a nice man, I think.

'Just because,' I say, and I hug him, wrapping my arms around his broad back and gazing out at the rooftops that lead to the sea. He feels safe, and solid, and like he's not going anywhere. Maybe that's a good thing, I think, looking sideways at Mum's place. Maybe that's what I should be aiming for.

And then Mum's phone rings.

'Yes. Oh, right. Yes. Of course.' Her face blanches whiter and whiter as she speaks until there are just two spots of high colour on each cheekbone, and something in my stomach drops down to the floor and I realise I'm clenching both hands into fists.

'Of course. Yes. We'll be there straight away.'

'Mum?' I squeeze the word out.

'We need to get a taxi to the hospital.'

'I've got the car,' says James, picking up his car keys.

'Of course. I need my bag,' says Mum, her words mechanical and stiff. 'Jess?'

'I'm ready.'

I don't even want to ask what's happened. If I don't ask, it can't be the worst thing. It *can't* be the worst thing.

Nanna's lying in a bed in the Coronary Care Unit. I see her through the window. She looks tiny, propped up in bed with wires coming from her arms. When the nurse takes us into the room I spin round, as if to walk away from it all, covering my face with my hands. It's Mum who puts a hand on my arm and says, 'Come on, love.' I turn back, and we walk in together.

The room is oddly silent. I don't know what I was expecting: beeps and machines and all the sounds you think of when you watch this sort of thing on *Casualty* on television, not just this weird, deathly silence. Mum sits down on the chair beside the bed and looks to the nurse as if to ask permission to hold Nanna's hand. The nurse who is checking something on the machine smiles and gives a brief nod. He looks exhausted.

'She's just sleeping. We did a procedure last night to unblock an artery and put in a stent.'

I glance up at him, horrified. 'Heart surgery?'

'Not the way you're thinking,' he says, gently. 'We went in through her arm, and removed the blockage that way. She should be okay to go home in a few days, although there'll be rehab and some lifestyle changes—'

'I'll look after you, don't worry,' says Mum, squeezing

316

Nanna Beth's hand. The nurse gives another reassuring smile and leaves us.

I watch him heading down the ward, checking the time on his watch. I stand at the other side of Nanna Beth's bed, stroking her fingers. There's a cannula coming out of her hand, and wires coming out of her arm. Across the way, in another bed, there's another woman, half awake, being helped upright by a nurse. It's weird to think of Alex in the same situation, doing that day in, day out. I wish there was reception in here. I want to message him and ask what he knows about all of this. I feel scared and powerless and—

'Hello,' Nanna Beth croaks.

'My God, you gave us a fright,' says Mum.

Nanna looks at me through heavy lidded eyes. 'Sorry,' she says. Her voice is not much more than a whisper. 'Didn't mean to cause a fuss.'

CHAPTER THIRTY-SEVEN

Alex

6th October, London

I'm so tired that I could just lie down here and have an emergency nap. The words on the screen of my iPad are swimming in front of my eyes. I'm supposed to be working on an essay, but my brain's gone on strike.

On a plus note, things at home are a bit less fraught. Now the whole Emma thing is over – and I've firmly ended my brief dalliance with being the sort of bloke who has a friend with benefits – I feel like I can breathe a bit. I mean it's all very well in theory, but it just wasn't me at all. Not even recovering-from-a-break-up me.

'Can't believe you got a first in that essay,' Jameela says, throwing her bag down on the floor of the nurses' station. I jump, because my overtired nerves are jangling on high alert at the moment, and she gives a snort of laughter.

She looks as shattered as I feel. Sometimes I think if

it wasn't for the others who are all in the same boat I'd struggle to believe this job wasn't just some sort of nightmare. We're all so tired we could fall asleep standing up, and we've got assignments coming out of our ears.

I watch her peeling off layers of coat, scarf and cardigan. She shoves them in her locker in a ball and, reaching over, grabs the cup of stewed tea I'm holding, then takes a slurp.

'Oi,' I say, laughing.

'I'm bloody freezing. And you got a first. Maybe if I nick your tea I'll soak up some of your magic.'

'Doubt it,' I joke.

We're waiting for one of the senior nursing team to appear and take us on an observation in theatre. My stomach's churning with excitement and nerves. The familiar ritual of boiling kettle, teabag in cup, milk and sugar steadies me. Before I'd started working in the hospital I'd taken tea with nothing more than a splash of milk. Now, working long hours, never quite sure when the next break is coming, I heap sugar in for extra calories to keep me going. We all do.

I make another cup and pass it to Jameela. 'Here. How did you do in the essay, then?'

'Sixty-eight.'

'That's basically a first.'

'No prizes for coming second.' She rolls her eyes.

I watch as Jameela sips her tea, flicking her hijab back over her shoulder.

'So what's happening at your place?' she asks.

'Nothing much.'

She gives me a meaningful look. 'Everything sorted with Emma?'

Jameela's a good listener. I told her the whole story one long boring night – she and I have ended up on the same rotation and it's made a real difference to have someone who actually gets how I'm feeling. And who doesn't mind if I doze off mid-sentence.

'Nope. She's got someone else. I've accepted my new life as a permanent singleton. Anyway, all that sneaking around in the middle of the night was a bit like being seventeen and on a school trip.'

'That sounds quite exciting.'

'It loses the novelty pretty bloody fast. No, I'm focusing on this—' I wave in the general direction of the ward '—and on getting decent grades.'

Jameela takes another sip of tea and looks at me for a moment. 'How's Jess?' she asks.

'Fine.'

'Fine?' She gives me a look.

'Fine. Well, she's in Bournemouth seeing her gran, who's had some blood pressure issues.' I take a green paper towel and dry the mug, hanging it back on the rack. I've been trying not to think about Jess down there in Bournemouth, with the perfect, super-capable James there for moral support. When they're not sitting hand in hand by Nanna Beth's bedside, they're probably taking romantic walks on the beach.

'And no news from Alice?'

I look at her sideways and arch an eyebrow. 'This is like the Spanish Inquisition.'

'Sorry. Your life's way more interesting than mine at the mo. Mine is basically work, study, sleep, work.'

I nod. 'Yeah. Mine is basically that with a bit of screwed-up relationship stuff added in. As for Alice, no. Nothing much. The odd text. But I don't think you can go backwards, you know?'

'God, yes.' Jameela sounds emphatic. 'Been there. It's like trying to revive someone who's come in DoA.'

'Nice image.'

'Sorry. I swear my entire life is nursing-focused since I started this course.' Jameela yawns so widely that the last words are smothered with her hand.

.

'All right?'

That evening I almost jump out of my skin as I walk into the sitting room after my shift and hear a voice from the dark. 'Rob,' I say, once I've got my bearings. 'God, I forget you're here half the time.'

'Cheers,' says Rob, sardonically. He lifts his legs off the coffee table so I can head over to the battered beige armchair beside the television. 'What's up? You look like you've had a shit day.'

'Just, y'know, life stuff.'

'Anything I can help with?' Rob leans forward. He turns the volume down on the television and inclines his head towards the door, and the rest of the house. 'Woman trouble?'

Does *everyone* know what went on with me and Emma?

'I dunno,' I say, picking up a cushion and hugging it. 'I was talking about Alice today at work and I got out of a surgery observation – open heart, ironically – and there was a message from her. I guess she's at a bit of a crossroads – she was seeing someone for a bit and it didn't work out.'

'Ah.' Rob nods briefly. 'That's a tricky one. You dinnae want to be the fallback guy.'

'Alice wants more than I've got. Not in a bad way – I mean I don't think she was only after my money when we met, but she thought she was marrying into a lifestyle. She wants kids, a nice house in the suburbs, all that sort of thing.'

'And you don't?'

Unbidden, an image of Jess pops into my head, laughing at something as we're walking along the canal path at Little Venice. I need to get a grip.

'I wouldn't say I don't, but I'm never going to be able to give Alice what she wanted, and – she's a nice girl, and all, but—'

'She's no' the one?'

'Exactly.'

Rob looks thoughtful. 'Well, you don't want to settle. I tried that, and here I am at forty-four, living in a basement with you lot.'

'What happened?' I ask.

'Oh, I liked her a lot; she was a nice lassie. We moved down here when I got the job as a commis chef at my first restaurant, and when things started falling apart we tried to fix it by getting married.'

'And it didn't work out?'

He shakes his head. 'Nah. She headed back to Glasgow, and I signed over the wee flat we had up there to her. Felt like I owed her that much.'

'So that's how you ended up here?'

'Yep. No property, no savings, not a bean to ma name. But I'd still rather have that than be stuck in a marriage where we were both miserable. You need to actually like the person you're with, no' just fancy the pants off them.'

'You're right.'

'Aye.' Rob looks at me, steadily. 'Mind you remember that. It's important.'

Suddenly, Becky crashes into the room. 'What's going on in here?' she asks.

'Just men's talk.' Rob waggles his eyebrows.

'Oh God, right, football and all that crap.' Becky laughs, looking at the screen where the weekend football fixture list is playing. It's a pretty good cover.

'Aye, something like that,' Rob says.

'Well, I have a treat in store, if you're not busy. A client's just delivered a massive crate of wine as a thank you, so I think we should celebrate the fact that we've made it to the end of the week – assuming none of you are doing anything tonight?'

'Nope,' I say. 'Well, I'd been planning an early night, and a bit of studying. But it won't take much to convince me to work on the assignment in the morning.'

'Or the afternoon, if you're hungover. But this is good wine,' Becky says, pulling a bottle out of the crate, 'and I was reading a thing today that said that you shouldn't get hangovers from expensive wine, so we can test it out. Rob, are you about?'

'I am.'

'Not working?' I ask, surprised.

'I've knackered my ankle.' He indicates the leg that was propped up on the table. 'Can't stand up for longer than about five minutes, and it's so manic in the kitchen on the weekends that I'm a liability, so I've been signed off sick for a couple of days.'

'We can have a party,' said Becky, looking cheerful. 'I've just helped on a case that looks like it's going to the High Court and we're going to win.'

She looks triumphant and exhilarated, the same expression on her face as I'd seen on the surgeon's earlier when they'd successfully completed a bypass operation. It was weird – instead of making me envious, it just underlines the fact that I don't miss law one bit. Doesn't make me want to be a surgeon, either, mind you.

'Em,' Becky calls up the stairs. 'Are you in?' She's opened the wine and is thrusting glasses into everyone's hands. 'Has anyone heard from Jess today?'

'She's coming back in a few days, I think.' I sip the red wine. It tastes expensive, and it's the kind that goes down way too easily, especially after the week I've had. I sit back and put my feet up on the coffee table.

'Shame she's not here for this,' said Becky, as Emma

comes down the stairs. I can see her through the open door of the sitting room. She's dressed for a lazy evening in a pair of cut-off jeans and a fluffy grey cardigan over a tiny white vest top. She pauses for a moment.

'This banister is seriously wobbly,' she says.

'The whole place is crumbling,' says Becky. 'Anyone any good at DIY?'

'I'll have a look at it tomorrow,' Rob says.

'With your foot?' Becky laughs.

'With my eyes.'

'I mean, should you be doing house repairs in your state?'

He chuckles. 'I know what you meant. I promise, I'll be safe.'

'Alex, want a top-up?' Becky pours more wine into my glass and hands one to Emma.

'It's Jess's birthday next Saturday. We should do something to cheer her up.' Becky curls up on the sofa beside Emma and Rob.

'Good thinking. Assuming she's free, of course,' I say.

I don't mention our plans to get together for a walk sometime soon. I haven't heard from her since yesterday, actually, which is weird. She's normally messaging stupid jokes or sharing things she's seen that she knows will make me laugh, although now James is on the scene that's tailed off a bit, obviously.

'I'm out of the loop a bit here. Is Jess okay? What's been going on?' Emma looks at Becky.

'Oh her gran's been sick, and she's been away. Didn't you notice?'

Emma shakes her head. 'I've been so busy with work, I thought we just hadn't crossed paths for a bit.'

It's weird how we can all scatter for days – weeks even – without really seeing much of each other. I watch Rob chatting to Becky about how to make the perfect chilli, arguing over recipes online, debating about whether dark chocolate is the perfect addition or an abomination. Emma catches my eye and raises her eyebrows heavenward.

We watch a crappy Netflix thriller and drink more wine. I nip out to get some snacks, realising halfway down Albany Road on my way to the corner shop that it definitely feels like winter's coming early, and a T-shirt and joggers is not enough to keep me warm. By the time I get back home my fingers and toes are like ice and the sitting room's empty.

'The secret's in the chopping.' Rob's preparing a very late-night dish of chilli-spiked vegetables and shredded beef. Becky's standing beside him, measuring out rice into a jug and boiling the kettle.

'They're doing competitive cooking again,' says Emma, passing me the wine.

We watch and wait, drinking and chatting. They work well together, despite the constant bantering half-arguments, and at quarter to midnight – all of us pretty much completely pissed – we're sitting down to dinner in the cosy, dilapidated kitchen.

CHAPTER THIRTY-EIGHT

Jess

7th October, Bournemouth

It's midnight. James is back in London, and I'm staying a bit longer, just because of the operation, and because I want to know Nanna Beth's okay before I leave. The people have been lovely at work – I think because they know she's like a mum to me. I said I'd take the time off unpaid, but got an email back telling me not to be so silly. I'll just have to work twice as hard when I get back. Meanwhile, the doctor and the nurses all keep telling us she'll be fine, and that she's doing well, but it doesn't seem to matter how many times I hear it.

I want to text Alex for reassurance, have him tell me she's going to be okay, and that I'm worrying about nothing. I can't take much more time off work. You don't get compassionate leave for grandparents, even if they're the ones who brought you up. I lie staring at the ceiling in Mum's flat, watching the hours go by on the clock, which ticks loudly on the mantelpiece, and wonder if I'll ever fall asleep.

Alex
7th October, London

'Morning.'

My eyes, which have been slowly and cautiously opening in the excruciatingly bright daylight, pop open in shock at the sound of a voice in my ear.

I close them again and screw my face up, because I think maybe I imagined it. But then I open them, and nope, there's a face beside mine on the pillow. And this isn't my pillow. It smells faintly of roses and the sunlight from the window's coming in at the wrong angle.

Emma rolls over to her side and props herself up on one elbow, and her hair falls down in a tangle. She pulls the cover up slightly, and I realise that she's got bare shoulders, which means it's more than likely the rest of her is bare as well.

I rack my brains. We were in the kitchen eating chilli wrap things, and there was wine, and . . .

'We drank the rest of the tequila. Did slammers. Don't you remember?' Emma says, clearly seeing my confused expression. She looks unperturbed.

'I—'

Vague recollections of Rob and Becky having a sword

330

fight with wooden spoons. Dancing. Music playing. It's slowly coming back to me.

'I feel like death,' says Emma, cheerfully. 'Thank God I've got today off. D'you fancy going out for breakfast to recover?'

I lie very still for a moment trying to piece it together. Rob juggling limes. Becky disappearing somewhere – probably to pass out due to an excess of wine and tequila. What a killer combination. I shift slightly in bed. It feels like my brain has come loose and is banging against my skull.

'Oh God,' I say.

'You all right?' Emma says.

I have a horrible moment of clarity. After Becky disappeared, Rob had tossed me the limes as he left the room, hobbling on his dodgy ankle. And Emma said, 'If life gives you limes, drink tequila,' and we'd finished the bottle, and . . .

For fuck's sake. Why on earth did I let my bloody libido drag me by the scruff of the neck up the stairs and into Emma's bedroom?

'I'm really sorry, Em,' I say, wriggling out of bed and grabbing my boxers and jeans, which are lying in a heap on the floor. 'I can't do this.'

'Breakfast?' She rolls over to face me, sitting up in bed and wrapping the duvet around her body. She looks like she's just woken up after an eight-hour sleep. If it was anyone else, she'd have the decency to look hungover.

'No.' I haul up my jeans, buttoning the fly. My T-shirt's

inside out and hanging over the bedside lamp. Bloody hell. 'Us,' I say, voice muffled from inside the T-shirt as I pull it on. This isn't who I am. It's not who I want to be. It's not about Emma – I like her a lot – and it's not about anyone else, either. It's just . . .

'Oh come on, Alex,' says Emma, in a cool voice. 'I'm not asking for your hand in marriage. We got pissed; we had sex.'

'Shh,' I say, putting a finger to my lips.

Emma laughs for a moment and then looks at me as if she's sizing me up, raising her chin slightly, her eyes narrowing almost imperceptibly.

'Jess isn't here, don't worry.'

'What d'you mean?' I say.

'Nothing.' She rolls over, lying on her back and staring at the ceiling. 'Just passing comment.'

'There's nothing going on with me and Jess.'

'Never said there was.'

I feel like a complete arsehole.

'It's just sex, Alex,' she says, in a clear voice, as I open the door to leave. I feel my cheeks stinging red. I am *so* shit at this whole relationship/no relationship thing.

Something's got to change. I stand in the shower, letting it run almost cold to try and wash off the hangover and the crappy feeling that I've made an idiot of myself. Afterwards I pick up my keys and my phone and head out into the autumnal drizzle. I walk up to the café in Little Venice, picking up a property paper on the way past the estate agent and sit brooding over the prices of houses until my coffee goes cold and I have to order another.

'Anything to eat?' Lona, the café owner, looks at me appraisingly. 'You look like you could do with something to soak up a hangover. Panini? Some soup?'

I thank her and order a panini, then sit in the corner by the window, looking out at the crowds of people bustling past wrapped up against a weirdly early cold snap. The leaves have turned already, and the slender poplar trees are already half-bare, their long branches reaching up to the sky like slender fingers. It's going to be a cold winter.

'Here you are, my love.' Lona slides a plate in front of me, the panini steaming hot. 'And I've made you another coffee on the house. You look like you've got the cares of the world on your shoulders.'

'Something like that,' I say. 'Thank you.'

I wait for my food to cool and stare into space. Something has to change. I saw Becky before I left, and she looked seriously shifty. She gave me an odd look and sidled past me in the hallway. I'm pretty sure she's guessed something is up. I've been taking the piss with the whole *no-relationships* thing, carrying on with Emma the way I have. I can't help wondering if it's time for a fresh start. I've screwed this up. Abeo and Oli, two of my friends from work, said the other day they were looking for a new place. We'd be on placements loads more in second year, and maybe living with other nurses would make more sense. But even if we found a grotty place the rent would be sky high compared to Becky's house.

Maybe I should look into that guardian thing that Jess's friend Gen does. But she moves house every few months, flitting from one place to the next quite happily. I've got enough going on with shifting placements. I want to feel settled, or at least feel like I can unpack my things and not be waiting for the next move all the time, especially with college stress going on as well.

I drop my head into my hands, closing my eyes and giving a quiet groan of desperation. Why the hell did I end up in bed with Emma? I don't even *like* her – well, not like *that*. I mean she's a lovely girl and everything. But – shit. The truth is, every time this happens, it feels like I'm doing a pretty good job of sabotaging something. I'm not sure what.

I look down at my phone. There's a message from Jess.

I am now a cardiac expert. Coming home to grill you and see if I know more than you do.

That wouldn't be hard, I type back in reply.

Feeling a bit better about leaving NB today – she asked for her lipstick to put on because the handsome nurse is on shift again, so think she's feeling better. X

Glad to hear it.

Oh and she patted the handsome nurse on the thigh in a slightly saucy manner earlier.

[eyeroll emoji] Yep, that's a sign she's on the mend. Happens to me all the time. x

I had no idea you were so popular. x

You'd be surprised.

I scroll through eBay as I'm eating. Jess's birthday's

coming up and I've had a brainwave – if I can find her a signed copy of *One Day*, I think she'd love it. Only reasonably priced signed copies are not that easy to come by. I disappear down an eBay rabbit hole of personalised *Game of Thrones* T-shirts and diamante dog collars, eating absent-mindedly. There's no sign of one on there or anywhere else online, so I finish lunch, and take a walk up to the second-hand bookshop. Despite my lack of success online, I have a good feeling they'll have a copy – they've got pretty much everything under the sun stacked up on the shelves there.

'*One Day*, you say?' The bookseller puts down the magazine he's reading.

'Yes. It's for my friend. It's her favourite.'

I've rummaged through the shelves, with no luck.

'As it happens, you've come to the right place.' He stands up, dusting off his sleeves in a curiously thoughtful manner. He's wearing tiny, silver-rimmed glasses and looks like he's stepped out of another century.

He beckons to me to follow him, through a little doorway and into a smaller room, where the air is heavy with that dusty, sweet, old-book smell. He waves to one of the shelves with a flourish.

'A whole shelf of David Nicholls books, right here. All signed.'

'Wouldn't they be better off out on the shelves in the actual shop?'

'Sell them through a book website,' he explains, shaking his head.

He wraps it up and I head out of the shop. I sit down when I get back to the house and find myself getting caught up in the story. I can see why she loves it, but God, it's like a jab in the ribs. All missed opportunities and second chances – appropriate under the circumstances.

By the time I get up, it's dark. I look out of the window to see a girl walking down Albany Road and for a second I think it's Jess and my heart leaps, but then she turns to check the traffic before she crosses the road and I realise that no, it's nothing like her. And I don't know why, but my brain spins me back to last December when we first met. God, I screwed up there. She'd laughed and wound tinsel round her hair, and we'd chatted about everything and nothing over fajitas and tequila. I could have been in a completely different situation if I hadn't been such an arse. If I hadn't fallen into bed with Emma – I groan and run my hands through my hair. If this year's taught me one thing, it's that I'm not ever going to be a casual fling sort of person. It's just too bloody complicated.

I keep thinking about what Rob said. He almost made me believe that if something was meant to be, it was worth all the struggle and the mess and the heartache. And with someone like Jess, I don't think I'd have to choose between the job and the relationship. She'd get it.

Sod it. When Jess gets back, I'm going to ask her if she'll come on that walk we've been planning, and then we can end up back at our favourite café, and Lona can make us a hot chocolate with rum. And I can give her the book, and – the idea makes me feel a bit sick – maybe I can find a way to tell her how I feel.

CHAPTER THIRTY-NINE

Alex

11th October

The week drags past. This module we're on is the most boring one so far – all health and safety issues in the workplace and risk assessments and protocols. I spend most of the time half-listening in lectures, doodling in the margins of my notepad, and feeling sick at the thought of seeing Jess.

And then Friday comes and I come back from college to find the front door open. Jess's red and white striped key ring is lying on the dresser, and her coat's hanging on the end of the banister. I try and act casual, taking the stairs one at a time. I don't want to look like I'm hurtling up there to see her but I realise I've got butterflies in my stomach. God, this is ridiculous.

I knock on the door and wait a second.

'Hello?' Jess says from within.

'It's me.'

'Alex!' She grins as I push the door open, popping my head round.

'Bloody hell,' I say. 'You're organised. Unpacking already? I always leave my case shoved under the bed for days after I get back from being away. Weeks, sometime.' *Shut up, you fool, you're gibbering nonsense.*

'Oh.' A strange expression flits across her face. She bites her lower lip and looks up at me. A long strand of hair curls across her face. 'I'm not unpacking. I'm packing.'

Her hair's escaping from a loose ponytail and falling in wavy tendrils around her face. She's wearing a huge fluffy jumper that hangs off one shoulder and her legs are folded underneath her. She looks adorable, and slightly frazzled, and I can't read the expression on her face at all.

'Packing? Didn't you just get back? Is your Nanna Beth okay?'

'She's fine. Really good, actually.' Her face brightens into a smile, and she adds, 'She's been misbehaving again.'

'She's going to get into trouble,' I say.

'I'm just glad she's back to herself. She's doing really well.'

'Oh that's good news. You must be relieved,' I say, conscious I sound stilted, formal.

'I am.'

'So what's the case for?' I ask.

She blushes slightly and drops her gaze. 'James. He

340

booked us a surprise trip for my birthday weekend. We're
going to Venice – tonight.'

Jess

I don't think – if I'm really, truly honest with myself –
I'd have let myself be as excited about James's
announcement, if it wasn't for something Becky said. Or
rather, what she didn't say.

Having dumped my stuff at the bottom of the stairs,
I had walked into the kitchen just as she made a slightly
pointed comment about *the other night* to Emma.

'I don't know what you're talking about,' Emma had
said, popping an olive into her mouth. She was standing
by the fridge, still wearing her coat. She'd turned around,
spotting me, and closed the fridge.

Becky was standing with her back to me. 'Just
saying, you and Alex sloped off without even saying
goodnight. Rob and I came back into the kitchen and
the two of you had buggered off. It's not exactly subtle,
is it?'

'Are you sure?' Emma sounded unconvincing. 'God.
I was so pissed I don't even remember. Oh, hi Jess.'

Becky spun around and looked at me with an odd
expression.

'When was this?' I tried to keep my tone of voice
casual. I felt a strange sort of dropping in my stomach.

'Oh we all had far too much to drink one night when
you were away, and it all got a bit messy.' Becky lifted

her chin slightly. Emma shot her a look. It was one of those looks – the *let's not mention this now* kind.

'Sounds like a good night.' I'd cleared my throat. 'I really need to get my stuff organised,' I'd said, making a rapid exit. I could hear my heart thudding in my ears.

When I got up to my room I'd flopped down on the bed with a groan. If things were back on between Emma and Alex, it was a fairly obvious sign. I needed to stop half-wondering if there was something between us, and work out what it was I wanted in my own life. And if a weekend in Venice wasn't a good way to start that, I didn't know what was. I opened my wardrobe and tried to decide what to pack.

'Oh my God, that's the most romantic thing EVER.'

Sophie hadn't even waited to message back when I shared the news on our little group chat. She'd dropped everything and called. I was on the train back from Bournemouth. I have to admit that it's sweet that James couldn't resist the urge to tell me before he saw me in person at the station when I got home to London. '

'How are you feeling?' I said.

'Like death.'

Oh yes. There's another thing – a pretty big one – that happened this week. It's clearly some sort of cosmic shift, or something. I can't believe it's happened. Sophie is actually pregnant. Eight weeks, which is early – I know that much, although I'm a bit hazy on the rest of the details – but she couldn't resist telling us. Sometimes I find myself wondering if she'd carried on doing headstands after sex, and if that had been the thing that had done the trick. It's a pretty weird image to have in your head.

'I feel like I've got travel sickness but I'm not moving.'

'That sounds awful,' I said.

'Ah, but it'll be worth it,' Soph replied, in a dreamy voice. I could already imagine Gen's sardonic comments. It's weird that we're friends when we're all so different. I guess that's why it works. Plus I bet Gen's going to be the best aunty you can imagine to Sophie's baby. She'll be taking it for exotic days out and introducing it to all her thespian friends at the theatre.

'So what are you taking to wear? Where are you staying? Oh my God, you don't think he's going to get down on one knee, do you?'

I felt a leaden thud of fear in my stomach at that. 'God, I hope not. I hardly know him.'

'Jess!' Sophie chided me.

'I don't mean "I hope not" like that, just . . .' I felt a weird sensation at the idea of it. I mean I like James, and everything, but – the idea of settling down fills me with a vague sense of terror.

'But he's lovely,' Sophie said. I know she's very keen that we end up together. It's very Sophie to want me to be with someone she's selected specifically for me.

'Oh yeah, yeah,' I replied, nodding so vigorously that the woman sitting opposite me on the train looked at me as if I'd lost the plot. 'Totally lovely. I just don't think we're quite there yet.'

I half-listened to Sophie chatting happily about odd, alien things, like nursery school waiting lists and house purchase timetables, making the right noises in the right places, staring out of the window as we passed the backs of suburban houses. The gardens follow a pattern. Untidy, stacked with miniature bikes and plastic toys and a huge trampoline on the grass. Neatly kept, with a greenhouse, tidy borders edged with hedges. Scruffy and chaotic, with uncut lawns and shaggy, overgrown hedges.

That's what our garden in Albany Road looks like. Becky's been saying she's going to hire someone to sort it out for ages, but it's funny, we all forget it's there. Sophie's going to be joining the trampoline and plastic toy society before long. When I think of that, I feel a pang of something I can't put my finger on – it's not jealousy, though. More the sense that she's going to disappear out of our lives. I resolved to call her and Gen when I get back from Venice and sort out a night out, maybe dinner or something, and we can catch up. It's ridiculous that we're all living in the same place and we go weeks and weeks without seeing each other.

Shortly after I'd finished talking to Sophie, the train ground to a halt at Waterloo and I'd bumped my bag out, walking up the platform towards the gate. As I was showing my ticket, I saw James, taller and blonder than almost anyone else, like a huge Viking (if Vikings wore suits and had neat, well-kept haircuts). His face beamed with a huge smile of welcome and I thought

344

to myself how lucky I am to be loved by someone who feels so safe, and solid, and sweet. He wrapped his arms around me.

'I didn't want to be one of those people who does the whole *pack your bag, we're going on a surprise trip* thing,' he'd explained, taking my case and wheeling it along as we headed for the tube. 'But I thought you'd had enough stress, and you could do with a break.'

He'd stayed on the tube and I'd kissed him goodbye, heading back to Queensway where I got off and bumped my case along the streets to Albany Road. There was a parcel in the porch, and I'd picked it up and opened the door, balancing it under my chin. Inside the house had smelled faintly of one of Emma's expensive scented candles.

It's weird. We've been living together for almost a year and I still feel like I know nothing about her. I've spent hours standing in the kitchen, helping Rob prep vegetables and learning how to cook some of his favourite dishes. Alex and I have walked so far over London that our Fitbits have given us all kinds of badges for effort. Becky – well, she's never here because she's always working, but I know her so well from uni that it doesn't count. But somehow, Emma and I have always kept each other at arm's length. I guess it's the Alex thing – not that there's an Alex thing from my perspective, I remind myself. We're just friends.

I told her I was off to Venice with James and she looked genuinely delighted for me.

345

'Oh, it's gorgeous. Hang on – I've been a couple of times with my ex,' she said, running up the stairs. 'I've got a couple of really good guidebooks.'

And then, once I'd gone into my room to get my stuff together, Alex appeared. And there was a moment when my heart leapt as his head popped round the side of the door and he stood there chatting to me. I felt weird, somehow, telling him I was going away with James. But he was his usual self, and waved me goodbye and wished me a happy birthday when it comes. I need to get over myself. And him. I've created a whole *thing* between us when there's nothing there, and there's a real live James who was messaging me that second. I clicked on my phone screen to read his message, telling myself to forget about Alex once and for all.

So now we're sitting in Terminal 5, drinking Prosecco and eating cashew nuts and looking at Emma's guidebooks.

'We have to do a gondola trip,' James says, pointing out a photograph on one of the pages. 'You can't go to Venice without doing that.'

I make a non-committal noise. There's something a bit weird, I've always thought, about sitting on a boat looking self-consciously romantic while a bloke stands at the end, trying not to look at you.

'How's Sophie?' James asks.

'Says she feels sick.' I've told James Sophie is pregnant – I checked it would be okay when she called and she said she didn't mind, but she's not telling anyone else at work.

'I'll cover her back in meetings,' he says, kindly.

We get on the plane; British Airways, of course. I don't know why I guessed it would be, but it's very James. We sit back and relax whilst they come round with champagne. It's a bit of a change from my last flight, which was a Ryanair last-minute job to Madrid with the girls.

And then, once the flight and taxi are out of the way, we arrive in Venice, and it is so – Venice-y. I mean Venetian. I *mean*, it's not like one of those cities where you get there and there are two streets that look like the brochure and the rest of it's all Holiday Inns and high-rises and dodgy-looking side roads. Literally everywhere you look it's so beautiful that it makes my heart ache. It's the most romantic city in the world.

Our hotel room is huge.

'D'you like it?'

James stands behind me as I look out onto the sparkling water of the canal. I can feel his breath in my hair. He wraps his arms around my waist.

'It's gorgeous. More than gorgeous.'

I turn around and he kisses me gently. 'I'm going to have a shower,' he says, dropping one more kiss on my temple before he goes. I turn back to look at the view, and a huge yawn escapes from somewhere deep inside me. I take a photo and share it on Instagram. Nanna Beth likes it straight away and leaves a comment:

Love you very much xxx

I feel tears prickling at the corners of my eyes. It's been such a long week, and I am so tired. Nanna's back in her sheltered accommodation, only with a carer popping in once a day just to make sure she's okay. She's got a ton of medication to take each morning and evening, but she's sorted it all out with neat little pillboxes – it's very her. But oh, I miss her. I wish I could be there – wish I didn't have to be so far away. Wish I wasn't so tired . . .

CHAPTER FORTY

Jess

12th October, Venice

When I wake up, it's with a start. And I realise it's morning, and the bed's empty. It's my birthday, and I'm in Venice, and I'm completely alone. It's not exactly what I'd been thinking of when James said we were having a weekend in a lovely hotel. I roll over, lifting the duvet just in case he's hidden underneath.

Shit.

'James?'

Silence.

I look in the bathroom and there's a hotel branded Post-it Note on the mirror.

Gone for a wander. Thought I'd let you sleep. J x

I think about breakfast in bed or a lazy brunch in a café,

and sigh as I switch on the little hotel kettle and make myself a cup of instant coffee. It'll have to do for now. When I look on the desk, James being James, he's left a fold-out travel map on the dressing table, and a note of where he's planning to be. He'd give Sophie a run for her money in the organisation stakes. I shake my head, laughing at how similar they are, and head for the shower.

Jess
13th October

Even on a grey October Sunday afternoon, the Piazza san Marco is heaving with tourists – and pigeons.

I drop a piece of the pastry I'm eating on the run on the ground.

'Shoo,' says James, as one hops up beside him when we stop to look at a carving on the wall.

I look at the pigeon and I swear it winks at me. It takes the piece of pastry and hops off, looking pleased with itself. I shiver, and pull the collar of my coat more tightly around my neck. I don't know why I'd expected it to be warm, but I've brought nothing but unsuitable clothes. The drizzle is relentless, and James's desire to inspect every building and tell me historic facts is . . . well, it leaves something to be desired. They do say you don't really get to know someone until you go away on holiday with them, and so far I've established that James is a *lot* more interested in Venetian architecture than I am.

I look longingly at a café with roaring patio heaters glowing in the doorway, and squeeze his hand.

'D'you think maybe it's time for a drink?'

Thankfully, he agrees, and as soon as we approach, the waiter takes my coat and pulls out my chair. We're in a covered dining area, and the plastic roof is rattling in the wind. A long stream of rainwater pours from the corner, splattering into a puddle, which is starting to seep underneath and spread below the chairs opposite us. It feels as if we're living underwater. I don't think I've ever been anywhere so damp in my life.

'Negroni?' James looks at me, his eyebrows questioning. I nod. He's been in a weird mood all afternoon. There's something about going away with someone – away from all the distractions of everyday life, from friends, and familiar places around you – that really underlines how your relationship is faring.

Or . . . *isn't?*

After I got up yesterday, and once I'd managed to get lost twice trying to find my way to the restaurant where we'd agreed to have lunch (Google Maps and I are officially on non-speaking terms again), we did the gondola trip that everyone has to do when they visit Venice. James told the gondolier it was my birthday, and he insisted on serenading me, which was – well, I think James thought it was romantic. If I'm truthful it was just mortifying. It finally stopped raining in the afternoon for an hour or two, and we went to a café and I sat, feeling awkward and self-conscious, trying to make conversation.

Somehow that pissed him off, and he was offhand and a bit moody for a while afterwards, as we squelched our way around sodden pavements, stopping for coffee again to try and dry off. The rain started about twelve hours after we arrived, and it hadn't stopped. We'd gone to bed after dinner, and I'd fallen asleep in James's arms and thought that actually it was rather nice. Then we'd woken up this morning, and I'd found him sitting, guidebook in hand, writing a list of places we could go. I made a joke about no more architecture spotting, and he'd been a tiny bit huffy about it.

'Cheers,' says James now, lifting his glass to mine. He looks at me with his big, soulful eyes, and seems to relax a little bit.

'Thanks so much for bringing me,' I say, taking a gulp of negroni. God, it's strong. He watches me, smiling fondly. An elderly couple sit down at the table across from us.

'I brought her here fifty years ago,' the man says, leaning over and smiling. 'We've come back for our anniversary weekend.'

James's eyes meet mine briefly and I am hit by a sudden panic.

'Just nipping to the loo,' I say.

'What if they come back to order?' James asks.

'Oh,' I say, clambering out of the chair and knocking over a candle holder at the table behind me, 'just tell them to hang on. Or get a pizza, or something.'

'What kind of pizza?' James calls after me, but I've

slipped through the plastic door and I'm standing in the Piazza San Marco, looking at tourists and Venetian people dashing, coats over their heads, trying to get out of the rain, which is landing in huge splashy drops on my head, covering my shoulders, dripping down my nose.

'Are you lost, *bella*?' The waiter appears, holding an umbrella over me. My reputation precedes me.

'Just looking for the loo. I mean the bathroom. Toilet?'

'Ah.' He beckons for me to follow him. 'This way.'

Standing in front of the mirror, I look at my mascara-smudged face. My hair has gone flop in the rain and is hanging in tragic limp strands. My heart is thumping because I have this terrible lingering sense of horror that something's going to happen. I put a hand to each cheek and hold them there, gazing at my own reflection. The feeling of trepidation doesn't go away.

What if James *has* brought me to Venice to propose?

I realise with absolute, incontrovertible certainty that I can't say yes. Not just because I've known him for about five minutes, but because he brings all his travel documents in a see-through plastic folder. And because he gets up the morning we arrive and goes for a walk instead of staying under the covers like any sane, normal person. And because he's – oh, God. Just because he's him. I love Sophie to death, but he's like the male version of her. And there is no way I could ever live with her. I think Rich needs a bloody medal.

I wash my face, wiping away the smudges of mascara with a paper towel, and run my fingers through my hair.

And then I square my shoulders, brace myself, and return to the Piazza, where James is sitting, waiting quite patiently, for my return. He's reading a guidebook. Obviously.

The waiter reappears and takes our order. I can't think what I want, because there are so many things on offer that my brain's on shutdown. Plus my heart is thumping with anticipation, and not in a good way. I choose a small margherita pizza, because it seems the simplest thing to go for.

James leans in, lowering his voice. I sit back slightly, curling my fingers into my palms. It's not him, I say to myself, it's me. He's lovely. I'm just . . . I don't know what I am.

'I wanted to talk to you about something,' he begins. I pick up a napkin and shake it out, taking it by the corners and folding it into neat squares.

'I wondered – I mean, the thing is – you said your lease is coming up soon. And I know you like living there, and Becky's your friend, and everything, but—' it feels like everyone in the room is holding their breath, waiting for him to carry on talking '—I've seen a really nice flat, and I wondered if you'd like to move in with me.'

There's a second where I exhale, and I feel so dizzy that it's as if I'm a balloon that's just been untied, and I can see myself whizzing round in circles, high above the Piazza San Marco, all the air flying out of me until I collapse back down, completely deflated, in my chair. Sitting opposite James – charming, nice, Golden Retriever James, with his big chocolate button eyes and his helpful, kindly nature, and his broad dependable shoulders and his good job. I look at him, and feel my shoulders sag with relief and guilt and a million other things I can't put a name on.

'I can't,' I say eventually.

'What do you mean, you can't? Have you signed another lease?' He looks at me, and I feel like I just kicked a puppy. But it's really just hit me. I'm thirty, and life is happening all around me. And I can't spend any more of it doing what looks like the right thing just to keep some imaginary observer happy. I've only got one life and I want to start living it, now.

'No,' I say, and I feel a bit sad, but not so sad I'd spend the rest of my life with someone who is nice enough, but not enough. 'I just . . . can't.'

The journey home is pretty hideous. James sits beside me, drinking gin and tonic and studiously reading the in-flight magazine and not saying much. I try to make things better by making stupid, pointless observations, and being extra lovely to the cabin crew, as if somehow that'll make up for the fact that I've just dumped James in the most romantic city in the world because I want . . .

What is it that I want?

We fly over London, the lights illuminating the darkness like a million tiny sparkles, and when we pass through passport control James turns to me, shouldering his bag, and says stiffly, 'I think maybe we could leave it from here?'

And I nod.

He strides off, his long legs eating up the floor of the airport, and I make my way back towards the station, and the tube, and home to Albany Road.

My phone buzzes with notifications as I get off the tube and the Wi-Fi connects. A million messages from work friends and Sophie and Gen, asking if I've had a gorgeous time, updating me on what's been going on, telling me they can't wait to hear all about it.

And there's a message from Becky, sent to the house group chat, calling for a team meeting.

When I walk into Albany Road there's a really weird, hushed atmosphere. Everyone – apart from Rob, who's (predictably) working – is sitting round the kitchen table, drinking coffee or tea. They look up at me expectantly.

'Nice time?' Alex says, first.

'Venice was gorgeous,' I say, truthfully. 'Lots and lots of water.' Also truthful.

'Loved your photos,' says Becky. 'Looks like you had the most amazing time.'

'It's so romantic,' Emma sighs. She glances across at Alex, and I can't read her expression. I want to tell them that what they see on Instagram isn't necessarily representative of my real life, and remind them that the main reason I share the photos isn't to try and become Instafamous or to get free stuff. It's because it's an easy way of sending a little pictorial *hello* to Nanna Beth and my friends from wherever I am, whatever time of day it is. And I suppose there's a bit of me that's felt like I had a point to prove – after all, I walked away from my life in Bournemouth and moved to London to have the dream career and the amazing house in Notting Hill, and all of that.

'Right. We're here for an extraordinary meeting,' Becky says, steepling her fingers and clearing her throat, 'because one of us is leaving the fold.'

I look at everyone. Before I have time to start trying to size up who it is, Becky laughs, and carries on.

'Alex is leaving to share a place with some of his friends from the nursing course, so we need to put our heads together and see if we can find someone to replace him.'

'Shouldn't be too hard,' Alex says, laughing and looking a bit uncomfortable. I try to catch his eye, but he looks down at the table.

'Have you got a place yet?' Emma says.

'Not quite,' says Alex. 'Got a couple of places to look at though.'

'I might know someone,' Emma says. 'She's a friend from work.'

'Do I know her?' Becky asks, looking interested.

I watch Alex, who is drinking his tea and looking out of the window. It's as if he's distancing himself already. I can't help wondering with a sinking feeling if he's moving out so he can make it easier for him and Emma to actually get together. Once again, I've gone away and come back to find that Alex has slipped through my fingers. Or the idea of him, anyway. I have to remind myself that all of this has been in my own bloody head. I need to get over myself and stop believing my life is going to turn out like a romantic movie.

It turns out Becky vaguely knows the girl through another friend at work, so it looks like the deal might already be done.

I stand up, faking a yawn. 'I'm really sorry,' I say, picking up my bag. 'I'm so tired, and I've got work in the morning. After a week and a half off, God knows what I've got waiting for me.'

I walk out of the room without looking back.

CHAPTER FORTY-ONE

Alex

20th November

Turns out it's not that easy finding a place in London. We've been trying for the last month but every time we think we've found somewhere that's the right price (cheap) and the right size (basically not a postage stamp) someone's got in before us with references and deposit. It's a full-time job trying to find somewhere, and we're all trying to juggle college work, agency shifts, and being in the same place at the same time. But I think at last we've done it.

The flat in Stockwell seems tiny compared to Albany Road. We take a final look at it as the letting agency guy stands in the hallway. The whole flat is approximately the size of the kitchen and dining room at Albany Road. The windows look out over a landscape that's grey and depressing. I give myself a shake, reminding myself that

it's pissing down with rain on a gloomy November afternoon, and anywhere would look miserable under those
circumstances.

'Everyone happy?' The estate agent does a sort of
shuffling motion, bobbing his head. He's wearing a shiny
grey suit and smells of Lynx Africa. It reminds me of
school changing rooms.

'Yep.' I look at the boys and we all nod.

'Excellent.' He puts out a hand. 'Let's shake. I like to
shake on a deal.'

We all go through the motions. I suppress a yawn,
because I'm exhausted after working a night shift.

'Assuming your references work out okay, you three
can be in just before Christmas.'

We're going to be working shifts, so the fact that the
sitting room is the size of a cupboard is a minor detail.
It's pretty unlikely we'll ever be in the room at the same
time.

We all stand and watch as the letting agency guy –
who's probably only twenty-one, at most – wanders back
to his little car, branded with the name of the agency.
He's already on the phone, organising his next deal. He
gets in and drives off, giving us a wave as he passes.

It's not exactly Notting Hill. Walking back to get the
tube we skirt a massive heap of rubbish waiting for
collection, and pass a house with broken railings, and
half a bicycle chained to a lamp-post outside. Music's
blaring from a window and a man wearing a vest is
hanging out shouting down to a boy on a bike below.

He circles, then disappears. It all feels a bit like something from a crime drama, and I half expect a flotilla of police cars to appear, blue lights on, and police officers to leap out and start surrounding the place. Still, it's all we can afford. And at least I'm getting out of my current house-share situation. Living in the same house as Jess has just brought it home to me that there's no way we can carry on the way we were before.

We walk down the road towards Stockwell. Some parts of it are unrecognisable now they've been poshed up, but it doesn't take long before you're in streets that look the way they've done for decades. Tattered shop hoardings and windows held together with thick layers of fly-posted adverts are interspersed with metal shutters graffitied with ornate spray-painted tags. We walk past a betting shop, which already has multi-coloured lights strung across the doorway and we hear a blast of 'Step into Christmas'. It's not even December. It gets stuck in my head and the words jam there, reminding me of this time last year when we were moving into Albany Road and I was still getting over Alice. It feels like light years ago. She sent me an email the other day, just to let me know she'd got back together with Paul, and that she hoped I was okay with that. I sent her a reply wishing them both well, and I meant it. I'm glad she's happy.

'Where are you headed now?' Abeo asks, checking his phone as we stand at the crossing, waiting for the lights to change. A recycling lorry groans and clatters past. It's got fairy lights strung across the dashboard and the driver's wearing a red and white Santa hat. I feel like the whole of London is lit up for Christmas. It's weird, then, that it feels like something inside me has been switched off.

'Back to my place,' I say, correcting myself mentally: *my old place.* I'll have to get used to the Victoria line, and find myself another café to hang out in on a Sunday morning. But it won't be the same without Jess. I've only seen her fleetingly since she got back from Venice – work is manic, by all accounts, and she'd messaged saying she'd have to put off the farewell walk we planned for Sunday morning. I chew my lip. I think she's probably avoiding me, and that makes perfect sense. Instead she'll probably be spending it tucked up in bed at James's place.

'Cheer up, mate,' a gang of suits say as they run past, tinsel round their shoulders, knocking me backwards. It looks like someone's cloned our estate agent. There's about ten of them, all in shiny-looking suits, ties loosened. They must be on an early Christmas lunch. A very early one. One of them pauses and drapes their piece of tinsel over my head, shouting, 'It's nearly Christmas, have a mince pie.'

God, London is oppressively cheerful at this time of year. I feel like the bloody Grinch. I must get a grip and stop moping. It's pathetic.

When I get back to Albany Road the house is deserted. There's a pile of post on the mat in the porch – mostly junk, none of it addressed to me. I stack it on the dresser and wonder if I should bother getting my mail redirected, or if I should just pop round once in a while and pick it up. That'll mean risking bumping into Jess. That's a good thing, and a bad one.

In the kitchen it looks like everyone's rushed out as usual. Someone's left the lid half-fastened on a carton of milk and it's fallen over sideways, leaving a leaky puddle on the fridge shelf. I pick it up, wipe up the mess, and bang the fridge shut. It never closes on the first attempt.

Upstairs, Jess's door's open. I pause for a moment outside her room, looking in at the unmade bed, the jumble of clothes on the chair beside her bed, and the snaking wires of hairdryer and straighteners tangled on the carpet. And then I notice the light of the straighteners is glowing green – she must've left them on in her rush to get out of the door and get to work on time. They're balanced on a pile of paper – she's always leaving stuff like that lying around – and I stand on the threshold, wondering what to do. Is it weird to go in? I can't ignore it. I decide to send a message to the house group chat. It's been quiet there for ages.

Just standing outside your door, Jess, and you've left your straighteners on.

Bloody hell, Jess 😨 , Becky shoots back.

Excuse me, Jess types, (I feel a little jolt of something. And then I shake my head. For God's sake.) *You did it the other day, Beck. Can you switch them off, Alex? Thank youuuu x*

I step in, carefully, and unplug them from the wall.

363

For the briefest of moments I look around at Jess's things – at her framed *When Harry met Sally* picture on the wall, and her fluffy pink coat thing. There's a striped woollen rug thing on the end of the bed, and a teetering pile of books on her bedside table. I step out of the room, realising that it'll probably be the last time I'm in there. It feels very final.

CHAPTER FORTY-TWO

Alex

18th December

There's a week to go before Christmas and I need to study for end-of-term exams. The prospect of lying in bed listening to Jess and James together isn't exactly appealing. I decide I might as well just head back, see my mum, get some decent work done and enjoy some meals I don't have to cook myself before next term starts. I pick up my notes and textbooks, and shove them in an overnight bag with a bunch of T-shirts, jeans and stuff. I message Mum to make sure she's okay with me turning up out of the blue. She doesn't reply. I think given past performance she'll probably be okay with it, and I pull the door on Albany Road closed behind me.

I always forget how full-on Christmas is in Canterbury. The market stalls are crammed with cinnamon-scented lebkuchen and painted wooden toys. Pubs are stuffed with people in striped Breton tops and deck shoes sipping mulled wine and having leisurely lunches. The university has broken up for the end of term, but the place is still full of students. And my mother is at home, where she's gone all out with a massive eight-foot fir tree decorated with tasteful silver baubles. She has a house full of guests from her art class.

'It's so lovely to have you here, darling,' she says as she shuts the door behind me, then pulls me in for a hug. The kitchen is jammed with people who all seem to know who I am. I'm touched that she seems to have got her head round the idea of nursing at last, and she's proudly telling everyone that yes, this is Alex, and yes, he's the one who's retraining as a nurse. It's sweet, if a little bit overwhelming. Eventually I escape upstairs. Mel texts to say she's checking in to make sure I'm surviving.

I point out that she owes me one. Or several.

20th December

I don't even manage a week before it all gets too much. I hadn't made any promises about staying for the whole of the holidays because of work. Mum's already got plans to spend the whole of Christmas Day helping at the soup kitchen in town, so I don't have to feel guilty about dropping her in it and leaving her alone. She seems pretty easy-going about it.

'You could always stay here for Christmas, darling,' she says, standing in the doorway watching as I shove things back into the overnight bag. 'I'll be back by six. Or you could come and help. They might need a spare nurse.'

I shake my head. 'It's all right, honestly. I need to go and say goodbye properly to the guys in the house and get myself settled in the new place.'

'What about Christmas?' She looked concerned. 'I hate to think of you sitting there in that place all by yourself when there's a perfectly good bed down here. And I've got the Bridge Club gang coming around on Boxing Day for a buffet.'

'I won't be alone, honestly.'

I don't have a clue if anyone's going to be around over Christmas. I'm half thinking I might just pick up some agency shifts and get a bit of money behind me before term starts. Thanks to Becky's ridiculously low rent, I've managed to keep a hold of a decent chunk of my back-up savings, but once I move they're going to be dwindling away rapidly. If I work all over the holidays, not only will I have a decent chunk of money behind me, but I'll have managed to avoid any awkward encounters with Jess and James too. Bonus. I'm a genius.

I head back home – well, home for now – to Albany Road and manage to lose the time leading up to Christmas in work and revision. Rob's working really long hours, Emma's nowhere to be seen, I think because we've both been skirting around each other a bit, and Becky's gone on a trip up north to see her parents, so there's a weird sense of anti-climax.

As I get to my room, I get a call to say that Abeo, Oli and I passed the landlord's reference checks without event. It feels a bit strange and final. We just need to sort a hire van so we can move in three days before Christmas, and then nip to IKEA and pick up the essentials. The thing I'd taken for granted living in Becky's place was that the house was fully furnished, with everything her grandparents had left there. We didn't have to buy so much as a can opener. I think I took a lot of things for granted in Albany Road.

Jess

The Christmas work lunch is legendary, apparently. Everyone comes, and they hire a whole restaurant and take it over for the afternoon. But I'm just not in the mood. A waiter passes as I'm escaping to the bathroom, offering me some sort of twiddly-looking canapé. I shake my head and lock myself in the cubicle, sitting down on the top of the loo seat. Elton John's playing through the speakers, and I listen as two of the women from editorial come in, chatting about an author they've had a nightmare time with. I sit, silent and patient, and they wash their hands, reapply their lipstick, and leave, still grumbling about how late he was delivering his last manuscript, and how it had screwed everything up for next spring.

Once I'm sure it's quiet, I let myself out of the cubicle and wash my hands and face, looking at myself in the mirror. I look tired, and a bit miserable. It's Christmas,

I'm living in London, and this is everything I ever dreamed of. I think about this time last year and how I was giddy with excitement, wide-eyed, ready to soak it all up. Right now I'd like to just slink off somewhere on my own and have a rest. It's probably just end-of-year tiredness, I tell myself, squaring my shoulders as I look at myself in the mirror. I add another layer of red lipstick as a protective barrier.

I make my way back downstairs and lean over the shoulder of Jav, who is wearing a purple Christmas crown.

'I'm feeling a bit sick,' I say, quietly. 'I don't want a massive fuss, so I'm just going to sneak off now before they do pudding. Will you let people know if they ask?'

She nods, waving the glass of Prosecco in her hand. 'You sure you don't just need another one of these?'

'Definitely not.' I shake my head.

As soon as I get outside into the fresh air I feel more human. I check the map on my phone to make sure I'm walking in the right direction, and decide I'll set off home through Hyde Park.

The bare trees are silhouetted against a silver-grey sky. Dogs scamper past, their owners carrying long plastic ball throwers and dressed warmly against the December cold. I'm in a dress covered in tiny, Christmassy stars, with my big red coat over the top. I've changed my work shoes for trainers, carrying them over my shoulders in a rucksack. I watch a couple walking past, his arm around her waist, and I feel a pang of guilt. Sophie says James

369

has been fine at work, but I still wonder if I should have let him down more gently. But I think about Nanna Beth, and how she told me to remember I only have one life and that I should leave it with as few regrets as possible. It's funny, but as much as Mum and Nanna Beth seemed to like him, I didn't love him – I mean *I* liked him, and he felt safe and secure, and all those things . . . but I definitely didn't love him. And being together with the wrong person was a million times worse than being single.

I walk past the bike hire rack where Alex and I hired Boris Bikes on one of our first outings together. I feel like he's been avoiding me, but when I tried to skirt around the question with Becky – trying to make it sound as casual as possible, she just made non-committal noises about him going back to his Mum's place to study.

'We've got someone coming to have a look at the room,' she'd reminded me that morning over breakfast. I'd looked up, confused.

'What about the girl Emma knew?'

'Mmm,' Becky had said, looking dubious. 'Dan's a friend from work. He's split up with his boyfriend and he's staying on a friend's sofa. I'd be doing him a favour. And after the whole – ' she'd raised her eyes towards the ceiling and waggled a finger back and forth, motioning in the direction of Alex and Emma's rooms '—Well, the whole *situation*, I think we want minimal drama, don't you?'

My eyes widened in surprise, and Emma had met my

gaze with a knowing look. I'd had no idea she'd known what was going on.

I stop to sit on a bench. My breath clouds in puffs in the freezing air. A family walk past, the children dragging sticks, the parents doubled over with laughter at their antics. That's the kind of family I want, I find myself thinking. And then it hits me. It's almost Christmas, and I'm here, alone, in London. I've got nobody. Publishing is full of women and gay men as far as I can see, so the chances of meeting someone at work are non-existent, and there's *nothing* on this planet that's going to convince me to try online dating again.

I'll just have to spend the rest of my life alone. Maybe I'll get some cats. Or a dog. Except I'm never going to be able to afford to buy a place. I give a massive, gusty sigh. Maybe I should just jack all this stuff in and go back to Bournemouth. If I went back to marketing, I could get a decent job and save up a deposit. I could even – I grimace at the prospect – move back in with Mum for a bit while I save.

I'd have to be pretty bloody desperate for that. I watch as two swans circle gracefully on the pond, and I pull out my phone to take a photo, editing it quickly then uploading it to Instagram. Sophie likes it almost immediately, and leaves a comment underneath.

That doesn't look like a publishing party.

I type a private message back.

I ducked out. Couldn't face it.

What're you up to now? Soph types.

Heading home. Having a bit of a walk and a think.

Sounds better than my afternoon, she types, after a moment's pause. *I've been on the bathroom floor hugging the loo for the last four hours. This is hideous.*

I look over at Kensington Palace as I walk towards Albany Road and think of the Duchess of Cambridge and her hyperemesis gravidarum. Imagine being in the public eye like that and just wanting to lie on the bathroom tiles dying quietly, but instead having to get up, plaster on a happy face, and shake people's hands. When I get closer, I realise there's a huge pine tree outside the Orangery at the palace, dotted with a million fairy lights.

There's a street vendor wearing a thick woollen cap and fingerless gloves, selling hot chestnuts. He offers me some, and I take out some money and buy a little bagful, stuffing them in the pocket of my coat. They glow in there, keeping me warm, as I head back to Albany Road. But something tugs my feet in another direction. I walk past shops lit up with decorations and buy a copy of the *Big Issue* from the man who stands outside Queensway station. My phone rings, and I almost drop it in surprise when I see it's Mum.

'Hello, love,' she says, 'I can't talk long.' She always starts calls like that. I don't know why she doesn't call when she's not busy, but she seems to like living her life pressed up to the edges of things.

'Hi,' I say, holding the phone with one hand and pressing the button at the traffic lights with the other. A little girl looks at me crossly and presses it again.

'I was supposed to do that, wasn't I, Mummy?'

I look at the mother and pull an apologetic face. She shakes her head, laughing. 'It's not a problem, honestly,' she says, taking the little girl by the hand and pushing the pram across the road.

'What's happening with Nanna Beth?' I ask.

'Oh she's fine, absolutely fine. I told her you and James might be coming down at Christmas to see her.'

'Just me,' I say, quietly. I walk past wildly expensive double-fronted houses with huge real Christmas trees in the bay of each matching window.

'Oh that's a pity,' says Mum, and she sounds genuinely distraught. 'What's James doing?'

'I don't know,' I say.

'What do you mean?' There's another pause, and I can almost hear her brain cogs whirring. 'Oh no, Jess. He hasn't finished with you?'

I give a snort, which I hope she can't hear.

'No, Mum, I finished it,' I say.

'For goodness' sake. Whatever for?'

She sounds completely astounded. There's no way on this earth that my mother, who likes to know which side her bread is buttered on, and who dreams of finding a nice, solid, stable sort of chap to rely on, could ever imagine ending things with someone like James.

'I just didn't think it was going to work out.'

'You didn't give it enough time,' she says, flatly.

'No, I just realised that I didn't actually love him. He's nice, but you can't just marry nice, and that's what I would have ended up doing.'

373

'Oh, Jess,' she says, again. 'What are you going to do now?'

'I dunno,' I say, stopping at the edge of Little Venice and looking at the canals. The late afternoon light is glowing on the water and it looks as if someone's spilled a pot of gold, which is floating on the top of the water, flashing dazzling soft light everywhere. I want to take a photograph before the sun drops down behind the buildings in the west.

It's weird. All this build-up to my glamorous new life in London, and I suspect I'll end up sharing Christmas lunch with Nanna Beth and Cyril and my mother (unless she got a better offer) in the sheltered accommodation dining room.

I say my goodbyes, and hang up. I snap several photographs and head for the café where Alex and I always liked to sit and share an after-walk coffee and a brownie. It's half three, and it closes at half four in the winter, just before it gets properly dark.

'Hello, my love,' says Lona, the owner. 'What are you after? Where's Alex?'

I shrug. 'Not sure, actually.'

'Haven't seen you two for a while. Have you had a falling-out?'

'No,' I say, taking a cup of coffee and tipping in sugar. 'Just busy with work and stuff. You know Alex is moving across town?'

She nods, thoughtfully. 'He's a nice boy.'

'He is,' I agree. But Becky let slip that things might be back on with him and Emma, and things are moving on. I wonder if maybe I should, too. Becky's never there, and while I like Rob, he's not around that much. Whoever moves in, it's going to feel pretty strange. I realise I'm going to miss Alex.

Maybe I should just head home for a bit. I sip my coffee and look out at the canal. Maybe I'm just having a wobble, because it's been almost a year and I still feel a bit like the new girl at work.

I look at my phone, and see a new message from Gen.

Oh my God I got the part. I GOT THE PART.

This is it for Gen – I just know it. It's a part in a West End show, and she's absolutely made for it. I feel a lump in my throat and realise that there's a tear sneaking down my cheek. I wipe it away with my sleeve. I'm so, so bloody proud of her.

CONGRATULATIONS! That's amazing! You're brilliant and you deserve this. Love you xxx, I reply.

Gen this is just the beginning. You are an absolute STAR xxx Sophie types. And then there's more coming. She's still typing something, then a moment later the little notification changes from 'Sophie is typing' to 'Sophie is recording'. I frown at the screen.

A second later a voice message pops up on our group chat.

'Hi,' says Sophie, 'It's me.' There's a pause. 'I mean obviously it's me. Anyway listen I have a confession to make and I was going to tell you today and you got in first with exciting news, Gen – congratulations by the way – so I thought actually maybe it's the day for it.'

375

And she gives a laugh, which sounds most unlike her. 'The thing is me and Rich did a thing today. A spontaneous thing. Well it wasn't that spontaneous really because we had to book it two weeks in advance but we didn't tell a soul – oh God, sorry, I'm gabbling – but we got MARRIED.' The last word comes out as a sort of shriek and then there's a giggle and the message ends.

I hit the record button.

'Bloody *hell*, Sophie. You did what? I mean congratulations! Oh my God.' I hit send, then add as an afterthought, 'I thought you were throwing up?'

Gen's typing a message.

OH MY GOD I MUST BE DREAMING.

Nope! Sophie types a reply. *You know how much Rich was dragging his heels over the whole setting a date thing. Well, we talked and it turned out that all he wanted to do was get married and not do the whole big wedding thing. Oh – and I am throwing up. But it's much nicer doing it in Paris.*

But you've been planning this since you were like NINE, Gen types.

PARIS??? I tap out.

There's another pause while Sophie records another message.

'I can't be bothered to type it,' Sophie says, and I can hear Rich laughing in the background. 'We're on the way to Paris on the train for a honeymoon. Turns out that being spontaneous is quite fun, actually. Love you both, speak to you when I get back . . .'

And she types in a string of kisses.

I sit back and put my phone down and for a second I think I'm going to cry again. I don't know what's wrong with me today. It feels like everyone is moving on except me. Yet again I wonder if I should just give up trying to be a London person, and head back to Bournemouth with my tail between my legs. I've got a million and one old school friends back there, and Gen and Soph visit all the time. Sophie's even muttered once or twice about moving back, because you get so much more house for your money, and she likes the idea of the baby living by the sea. But I don't know.

I begin to type a message to Becky, just to see how it feels if I see it written down.

Hi Beck, I begin. *I've been thinking that maybe London life isn't for me. I've decided to hand in my notice on the room, and head back to the beach.*

Alex

How anyone could amass so much random stuff in the space of a year is pretty amazing. I shove a pile of scrappy course notes into a box, and tip the contents of my desk drawer out to see if there's anything in there worth salvaging.

'All right, mate?'

I look up to see Rob in the doorway. He's in chef's trousers and a black T-shirt, and he's growing a beard. He's looking good. Happy.

377

'No' going to be the same without you here. D'you reckon you'll come back and see us now and then?'

I grin up at him, touched. Not only has Rob given me a decent bit of life advice here and there, he's also taught me how to make a mean lamb jalfrezi and all the trimmings.

'Now and then,' I say, feeling a bit sad, knowing it's not that likely. I can't face coming back to see Jess and James all loved up and cosy. It already feels weird, because I haven't seen her in weeks. I miss our talks. London felt different when I was sharing it with her – as if I was seeing it for the first time all over again. But – I shake myself, mentally – that's over. 'But I've got a really busy year coming up with college.'

'Aye,' Rob says, nodding. 'I bet. Have you seen Jess recently?'

'Not really,' I say, looking down at the stuff on my desk. I pick up a jade green stone I was given at a fortune-telling stall when Jess and I were wandering around Camden, and I shove it in my pocket.

'You know her trip to Venice didn't go all that well?'

My head snaps up and I look at Rob, saying more sharply than I mean to, 'What d'you mean? Is she okay?'

'Oh she's fine, I think. Wee bit quiet. Less of the romantic break, more of the break-up.'

My heart bangs against my ribs. 'Break-up?' It feels as if the blood is rushing in my ears.

'Aye.' Rob looks at me, levelly. 'Told me a while ago when we were having breakfast. We were talking about this and that, and she just came out with it. Said she realised she didn't feel anything for him but friendship, so when he asked her to move in, she gave him the heave-ho.'

'Ouch,' I say, to cover my elation.

He nods. 'Aye. Anyway—' Rob sticks his hand out, and I stand up and make as if to shake it, but he pulls me into a bear hug and slaps me firmly on the back. As he lets go, he murmurs in his gruff Glasgow accent, 'Reckon you should be having a wee think about telling Jess how you feel.'

'Me?' I'm surprised that Rob seems to have picked up on what's going on – or should I say, what's *not* going on. I sigh.

'Aye. You. No point missing the boat, eh? I'll see you later, pal.'

And with a wave of his arm, Rob pulls the door closed behind him and leaves me standing in a sea of cardboard boxes and half-packed bags, my mind whirling in confusion.

I pick up my phone and scan my messages. The last one I got from Jess was a photo of a terrier in a Christmas sweater walking on a lead in Hyde Park a couple of days ago. No message, just the photo and a laughing face.

Maybe I should message her now. And say what?

Oh hi, I hear you've dumped James . . . what about it? Hardly. My heart seems to have gone into overdrive and it's banging so loud in my chest I feel like it's about to crash out. Of course—

I click on Instagram, checking to see if she's updated

her whereabouts. I'm always teasing her that she can't resist documenting every second of her day.

'If a serial killer was after you,' I've told her, 'all they'd have to do is check Instagram and they'd be on to you in a second.'

I scroll down the main page and her face flashes up on the screen. Sure enough, there's a photograph – I zoom in on the picture, looking at the golden light on the water, and the sun setting over the canal at Little Venice: 3.30 p.m., the time stamp underneath says. It's ten to four now. Surely she'll still be there?

I grab my wallet and pull the bedroom door behind me. I hurtle down the stairs two at a time, almost tripping over my own feet, and yank the front door open. Then I have a brainwave and run back up the stairs and into my room. I grab the book I never got the chance to give her and shove it in the back pocket of my jeans, before hurtling back out of the door again.

Outside on Albany Road the light's already fading, and the sky's a strange blue, tinged with orange. It's freezing cold. My breath clouds as I sprint up the street, jumping over a pile of cardboard boxes folded up by the red letterbox, and head towards Little Venice. The strains of carol singers on the corner of Talbot Road drift towards me as I stop for a minute, doubled over, catching my breath. God, I really need to get back to the gym.

'Mummy,' says a little girl, wrapped up against the cold in a bright red woollen coat, 'do you think Father Christmas gets cold living at the North Pole?'

'Definitely not,' I say, straightening up and looking at the solemn-faced little girl. 'I think he's got a nice warm coat like yours to keep him toasty.'

'Exactly,' said the mother, giving me a conspiratorial smile. 'See. That nice man knows, too. Everyone knows.'

I set off again at a jog. The streetlights are on, and cars line up with red buses and chunky black London cabs along Delamere Terrace as I head towards the trees and water of Little Venice. Running to the end of the road, I stand on the footpath and shade my eyes, realising that tiny pinprick flakes of snow are starting to fall.

Is that – I screw up my eyes—

It's definitely her.

'Jess!'

I can see her, sitting outside despite the freezing cold, a black bobble hat on her dark hair, a thick scarf wrapped around her neck. She's in her red coat, and she stands out in the crowds of people – as if she's the only one there. She's standing up, putting something in her bag.

'Jess!' I call again, and she half-turns, as if she'd almost heard, but isn't quite sure.

Jess

I shove my phone back in my bag and stand up, putting the coffee cup and sugar sachets back on my tray. I can't decide what to do.

And then I think I hear someone calling my name. I

look around, wondering if I'm imagining things. And a second later, more urgently, I hear it once more.

'*Jess!*'

Standing at the top of the road is Alex, his T-shirt hanging out from under the huge blue sweater he wears around the house, no coat on despite the fact it's zero degrees and starting to snow. My heart feels as if someone's shot it with about a million volts of electricity and I walk towards him as he weaves his way through the meandering tourists, bumping into them and apologising, his face – his lovely face – one huge ridiculous grin of happiness.

We reach each other and stand on the canal path, beside the houseboat we've both said we'd love to live in, and we stare at each other for a moment.

'Hi,' says Alex, after a moment.

'How did you know where I was?'

'You leave a trail,' he says, and reaches across, unfurling one of the tassels of my scarf. 'I got you a birthday present. I mean, I'm sorry it's late, but—' he says, pulling a book out of his back pocket. He hands it to me. It's wrapped up in brown paper and string. I tug at it and the wrapping comes away.

'Look inside,' he says.

It's a signed copy of *One Day*. I feel my cheeks going all pink with happiness. 'That's so lovely.'

'Is it okay? I thought . . .' He looks a bit shy.

I look up at the sky. 'It's snowing,' I say, for no reason at all. As if he hasn't noticed. As if it actually matters. My brain isn't working properly.

382

He nods. 'The thing is, I spoke to Rob,' he starts to say.

He's gazing at me intently. I put a hand to my face.

'Have I got chocolate on my nose, or something?' I ask.

He shakes his head. 'You broke up with James.'

I nod. Something inside me gives a gigantic whoosh, as if I'm a firework display and someone's lit the first match. It's freezing cold, but I drop my gloves on the footpath beside the canal and take a step towards him. My heart is going to explode in a moment and I think if I don't just do something about it right now I don't know what'll happen—

'What about – I mean . . .' I open my mouth and try and find a way to say what I want to, but there doesn't seem to be a way to ask.

'Emma?' He reads my mind. I nod.

'Friends.'

I raise my eyebrows slightly.

'It wasn't ever really a thing. I mean we're friends. That's all. I mean the thing is, it couldn't be, because . . .' He stops and puts the heels of his hands to his forehead, closing his eyes, as if he's trying to concentrate. 'Because the thing is—'

· 'What is the thing, Alex?' My heart is beating so loudly in my ears that the outside world seems to have just disappeared. I watch as he bends down and picks up my gloves, holding them in one hand.

He's closer to me now, so close that I think it's possible

that he can hear the sound of my heart banging in my chest.

'The thing is—' He takes a breath and looks at me with those huge brown eyes. 'I love you, Jess.'

My breath catches in my throat. A couple walk past and I see them looking at each other and one says 'aww' to the other. There's a snowflake on Alex's eyebrow and I reach forward to brush it off and he catches my hand in his and there's a moment where I feel like all the snowflakes in the world have paused, just for a second, and I look into Alex's face – and I see his beard and his melty brown eyes and the way one eyebrow sticks up untidily and his hair is scattered with snow and—

'That's funny.' And I don't know why but I feel like my whole face is one huge beam of happiness. 'Because I love you, too.'

And I stand on tiptoe and for a second I brush a kiss on the side of his mouth and I breathe in the familiar scent of him and I think my legs might give way. And then he drops my gloves and I drop my bag and he pulls me close so I can feel that underneath his jumper his heart is thumping even harder than mine, and we kiss. And the snow starts falling again, and I don't even notice. I reach my hands inside the warmth of his jumper and feel the skin of his back under his shirt and it's burning hot.

'Your hands are bloody freezing,' he says, pulling back and laughing.

'I think maybe we should go home,' I say. And I take his hand, and we walk back through the darkness, past

384

the cinnamon-scented coffee stall, and through the shortcut past the Dog and Ferret, where they're playing 'Last Christmas' on the speakers and we hear a blast of it when someone pushes the door open. And he looks at me and swings my hand for a second, and smiles.

EPILOGUE

Jess

One Year Later

'You sure you want to give up the room?' Becky says, still dressed in her work clothes, which look incongruous because she's got a Santa hat balanced on the top of her hair. The kitchen's covered in paper chains, which I can't stop making. I found a kit in the craft shop round the corner, and it's very therapeutic. Alex said earlier that he's worried that if anyone stands still for too long they'll be decorated with baubles and strung up with Christmas lights. I can't help it. We've been together a year, and I'm so revoltingly happy that I even make myself slightly queasy sometimes. Nanna Beth's doing really well. She's completely Team Alex – in fact she loves him to bits, probably because she's got her very own male nurse to harass. And even my mother – grudgingly, because she still secretly thinks James was a better bet – has conceded that Alex and I seem very happy together.

'Yes. I definitely want to give up the room,' I say. If someone takes it over and has as good an introduction to London as I've had, they'll be lucky. I look around the kitchen, which is still as tumbledown and dilapidated as it always was. I've loved living at Albany Road, but it's time to move on.

'We could put up with a couple if it was you two, I reckon,' she says, looking across at Rob. He nods. I look at Alex fleetingly. There's something in the air. I've suspected for a while that maybe she and Rob are more than just friends, but they still haven't gone public, and I'm not going to be the one to push her to admit to anything if she's not ready – I mean, it took us long enough. But if they're just good friends, they're *very* good friends. And I love watching the way they wind each other up, and the way they spend hours in the kitchen cooking Sunday roasts. They're like the parents of the house.

'Well we're going to have two rooms to fill, then,' Becky says, looking at Rob.

'Two?' I frown.

'Oh, Emma's moving out in January – didn't I tell you? She's off to manage the entertainments section on a cruise ship.'

When we first came out and told everyone about our relationship, I'd been nervous about her reaction. She'd been a little bit frosty to start with, but it only lasted a few days. I tried to talk to her about it but she shook her head and told me that it hadn't ever been anything more than a hook up with Alex, and that she hoped we'd be very happy together. And that – amazingly – was that. Things had been pretty much plain sailing after that.

'A cruise ship?' I look at Alex, who is sitting at the kitchen table where we first met in December last year. This time, though, he's not making margaritas, but scrolling through his phone looking at online baby shops. He makes an impressed sort of face. I half wonder if she'll end up working alongside my mum, if she ever manages to get her dream job.

'If you and me and Gen club together,' he says, thoughtfully, 'we could get this for Lottie as a christening present.'

Becky peers down at the screen. 'A rocking horse? Didn't you say she was only six months old, Alex?'

'Yeah, but Jess and Gen are joint godmothers. They should get something she can keep.'

'You're such a softy,' says Becky, ruffling his hair. He ducks away, laughing.

'I think it's a lovely idea.' I drop a hand on the back of his neck, feeling the heat of his skin underneath my fingertips. And then I want to leave the kitchen and head upstairs with him as soon as I can. I take my hand away, trying to focus on what we're supposed to be doing.

'Becky, did they get in touch about doing references for our new place?' Alex asks.

'Yeah, it's all done. Can I see the pics again?'

I click on the link on my phone. I've saved a load of photos, but I won't be uploading them anywhere until we've got the keys in our hands. It's the tiniest flat you can imagine, one bedroom and a kitchen/sitting room in Queen's Park, the closest we could get to Little Venice, which is always going to be special to us.

'It looks so sweet,' Becky coos, looking back at Alex. 'How long do you have left 'til you qualify?'

'Another year.'

I look at him then back at Becky. It's going to be tight, but I don't care. 'But I've been promoted, so we'll manage – just.'

'I get the feeling you two would be okay whatever happened, anyway.' Rob looks pleased with himself. He's still revelling in his Cupid role, a year later.

Alex swivels round in his chair and looks up at me. 'I think you're right,' he says to Rob, but I'm the one who gets the full benefit of those gorgeous chocolate-drop eyes. He gives me the ghost of a wink.

'Took you long enough to work it out,' Becky teases. 'I thought you two would be perfect for each other the moment you met.'

'We were,' I say. Alex stands up, taking my hand, and as I finish my sentence we're disappearing out of the room.

'It just took us a while to figure it out.'

Acknowledgements

Like Alex, when I was a teenager I spent a lot of time wandering around London while my dad was working, so it's been absolutely lovely to write a whole book about one of my favourite places in the world. Huge thanks to everyone in the hardworking Avon gang for being so welcoming, and making this book such a joy to write – particular thanks to my brilliant editor, Rachel Faulkner-Willcocks. Thanks also to Amanda Preston, brilliant agent, moral support and cheerleader. You deserve a medal.

To the Millionaires, Hooters, and the Book Camp gang – thank you all for keeping me (relatively) sane, making me laugh with publishing gossip, and for celebrating with me every time I think I'm finished a book, and then again when it's finally done. You are all the best.

To my gorgeous children Verity, Rosie, Archie, Jude

and Rory – I love you enormously, and I'm so proud of the kind, lovely, thoughtful people you are. Sorry we've had pasta for dinner eight million times this year, but on the plus side, at least it's not risotto. Also please tidy your rooms. (If I put it down on paper, maybe you'll listen.)

To my family – Ross, Zoe, Mae, Mum, Chris – and my dear friends – Jax, Elise and Rhiannon – who put up with my vagueness, disorganisation and promises to call back when I've finished one more chapter, I love you all.

To my dogs, Mabel, Martha and Tilly – love and ear rubs. (But do please stop eating the furniture/chasing the guinea pigs/barking when I'm trying to edit.)

Last of all and most importantly – to you, reading this. Thank you for picking up this story. I hope you enjoyed reading Alex and Jess's story as much as I enjoyed writing it!

About the Author

ROSIE CURTIS was born in the Highlands of Scotland, and now lives with her family in a 150-year-old house by the sea in the northwest of England. She loves travel, happy-ever-after stories, and daydreaming. Her favorite book character is a toss-up between Anne Shirley and Jo March. Rosie also writes adult and teen fiction as Rachael Lucas.